AGAINST ALL FIERCE HOSTILITY

BOOK 6 ✣ THE MONASTERY MURDERS

DONNA FLETCHER CROW

Verity Press

Against All Fierce Hostility
Copyright © 2020 by Donna Fletcher Crow

All rights reserved as permitted under the U.S. Copyright Act of 1976.
No part of this publication may be reproduced or transmitted in any form or by any means, electronic or mechanical, including photocopy, recording, or any information storage and retrieval system, without permission in writing from the publisher. The only exception is brief quotations in printed reviews.

Verity Press an imprint of Publications Marketing, Inc.
Box 972
Boise, Idaho
83701

Cover design and layout by Ken Raney
Edited by Sheila Deeth
This is a work of fiction. The characters and events portrayed in this book are fictitious or used fictitiously.

Published in the United States of America

❦ Created with Vellum

Praise for the Monastery Murders

A Very Private Grave

Like a P.D. James novel *A Very Private Grave* occupies a learned territory. Also a beautifully described corner of England, that of the Northumbrian coast where St. Cuthbert's Christianity retains its powerful presence. Where myth and holiness, wild nature and tourism, art and prayer run in parallel, and capture the imagination still. All this with a cinematic skill.

A thrilling amateur investigation follows in which the northern landscape and modern liturgical goings on play a large part. The centuries between us and the world of Lindisfarne and Whitby collapse and we are in the timeless zone of greed and goodness.—Ronald Blythe, *The Word from Wormingford*

With a bludgeoned body in Chapter 1, and a pair of intrepid amateur sleuths, *A Very Private Grave* qualifies as a traditional mystery. But this is no mere formulaic whodunit: it is a Knickerbocker Glory of a thriller. At its centre is a sweeping, page-turning quest—in the steps of St. Cuthbert—through the atmospherically-depicted North of England, served up with dollops of Church history and lashings of romance. In this novel, Donna Fletcher Crow has created her own niche within the genre of clerical mysteries.—Kate Charles, *False Tongues,* A Callie Anson Mystery

A Darkly Hidden Truth

In *A Darkly Hidden Truth,* Donna Fletcher Crow creates a world in which the events of past centuries echo down present-day hallways—I came away from the book feeling as though I'd been someplace both ancient and new. Donna Fletcher Crow gives us, in three extremely persuasive dimensions, the world that Dan Brown merely sketches.—Timothy Hallinan, *The Queen of Patpong,* Edgar nominated Best Novel

With *A Darkly Hidden Truth* Crow establishes herself as the leading practitioner of modern mystery entwined with historical fiction. The historical sections are much superior to *The Da Vinci Code* because she doesn't merely recite the facts; she makes the events come alive by telling them through the eyes of participants. The contemporary story is skillfully character-driven, suspended between the deliberate and reflective life of religious orders in the UK and Felicity's "Damn the torpedoes, full steam ahead" American impetuousness.

Her descriptions of the English characters read like an updated and edgy version of Barbara Pym. *A Darkly Hidden Truth* weaves ancient puzzles and modern murder with a savvy but sometimes unwary protagonist into a seamless story. You won't need a bookmark—you'll read it in a single sitting despite other plans.—Mike Orenduff, 2011 Lefty Award Winner, *The Pot Thief Who Studied Einstein*

An Unholy Communion

A truly great mystery that had me guessing throughout the entire book. It was full of twists and turns and I learned a great deal of new information about the occult and spiritual warfare as well. The author most definitely did a lot of research and, although this book is a work of fiction, has included much fact so that it is not only a fun read but also a learning experience.—Alicia, *"Through My I's"*

Erie feelings, strange happenings, premonitions and unexpected occurrences mark the many events depicted within this well researched, documented and crafted novel. When all of the clues, the pieces and the final reveal come together you will not believe who is behind everything.—*"Fran Lewis's Book Reviews"*

Ingeniously plotted by a master of contemporary suspense, *An Unholy Communion* weaves Great Britain's holy places and history with an intricate mystery that will keep readers guessing to the very end. An exciting book that will keep you engrossed in the characters as well as life in England. A wonderful series.—*"Vic's Media Room"*

A Newly Crimsoned Reliquary

Skillfully builds tension from one peril to another, leading to a thrilling climax and satisfying denouement. But more than just a mystery, Crow weaves in rich and colorful details of English church and political history.—Donn Taylor, *Lightning on a Quiet Night*

If you like *Midsomer Murders*, *A Newly Crimsoned Reliquary* will be a comfortable read to sink into. Especially for the reader who loves centuries of English history. Perfect to read while on your vacation flight to the UK.—Mary E. Gallagher, *Gallagher's Travels*

A thoroughly enjoyable read from beginning to its suspenseful end. I could barely put the book down.—Janelle Watkins, *The Scene in TO*

A worthy addition to *The Monastery Murder Series*. Highly recommended.—Jeff Reynolds, *Sleuths and Suspects*

A really enjoyable, fast-read. It's obvious the author really knows her stuff. Great book.—Dolores Gordon-Smith, *The Jack Haldean Mysteries*

An All-Consuming Fire

Watch the pageant and take a front seat as the youth prove that when someone has faith they will shine to the top. Characters that are unique, true to life and interesting as Felicity, Antony and Cynthia take charge and will once again fill your heart.—Fran Lewis: *Just reviews/MJ magazine*

Wedding preparations, traditional Advent celebrations, threats to their lives, oh, and several murders, make for a true page-turner. The suspense lover will not be disappointed and the history buff will come away with a greater sense of 1300s England and its spiritual climate.—Alexis Gorin

A monastery, a documentary, romance, and multiple murders all combine to make a masterful read. Set against the backdrop of a beautiful English countryside, the story unfolds with ever mounting suspense. As with all the books in this series, church history is an added bonus, and it blends wonderfully with the narrative. One learns without lecture and is entertained at the same time. With a mystery and a marriage, what's not to love? Donna Fletcher Crow has produced a masterpiece once again. —James West

A totally gripping read. There's a fascinating mix of medieval church history, seamlessly woven into a very modern plot of a series of murders surrounding the shooting of a film, in which Antony is the polished but somewhat reluctant narrator. Naturally, the main thing on his mind is his forthcoming wedding to the irrepressible Felicity, but Felicity herself is in danger as she becomes a target for murder. There's a great cast of characters including Cynthia, Felicity's very polished, very professional and totally captivating mother. Yorkshire in winter is excellently portrayed, as is Monastery life, with the church calendar of the Christmas season adding a fascinating framework to the action. Highly recommended!—Dolores Gordon-Smith, *The Jack Haldean Mysteries*

*To Jane Elizabeth and Adela Marie,
My favorite ballerinas,
Thank you for helping Felicity
Update her rusty skills*

Acknowledgments

Thank you so much to all my Canadian friends who have made my many visits there such a delight over the years. A special thanks to: Alex from Lokafy, our knowledgeable Toronto guide; the charming Jane and Judy at Saint Thomas More in Toronto; the real-life Yoan and Lynda and all the excellent staff of the *Canadian*; the monks and nuns at Saint Benoit-du-Lac, Villa Sainte-Scholastique, Westminster Abbey, and the House of Bread—all who provided completely murder-free hospitality.

As always, thank you to my wonderful team, especially my careful editor Sheila Deeth and my cover designer Ken Raney who went to considerable lengths to find a photo of the right train. And a special thank you to the award-winning Canadian author Eva Maria Hamilton who contributed her extensive local knowledge. Any mistakes that remain are my own.

Finally, special thanks to my husband Stan who accompanied me every step of the way, and to my favorite Canadian family, Father Lee and Elizabeth Kenyon with my beloved English/Canadian/American grandchildren.

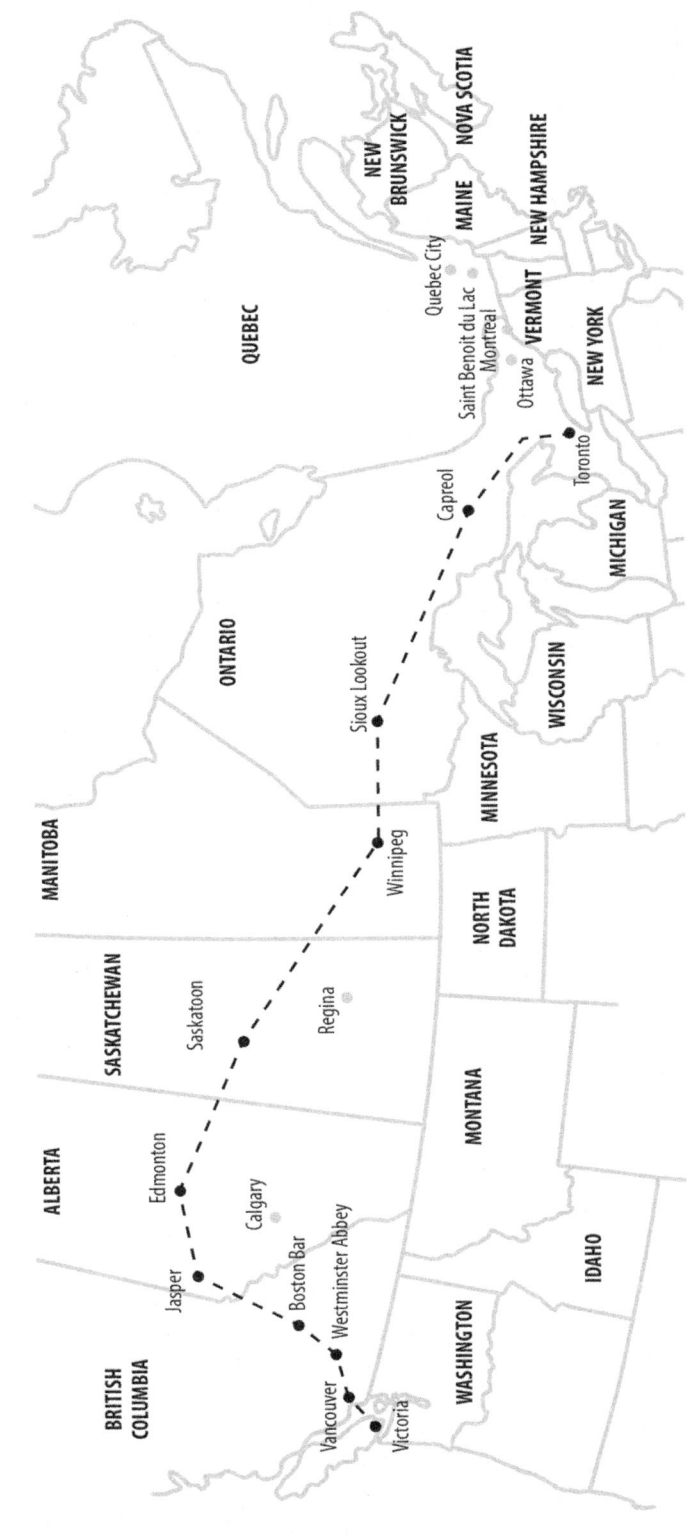

Saint Patrick's Breastplate

I bind unto myself today
The strong name of the Trinity,
By invocation of the same
The Three in One and One in Three.

I bind unto myself today
The power of God to hold and lead,
His eye to watch, His might to stay,
His ear to hearken to my need.
The wisdom of my God to teach,
His hand to guide, His shield to ward;
The Word of God to give me speech,
His heavenly host to be my guard.

Against the demon snares of sin,
The vice that gives temptation force,
The natural lusts that war within,
The hostile men that mar my course;
Or few or many, far or nigh,
In every place and in all hours,
Against their fierce hostility
I bind to me these holy powers.

Timeline

- 5 BC – Nov 30, 60 AD St. Andrew lived

- 303 AD St. George Martyred by Diocletian

- c. 435 St. Patrick goes to Ireland as a missionary

- 461 St. Patrick dies in Ulster

- 494 St. George canonized

- 1098 St. George named patron saint of England

- 1320 Scottish independence, St. Andrew named patron saint

- 1685 Wigtown martyrs executed

- 1793 City of Toronto Founded

- 1834 Toronto Municipal Wards founded

Characters

Felicity Margaret Sherwood—newly graduated, Community of the Transfiguration

Father Antony Stuart Sherwood—former Church History lecturer, Community of the Transfiguration

Family members:
Cynthia Howard—Felicity's mother

Andrew Howard—Felicity's father

Jeff Howard—Felicity's older brother

Charlie Howard—Felicity's brother

Judy Howard—Charlie's wife

Gwendolyn Sherwood—Antony's sister

Beryl Sherwood—Aunt who raised Antony and Gwen

From the College of the Transfiguration:
Father Anselm—Superior

Father Peter—Precentor

Police:
Detective Inspector Nosterfield—West Yorkshire Police, Huddersfield

Sergeant Mark Silsden—West Yorkshire Police

Inspector Langdon RCMP—Mission, BC

In Toronto:
Dr. Spaulding—Conference director

Zack—Dr. Spaulding's assistant

Surindar—Music director, St. Patrick's

At Saint Benoit-du-Lac:
Père Denis—Precentor

Sister Bernadette—Guest Sister, Saint Scholastica's

Mother Anne-Marie—Mother Superior, Saint Scholastica's

Cerise—her sister

On the *Canadian*:
Yoan—Steward

Prof. McKinnon—Archeologist

Lynda—Steward

At the House of Bread:
Sister Emma Grace

Mother Mary Joy

At Westminster Abbey:
Frère Sylvester—Guest master

Father Conall—Precentor

Dr. Penhaligon—Archivist

The Lighting of the Fire

c. 425 A.D.
Ireland

The April countryside slid past the little line of coracles gliding up the River Boyne. All was a patchwork of every imaginable shade of green, from the forest black of ancient hill junipers to the tinted yellow of newborn shoots of spring wheat. And around every rath and on every hillside, baby lambs bleated, tottering after their mothers. Rocks, trees, and clouds shaded the land with blue, purple, and gray shadows, and Patrick thanked God that he and his fellow missionaries should have arrived at this wonderful season of the renewing of life.

Patrick took a deep breath of the fresh, moist air and shook his head at the wonder that he should be returning here—to the very land where he had been held as captive; to the very people for whom he had labored as a slave for six years. Renewed life, indeed. A time of studying in a monastery in France had kindled his passion to bring the light of Christ to these people who once enslaved him. And here he was back in Ireland on the very eve of Jesus' victory over death. Tomorrow would be Easter.

Tonight he and his companions would camp near a hill where they could light their Paschal fire, as was always done to mark the rekindling of the Light by Christ's resurrection. Then, at dawn's first light, they would celebrate the most joyful, most holy, Mass of the year to inaugurate their mission.

Patrick turned to his bandy-legged little boatman who sat paddling with sure strokes in the back of the boat. "Do you know if King Niall is in residence at Tara just now?"

Righ, the boatman, shook his head. "Niall sleeps with his fathers these three years and past. Leoghaire, son of Niall, is now king in Tara."

Patrick closed his eyes at the news. He had not thought of the changes that would have occurred in his absence. Leoghaire. Patrick remembered him—taller, broader, louder than his father. And he remembered the tales he had heard of his cruelty. Leoghaire did not take hostages as his father had; he killed all his enemies in the most painful manner he could devise.

"And who are his chief druids?" Patrick asked.

"Lochru and Lucetmal, as served his father." Righ dipped his paddle into the river and slipped it skillfully through the smooth water.

Patrick nodded. He remembered their names. Men of great power. If he could reach these men, he could then preach anywhere in Eire. He looked across the garden patchwork of the countryside. Ahead and to their left, as on his first time here, Patrick saw the Hill of Tara crowned with ancient buildings. Closer, to their right, was another hill, slightly smaller, but open to view on every side. There could be no better spot to light their Paschal fire.

He knew of it from his time before—the Hill of the Slain where the mighty Cúchulainn had slaughtered his foes. The bards of Eire still sang of the deeds before the feast-fires. Yes, here Patrick would also light a victory fire that would burn forever throughout the land. He pointed. "We will camp there tonight. This is the eve of our greatest holy day. Tonight we will burn a fire on that hill in honor of the resurrection of our Lord, whose truth burns in our hearts."

The boatman's eyes grew large with fear, and his patchy beard seemed to bristle. At first, Patrick, who had gone these six years without speaking Gaelic, thought he had said something wrong, but then he realized Righ had understood perfectly. "On the Hill of the Slain? You build a fire? Tonight?"

Patrick nodded calmly. "I don't understand your alarm. Fires on hilltops are common here—I remember well seeing them in the distance when I watched over the sheep in Slemish."

"Ah, but not on that hill. It is forbidden. Only druids may go onto the Hill of the Slain. Only they are safe from the snakes."

Patrick frowned, struggling to recall. Where had he heard that before? Ah, yes, he remembered. The druids kept all from the hill by calling it the habitation of snakes.

Righ nodded with such energy he broke the rhythm of his rowing as he urged his point. "The druids go there at the dark of the moon to make kill-offerings to Dagada that his cauldron of plenty will not fail our land. Only then the snakes will not harm them."

Patrick shook his head. "Our God is stronger than Dagada. We are not afraid."

The boatman persisted. "But not tonight. You must not light your fire tonight. There are no fires in all of Tara on this one night of the year."

"And why is that?"

"Tomorrow is Leoghaire's birthday. All fires save the king's feast-fire are to be cold in Tara tonight until the High King himself sets the first blaze in the morning. Then all will light their fires in honor of the day that gave our king birth."

"No. We will ignite our fire first, as do all Christians on this night, in honor of the day that God gave the new birth to mankind."

The boatman leaned forward and gripped Patrick's arm. "But it is a dying matter to disobey the king in this."

Patrick had not expected such a violent confrontation to come so soon. But this solved one problem that had been puzzling him for days—how was he to gain admittance to the High King? Now, if he were to be brought before Leoghaire for judgment, he would have an opportunity to speak.

Patrick walked a bit apart from his men who were setting up their camp. Sitting at the foot of the hill, he repeated the words of the prayer song he had been forming for many days—ever since he knew he would be returning to Ireland. Half in his mind, half aloud he repeated:

I bind unto myself today
The strong name of the Trinity,
By invocation of the same
The Three in One and One in Three.

I bind this today to me forever
By power of faith, Christ's incarnation;
His death on cross for my salvation;

Patrick paused and lifted his eyes to the top of the hill. He had uttered brave words to the boatman, but was he truly ready for such an encounter? Was it possible that his mission should end in death after barely twenty-four hours? Then he saw his error. He had left Christ in his tomb.

He added another line:

His bursting from the spicèd tomb,
I bind unto myself today.

And now the words tumbled from him:

Against the demon snares of sin,
The hostile men that mar my course;
Against their fierce hostility
I bind to me these holy powers.

Against the wizard's evil craft,
Against the death-wound and the burning,
Christ be with me, Christ within me,
Christ behind me, Christ before me,
Christ in quiet, Christ in danger.

I bind unto myself the name,
The strong name of the Trinity,

By invocation of the same,
The Three in One and One in Three.

After another moment, he stood. He was ready. Even if the death sentence followed, he would speak first. Leoghaire would hear God's message.

Chapter One

Petertide

The Ordination of Deacons

F elicity took a deep breath and lifted her chin just a fraction. Who would have guessed it would take so much courage just to walk up the aisle of the cathedral?

Pour out thy Spirit from on high;
Lord, thine assembled servants bless;
Graces and gifts to each supply,
And clothe thy ministers with righteousness.

The congregation sang with the pealing of the organ and the procession started forward. *Graces and gifts*, indeed, Felicity thought. How could this day have arrived so quickly? And how could anyone who was so sure she knew it all when she began this journey three years ago possibly feel so unsure now?

Her black cassock and white surplice swayed with each step she took in rhythm with the eight other ordinands being deaconed today. A strand broke free from the black velvet bow clasping her long blond hair loosely at the nape of her neck. She raised a hand to brush it back, then the motion turned almost into a wave as her eyes connected with Antony, standing in the congregation just ahead to her right. *To teach the truth as...* she stumbled over the words of the hymn as her throat constricted at the sight of his dear, lopsided smile.

She steadied and her gaze moved on down the row to her mother and father, thankfully reunited, and to her brothers Jeff and Charlie, Judy, Charlie's wife—her family who had come all the way from America just to support her in this big moment. She mustn't let them down now. *Wisdom, and zeal, and faith impart...* she picked up the lyrics. Well, she had always had plenty of zeal, but dear Lord, give her wisdom. She took her designated seat in the second row of chairs before the altar.

"God our Father," the bishop intoned. "Hear our prayer for your faithful people, that each in their vocation and ministry may be an instrument of your love, and give your servants now to be ordained the needful gifts of grace..."

Responding with a fervent "Amen," Felicity was at last free to sit down.

The service moved on to the Old Testament reading from Isaiah. "In the year that King Uzziah died, I saw the Lord sitting on a Throne..." Try as she might, Felicity found it impossible to concentrate on the words. It was all very well for Isaiah—he had a vision of God—high and lifted up. She had a head stuffed with information, a plethora of amazing experiences, both good and bad, and a whole new perspective on life to show for her time in seminary. But no plan for the future.

She, who always knew exactly where she was going and how to get there and what to do when she arrived. She stole a sideways glance over her shoulder—fleeting, but enough to tell her that her earlier impression had been correct. Antony and her parents were glowing with pride at the accomplishment of their wife and daughter—her. Not surprising that dear Antony would be well-pleased with her; after all, he had mentored her through it all—including marrying her for better or for worse. She smiled to herself—it had certainly been better for her; she could only hope it wasn't worse for him than he might have expected.

The real surprise for her though, was that her mother Cynthia should be so radiant. Felicity's decision to enter the church had been almost as traumatic for her mother as for herself—although their often stormy relationship had improved greatly these past couple of years. And now, thanks be to God, Cynthia was reconciled with Andrew, Felicity's always supportive father.

Further ruminations were interrupted as the voice of the reader penetrated her consciousness with Isaiah's words, "Woe is me! I am lost..." Isaiah, too? One of the greatest, maybe *the* greatest, of the Old Testament prophets? Had the bishop selected this reading with Felicity in mind—as if he knew her conflicts? Or did he suspect some of her fellow ordinands to have similar anxieties? She looked to each side of her and saw only serenity on the faces above the white surplices. Did they all know exactly what they would be doing next? What they were going to do beyond this milestone they had worked so hard to achieve?

The reading ended with Isaiah hearing the voice of God. *Nice for some*, Felicity thought.

Then the choir set the response for the Psalm, "Teach me O Lord, the way of thy statutes." Ah, here was a refrain she could sing with gusto.

Of course, the normal career path at this point would be to serve as a curate in a parish for a year, then go on to be ordained a priest and take over one's own parish. A strange thing had happened to Felicity over the course of her time in theological college, however. After all, she had started out with a clear goal to become Pope—well, okay—Archbishop of Canterbury.

Recently, though, she was finding it harder and harder to picture herself leading a parish. Surely she wasn't developing a modicum of humility—or worse yet—caution? Was that why she hadn't put her name forward for a parish position? No, her reluctance had started with Antony's decision to leave his position as church history lecturer at the College of the Transfiguration and return to parish ministry himself. This autumn he would be taking up his new position in the diocese of Blackburn—a role he was all too excited to jump into. And well suited for, Felicity believed. Unlike herself.

That seemed to be the crux of the matter—seeing Antony's anticipation had shown her how reluctant she would be to take on a similar role.

Not wanting to dampen his enthusiasm, however, she had refrained from voicing her own conflicts. Of course, she wanted her husband to follow what he felt his calling to be. And it was lovely to see him abandon some of his earlier reticence as he made plans for what he wanted to accomplish in his ministry. She simply couldn't see how she fit into the picture. Whatever she did, she would be the vicar's wife. Did that entail donning a frilly apron? It certainly would involve brewing massive pots of tea—fine—but she blanched at the thought of making the accompanying scones.

After today Felicity would be a full member of the clergy—qualified to be called "the reverend" and to wear a clerical shirt (she put a finger under the stiff, white collar rubbing the top of her neck). But the possible duties were far-ranging. She knew most of her fellows had already been assigned curate positions back in their home dioceses—serving their title, they called it. Others would serve as minor canons in their diocesan cathedral, or as assistant chaplains in schools or hospitals. One of her classmates, who had always been wild about airplanes, was even to work with an airport chaplain.

Neither she nor Antony—nor the bishop, for that matter—

had been so foolhardy as even to mention the fact that she would actually be qualified to serve as Antony's curate.

But performing a similar function in a nearby parish seemed almost as unimaginable to her. So what would she do? The church dressed such a quandary up in a fancy name—discernment. It did sound better than "dithering" but Felicity knew it came to the same thing.

The realization that everyone around her had come to their feet brought Felicity back to the present moment. "We believe..." She stood hastily and recited the creed, bowing and crossing herself in the appropriate places with the others. "Amen."

The archdeacon stepped forward and began announcing the name of each person to be ordained deacon, and that of the place where they were to serve. "Felicity Margaret Sherwood, Blackburn." Felicity had been named for her mother's two best friends, but it was a mere fortuity that she had wound up with the names of two saints. A few from her class had chosen to be ordained with new names, symbolizing the spiritual life they were taking on. Felicity, though, was only too aware that it would be enough of a challenge to live up to the names she had already been given.

The list came to an end and the archdeacon continued. "Reverend Father, I present these persons to be ordained to the office of deacon in the Church of God."

The bishop stepped forward and addressed the congregation. "Those whose duty it is to inquire about these persons and examine them have found them to be of godly life and sound learning, and believe them to be duly called to serve God in this ministry. Is it therefore your will that they should be ordained?"

Felicity's mind flitted back to her interview with the committee, her "chat" with the archdeacon, the endless forms she had filled out, even her psychological examination. Well, apparently she had passed. To say nothing, of course, about three years of study, writing papers and taking exams. She must be good for something.

She stole a sideways glance at her mother as the congregation responded, "It is." Again, the unmistakable look of pride on Cynthia's face made Felicity catch her breath. She had spent all of her life believing nothing she did was good enough for her mother. The thought that she had at last come up to the mark as a daughter made her grab the chair-back in front of her for support. Then Cynthia leaned over to say something to Judy, Charlie's wife. The brims of their hats bumped, bringing an even broader smile to Cynthia's face.

And Felicity understood. At last, her mother had her royal wedding. The mother-daughter conflicts over Felicity and Antony's wedding had never been entirely resolved—another failure of Felicity's to come up to expectations. But now, with the cathedral gleaming, the clergy splendid in their best white and gold vestments, and all in attendance dressed to the nines, Cynthia's daughter had scored a success.

"Will you uphold them in their ministry?" the bishop continued.

Felicity's gaze shifted. Antony's fervent, "We will" reached her as if he had been the only person responding. And she knew he would. Whatever she decided. Whatever she did or didn't do, she had Antony's complete support. And with that, she exhaled as if she had been holding her breath for hours. She felt her shoulders drop and the tension leave her body. Antony gave her just a ghost of a wink as he sat down with the congregation. Had he known of her struggles all along? Had his silence on the subject of her future not been absorption in his own up-coming change, but rather merely giving her space? Time for her own discernment—that word again—while he prayed silently? What a very Antony-like thing to do. With that tiny gesture he was saying to her "all shall be well." And she believed it.

If it wouldn't have been so inappropriate, she would have blown him a kiss, but she could feel every eye in the cathedral turned to the row of candidates still standing before the bishop as he instructed them. "Deacons are called to serve the Church of God, and to work with its members in caring for the poor, the needy, the sick, and all who are in trouble. They are to strengthen the faithful..."

The bishop paused and regarded those standing before him. "Do you believe, so far as you know your own heart, that God has called you to the office and work of a deacon in his church?"

"I believe that God has called me." It was the response printed on the page in front of her, but it came from Felicity's heart. And with that knowledge came freedom. That was all she needed to know. The rest would work itself out. In time.

The catechism continued, and to each question Felicity was able to answer an ardent "By the help of God, I will."

Antony knelt as the dean of the cathedral lead in prayer for the candidates. He didn't need the adjuration the bishop had just given that they pray for those to be ordained. He did that for the special ordinand in his life with every breath, but he was glad of the dean's invocation, "Bless your servants now to be made deacons, that they may serve your church and reveal your glory in the world."

"Hear us, good Lord," all responded. As the litany continued, Antony looked back over the past three years. The three years with this whirlwind of a woman that had turned his life upside down and set him on such an amazing new path. Or, perhaps, kept him steady on what he hadn't realized had been his path all along. It was impossible to say whether Felicity was a steadying influence or a cyclone; he just knew he couldn't imagine life without her. And was incredibly thankful that her eruption into his life had shown him how wrong he had been to suppose he should become a monk.

Now the ordinands were kneeling before the bishop. "We give you thanks, that you have called these your servants, whom we ordain in your name..." The bishop went down the row, laying his hands on the head of each candidate. Antony felt the warmth on his own head when the bishop's hands rested on Felicity. Antony knew the rightness of it. It was as if his own deaconing were being renewed, and that certainty made him smile. That was part of what the "one flesh" of marriage was all about—whatever either one of them did, they were in it together.

Hopefully the new ventures he was to undertake would be right for Felicity as well: their new home, new responsibilities in a parish; and before that, their journey across the water for his lecture tour of Canada. Their honeymoon, coming as it had, on the heels of the unveiling of a murderer that almost cost Felicity's life—a year and a half later, he still couldn't control a shiver at the memory—and sandwiched as it was between the Christmas holidays and the start of a new college term—had been a brief, if very special, few days in York.

They had been denied the true sense of a secluded getaway that most newlyweds enjoyed. That was what he was hoping for on this journey. He pictured in his mind the visions he had cherished ever since he had booked their passage from one side of the vast North American continent to the other aboard the *Canadian*. Four days on the train, just the two of them, only obliged to leave their tiny roomette to go to the dining car. Well, and for other basic necessities. If only he could have managed a higher grade compartment with *en suite* facilities. Still, the view would be the same. And most importantly, the time secluded with Felicity would be the same.

The same except for the bunk beds. Still, with only a few lectures to give at each venue—and on topics he was so well acquainted with—he would be truly free to concentrate on Felicity. And the manuscript they—well, Felicity—had agreed to work on for Father Peter... he shook his head at his beloved's ready willingness to get involved. Still, she had assured him the translation work would require hardly any of her time. All the rest would belong entirely to them.

Bishop Nicholas' penetrating voice saved Antony from the temptation to let his mind stray to the talks he was to give. "Almighty Father... grant that, always having full assurance of faith, abounding in hope, and being rooted and grounded in love, these your servants may be faithful to fulfill their ministry. May they continue strong and steadfast..."

At the end of the prayer each newly ordained deacon stepped forward with a gold stole draped over an arm. When it was her turn Felicity smiled as the bishop slipped the stole over her left shoulder and clasped it together over her right hip—the vestment of her new office. The Bishop then put a Bible into her hands. "Receive this Book as a sign of the authority given you this day to speak God's word to his people, build them up in his truth, and serve them in his name."

Felicity returned to her seat and clasped this symbol of her new office to her chest with both hands. *Always having full assurance of faith, abounding in hope...* The words of the Bishop's prayer rang in her mind. The assurance of faith she wasn't always so certain of, but hope—ah, she liked that. She was always hopeful. Well, maybe not in the full theological sense that carried an element of certainty, as "in the sure and certain hope," as the prayer book said. But at least in the more common usage as aspiration. She was great at being a cock-eyed optimist. Which was what made her current case of ambivalence and doubt so difficult.

Still, the bishop believed in her, Antony believed in her, and suddenly, it seemed that her mother believed in her. That should be enough to go forward with. She had always adored Dickens' Mr. Micawber: "Something will turn up."

That cheerful confidence carried her through the Liturgy of the Sacrament and all three communion hymns to the final prayers. "Father, you have taught the ministers of your Church to be the willing servants of others. Give to these your deacons skill and gentleness in the practice of their ministry..." Oh, dear, gentleness had never been at the top of her skills. It looked like she was going to have to start by practicing her ministry on herself.

And then, the cathedral was ringing with the pealing of the organ and the singing of the recessional. The movement all around her carried her down the center aisle, processing with her fellows. She smiled, head held high, all the way to the great west door, keeping in her mind's eye the snapshot of Antony's look of love and the pride on her mother's face she glimpsed as she passed them.

Once in the flagged courtyard before the cathedral, she barely had time to blink in the early afternoon sunshine and take a deep breath in the midst of the milling crowd, before her family was upon her.

"Darling! I could never have imagined! Why didn't you tell me it would be like this?" Not surprisingly, Cynthia reached her first. "It was magnificent! You were magnificent! My little girl." Her voice was only slightly muffled by the hug with which she engulfed her daughter.

Felicity did her best to return her mother's fervor. "Thank you, Mom."

"I mean, I was so proud. As you know, I thought you were throwing your life away. Burying yourself. But I can see you were right. You'll be the most magnificent success. I just know it." Another overwhelming hug followed.

"Thank you, Mom." Felicity struggled to suppress her embarrassment as Cynthia's commanding American voice seemed to echo off the stones and carry to the groups of English families politely exchanging handshakes. "Dad!" With relief Felicity saw her soft-spoken father approaching behind Cynthia.

The congratulations continued around the family circle, her brothers Jeff and Charlie and Charlie's wife Judy, then Gwena, Antony's sister, who was opening in a new play in Manchester next week. "Gwen, Thank you so much for coming. I'm so happy you could get away from rehearsals." She embraced the sister-in-law she hadn't seen since the wedding.

Antony stood a little apart, chatting quietly to his beloved Aunt Beryl who had raised him and Gwena after their parents died. He stepped back to make room for Felicity and his warm brown eyes caught hers. Her heart fluttered in her throat, as it always did when she came unexpectedly on his special look. But she had to go to Aunt Beryl first. She embraced her gently, feeling the frail bones through the fabric of Beryl's lightweight suit jacket. "Thank you so much for coming. It means so much to me." Felicity wished she could offer the octogenarian a place to sit down, but the best she could do was to shift from her brief hug to keep a supporting arm around the thin waist, hoping it would be of some aid.

Felicity looked longingly at the one person in their group she hadn't yet spoken to, but she couldn't leave Beryl alone. And then her father was beside her. "Felicity, let me do the honors with Mrs. Sherwood. Your mother wants to get a picture of you and Antony." At last she was free to stand by Antony—with his arm around her—even if only in a most proper pose for the camera.

"And now one with the bishop, darling. He does look so splendid in all that gold. What do you call that hat thing he's wearing?"

"A mitre, Mother," Felicity hoped her own near-whisper would serve as a signal to Cynthia to lower her voice.

No such luck, however, as Cynthia continued eagerly. "And his cross—isn't that simply gorgeous. Darling, why don't I get something like that for you? It would look lovely with your gold banner thing."

"No, Mother. It's a stole. And only bishops wear pectoral crosses."

Suddenly, Cynthia seemed to get it. "Oh, sorry, darling. I'm embarrassing you again." She lowered her voice a decibel. "But

I'm sure he won't object to a picture, will he? I know I saw others."

Felicity smiled. "Of course, Mother. It's fine."

Bishop Nicholas matched Cynthia's exuberant smile and made complimentary remarks about Felicity for the course of three photos with Cynthia purring delightedly.

"We should be moving on, if you've finished here. I took Mrs. Sherwood to the car, and we don't want to be late for our dinner reservation."

Once again, Andrew rescued his daughter. Now she could really relax.

Chapter Two

At Felicity's suggestion Andrew had booked a table at the Three Nun's pub back in Kirkthorpe, just up the road from the Community of the Transfiguration which had been home to Felicity for three years. As they drove past the high stone walls around the community and college, Felicity reflected on how she had come to love and value the peace that had engulfed her inside that solid barricade. At first, she had chafed at the enforced quiet, at the discipline, at the unending routine of study and worship. Until it got hold of her. Became part of her daily rhythms. Part of her breathing. Now she wondered if she could learn to live outside in the 'real' world. To her, that enclosed life had become the real one—especially when it had repeatedly served as a refuge after the various dangers and escapades that had interspersed her life of study and prayer.

As soon as they were settled and had given their orders, Cynthia turned to Antony, sitting on the other side of Felicity. "Now, do tell us more about this lecture tour you're undertaking. It sounds absolutely glamorous. I am so thrilled that my son-in-law is becoming so famous."

Antony blushed and ducked his head, as a waiter entered

with the jugs of ice water the Americans had requested. Still, he managed with barely a stammer, "No, no hardly that. Really—um, er... merely a few talks. About British saints who are patrons of Canadian foundations." He paused. "At conferences in Toronto and near Vancouver. In support of the Ecumenical Commission. To strengthen ties between Britain and Canada..." He ground to a stop and ran his hand backward through his hair.

Well aware of his discomfort, Felicity took up the thread. "It really is fun how many times Antony has been asked to speak to groups since he did that series on the telly." She turned to him and said so only he could hear, "I always wanted to be married to a media star." He merely ducked his head again—as she knew he would. But she had seen the pleased look cross his face. Besides, she couldn't resist a little gentle teasing, and she was so proud of the enthusiastic reception the series he narrated on the English Mystics had received.

"Really, your daughter's scholarship deserves a great deal of the credit." Antony was always quick to shift the attention from himself. "Has Felicity told you about the rare manuscript she has been asked to work on and share with monasteries in Canada?"

Felicity grinned. Her husband's eagerness to move her family's focus to her had led him to bring up a topic he had repeatedly warned her to be cautious in speaking about. Father Peter had given her to understand that not only was the manuscript extremely valuable, but also the presentation at the Gregorian chant conference was to be something of a surprise.

"What's this, darling? Why didn't you tell us?" Cynthia was first to respond.

"I haven't had a chance. Father Peter only asked me yesterday, but I think it will be quite fun."

"Tell us more." Felicity was especially pleased with Jeff's interest. She always suspected that her older brother persisted in seeing her as merely the little sister. "Working on a rare manuscript?" His voice only slightly hinted at wonder that anyone would let her out with a valuable antiquity.

"Well, not directly of course. I'm working from a copy, but taking the real one to show to colleagues of Father Peter's in Canada." Pleased with her brother's apparent interest, she explained further. "It's to be used at some conference thing Father Peter is going to next year. The document is thought to have been written in Ireland, but it was discovered in Canada—at least, that's the theory because an elderly monk who had come to the Community from Canada after the war died recently and they found it among his belongings. Anyway, it's really interesting for me because I've never done anything like it since it's in Gaelic."

Jeff's eyebrows shot up at her somewhat garbled tale. "You know Gaelic?"

"No, not really. I did take one class on Latin-derivative languages, of which Gaelic is one. Well, within the Indo-European family of languages, that is. Gaelic borrowed lots of words from Latin because the Church spread to Celtic lands during the early Middle Ages. Like when Saint Patrick evangelized Ireland. Gaelic-speaking monks learned Latin and copied Latin books." Her brother's eyes began to glaze, but she did want him to understand.

"I do have an English translation to help me along, as well. I'm putting it into Latin. For the monks to sing in Gregorian chant at some big conference or something."

As a cork popped and waiters began filling glasses, all attention shifted from ancient scholarly topics to the champagne Andrew had ordered. When the glasses had been charged, Felicity's father raised his glass and said simply, "To Felicity."

When the ritual responses, clinking of glasses, and sipping were complete, Jeff cleared his throat. "Well, as we all know, the guy who comes up with an idea gets stuck with delivering the goods, and it looks like that's me." He pulled a long, white envelope from his breast pocket. "Actually, it's an honor to represent the family on this. I'm truly proud of you, Lissie."

"Of course, no one ever doubted your ability to get where

you were going—no matter how many times you might have skinned your knees on the way." Soft chuckles and knowing nods from Felicity's family filled his pause. "But your choice of vocation and persistence have been—well—rather amazing to observe." He cleared his throat.

"So, what I'm trying to say is that I passed the hat around, and we want you to have an upgrade on that trip you're taking." He handed the envelope to Felicity.

She stared in amazement for a moment, then lifted the flap on the envelope. The pictures of the elegant service accompanying the new train ticket made her gasp. "Thank you." It was inadequate, but that's all she could think to say.

"Nothing but the best for my daughter. And for you too, Antony," Cynthia added hastily. "I was delighted when Jeff came up with the idea. We couldn't have you spending all that time sleeping in separate bunks as if you were back in summer camp."

Felicity didn't know what to say. She was delighted with the prospect of comfort, and touched by her family's gesture. But what would Antony think? She knew he had stretched to the limit to provide sleeping compartments at all. She handed him the envelope.

She let out a sigh of relief at his instant smile. "Thank you very much. That's most kind." He looked at Cynthia, "Actually, I had been a bit worried about the accommodation. You're all very thoughtful."

Their starters arrived and the conversation became general. Antony turned to Aunt Beryl and asked her about the new vicar at her church in Blackpool. Across the table, in response to a question from Judy, Antony's sister was telling about the new production of "The Ladykillers" she was starring in. "Imagine me playing Mrs. Wilberforce—60, if she's a day. It's a great challenge." Gwena bent over, her shoulders rounded, head thrust forward, her brow wrinkled, and suddenly she did appear a good twenty years older.

"Yes," Judy applauded. "Mrs. Lopsided to a tee. What fun! I love the old Alec Guinness movie."

They moved on to talk about classic films while Jeff brought Charlie and his parents up to date on his latest project working for Mckinsey in London. "It's great, but I think it's about time for a move. I've been offered a position with the Los Angeles office that starts in the fall."

"That would be wonderful, darling! You need to come home and find a nice girl..." Cynthia continued to hold forth on her pet theme with her oldest son.

The room was getting stuffy. Conversations from diners at tables beyond their semi-private room swirled around, raising the noise level. The champagne made Felicity's head swim. "Excuse me," she muttered and left the table.

She had thought to go to the ladies' room, but then she glanced out a window and the peace of the woods beyond the pub property beckoned to her. A shady path led into the green with a promise of a cool refuge away from the noise and the pressure of the day. She slipped out the back door.

Just a few minutes, she promised herself as she strode across the grass. *Just to clear my head*. She would be back before the main course was served.

The air cooled several degrees as she entered the woods. Her breathing slowed and deepened. Her stride relaxed. Birds chirped in the branches overhead, and filtered sun highlighted the ferns and brightened the scattered wildflowers along the path. A rustling in the underbrush ahead indicated the presence of small animals. A few yards on, and the sound of traffic on the Leeds Road behind her faded. Perfection.

A mossy rock a few steps off the path was irresistible. Felicity sat down with a sigh and let the peace of the moment fill her. Now the intermittent birdsong was accompanied by the murmur of a small brook tumbling over stones in the ravine a small distance beyond.

Her mind strayed to the adventure ahead. She hoped she had

done the right thing in agreeing to Father Peter's request. But then, really, what else could she have said to a request from the precentor of the Community? And it did sound simple enough.

The request had followed on the heels of Felicity's readily agreeing to Father Peter's appeal for her to do a spot of translation for them. She could see him now, holding out two sheets of paper. The lovely illumination down one side of the first page immediately attracted her, but the text was in a language she had never encountered before.

"Oh, sorry. I'm afraid I can't translate that. What is it?"

"Old Irish—a form of Gaelic." Father Peter smiled. "No, no, of course not." He held out more sheets of paper. "You'll see it's well known in its English form."

She looked at it. "Oh, 'Saint Patrick's Breastplate.'" She turned back to the photocopy she held of the illuminated sheet. "Is this from the actual original?" Could she be holding a copy of Saint Patrick's own handwriting?

"Unlikely. Sadly, most unlikely. But it does seem to be a very early copy. I thought you might find it inspiring to have that alongside the English."

"So you want a Latin version from the English rendering of a poem written in Gaelic?"

"That's right. And if you could then just leave it with Father Conall, my counterpart at Westminster Abbey, which I understand you will be visiting in western Canada. He can begin work on setting your translation to a chant line and training his choir —as well as sending it on to Père Denis at Saint Benoit-du-Lac, who will likewise train his choir. The presentation is scheduled to be the centerpiece of the colloquium of the Gregorian Chant Institute of Canada to be held at Saint Benoit's next year."

Felicity thought for a moment. Yes, that was clear. She looked at the two pages of English in her hands. Adapting that to Latin shouldn't be any problem at all. "Certainly. Happy to." She smiled.

And then had come the codicil. "And just one other thing." He took a leather case off his desk and held it out to Felicity. "Of course you'll be working from the copy, but if you and Father Antony would be willing to take the original to show to my colleagues, it would be of great service to them."

"The *original* original? Where did you get it?"

"You remember a few months ago when our beloved Brother Finbar died."

Indeed, Felicity did. The ninety-some-year-old monk had never missed a single Office in all of her three years there. Always first in his stall; always last to leave. A life of perpetual prayer. Even now, she was certain his prayers were still with them.

"He brought it with him from Londonderry—the one in Nova Scotia, that is—when he made his profession some seventy years ago. Technically, as the property of the Community, it should have been in the library, but he was always allowed to keep it in his room. Now, though, it must become more widely available to scholars."

"And you want us—Antony and me—to carry it?"

"Of course I could just send copies, but it can be of great help to my colleagues if they could see the original."

Felicity shrugged. Just show it to them? How hard could that be? No problem at all.

The crash of a large animal plunging through the woods made Felicity turn. Could it be a deer? Or two? Then the sound of angry male voices made her realize her intruders were human. She slipped from the rock and drew back into the trees just in time as two men came around the corner.

The shorter, younger man shook the other's restraining hand

off his arm and growled an obscenity. His features flushed as red as his hair and he turned to walk away.

The taller man grabbed and jerked him back roughly. "No, you don't! I warned you what would happen if you refused." A shaft of sunlight glinted off the attacker's glasses, emphasizing the size of his nose, increasing the impression of a granite carving.

His large hands shot out and grabbed the other by the neck. Seeming without effort, he lifted the smaller man off the ground and shook him like a rag doll.

"Stop! You'll kill him!" Felicity shouted as she darted forward. The limp form falling to the ground told her it was too late.

And she would be next.

Felicity spun and blasted her way through the underbrush. Ever thankful for her long legs and ballet training, she leapt stones and fallen branches. An enraged bellow and the sound of branches snapping under thudding feet told her that the assailant wasn't far behind.

Feeling her lungs would burst, and praying she didn't stumble in the rough terrain, she broke out onto the path. Her own breathing was so loud she couldn't tell whether she was still being pursued. Her throat burned and she felt her lungs would explode. Still, she forced herself to increase her speed back to the pub.

Shaken and tattered, she burst through the back door she had exited so quietly such a short time ago. "Police," she gasped. "Call them!" She pointed at a guest at the closest table, absorbed in checking her email.

Then she collapsed.

Chapter Three

"No, I didn't see him that clearly." Felicity shook her head in reply to Detective Inspector Nosterfield's suggestion that she might describe the assailant to a police artist. "Tall. Very tall." She shivered, recalling how that height had meant long legs pounding after her.

"Yes?" Nosterfield waited.

Felicity tried to think. Did he have cold, blue eyes, or did she just imagine that? She shook her head, then remembered. "He wore glasses."

The pub owner had hastily installed the police in his office, as far away from his customers as possible. Sergeant Silsden, whom Felicity had met before, as she unfortunately had Nosterfield also, stood in a corner taking notes while the ever-bullish Inspector towered over his witness in the middle of the floor.

Nosterfield regarded her skeptically. "And that's the best you can do with a description—he was tall, maybe middle-aged, and had big hands?" He scowled as if he thought perhaps she had strangled the victim with her own hands. "Very convenient, too. You just 'happened' to be sitting on the one rock in the entire Thorpeside Wood that gave you a ringside seat to a murder." He raised a bushy eyebrow above a bulging black eye. "Back to your usual tricks."

Well, she had moved off the rock, but never mind. Felicity tried to focus. Surely she could think of something useful. They should be grateful that she could inform them about the crime before some child was traumatized for life by stumbling over the body. "Somehow, he looked old-fashioned." She closed her eyes and tried to see it all again—as much as she would have preferred to put it out of her mind. "Yes, that's it. He was wearing a hat. What do you call them?" She paused. "Like in an old movie. That's it—a Panama."

"Not much help, that. Is it? All he has to do is change to a baseball cap and he's home free."

But Felicity was still working on that picture in her head. "Oh, and he had a big nose." She drew a beaky nose in the air beyond her own face.

"Well, now, that narrows it. Probably not more than half the population of England has what they call a Roman nose." Nosterfield turned his own red, bulbous nose toward his sergeant. "Put away your book. We'll get nowt more here. Tell them they can go."

He was obviously so disgusted with Felicity he didn't even want to bother dismissing her himself, but she needed to explain. "Inspector, you need to know. When you say 'go'... That is, we're off to Canada."

The Inspector looked pleased for the first time. The jerky nod he gave to her statement gave her the feeling he was barely restraining himself from asking if they couldn't go someplace further. Or better yet, emigrate, maybe?

Antony and her parents were still waiting for her in their private room; the others had gone home. Felicity's dinner sat in the take home box Cynthia had requested. Felicity emerged regretfully from Antony's comforting hug. "Was it awful?" he asked.

"Nosterfield, you mean? No worse than before. The same bullying manner. I couldn't solve his case for him, so he doesn't want anything more to do with me."

"He's right about that! We certainly aren't going to have anything to do with his case." She could tell by the sound of Antony's voice he was worried. Going on past record, that was understandable, of course. He drew a breath. "We *can* leave?"

"The sooner we go, the happier he'll be. I think he's relieved we won't be around poking our noses into his investigation." She gave Antony a quick peck of a kiss before moving fractionally away. "Not that we ever did such a thing," she added hastily. "Well, not on purpose. It was always more like events involved themselves in us—not that we chose to involve ourselves in them."

"Nevertheless, darling," Cynthia stepped forward and enveloped Felicity in a hug. "I'm glad you'll be far away from any such danger."

Chapter Four

The minute they stepped off the plane and into Toronto's Pearson International Airport, Antony felt that he was, indeed, in a New World. Watching films made in Canada and America was as close as he had ever come to crossing the Atlantic. Truth to tell, he had hardly been out of Britain at all. He had only the haziest impressions of trips with his parents when he was young. Spain, France—mostly just memories of a dazzling sun feeling hot on his head, and Gwena burying him up to the neck in warm sand... They had gone to places his parents could sail to. Then, after the disastrous accident, his memories all seemed drenched in grey, drizzling rain in Blackpool. Aunt Beryl and Uncle Edward certainly hadn't traveled to foreign parts. Antony's traveling—in both time and space —had been in books.

Blinking at the clear light that filled the modern airport, Felicity and Antony pulled their roller bags past the barrier beyond customs and emerged into the crowded, glass-surrounded terminal. A tall, solidly built man with a fashionable stubble beard emerged from the mass of people waiting for friends and family to arrive. "Father Antony and Mrs. Sherwood, I assume." He came toward them with an easy stride, his hand held out. "I understand it's the Reverend Sherwood now." He grinned as he shook Felicity's hand. "Does that make you Father and Father?"

"I haven't had time to figure out how that works, but please call me Felicity."

"I'm Zachary Dundalk—call me Zack." He shook Antony's hand.

"Ah, Scots?" Antony asked.

"Father Scottish, mother French. That makes me a hundred percent Canadian."

Antony consulted the instructions he had received by email, regarding their arrival. "I was expecting Dr. Spaulding."

"Right. I'm the B team. General dogsbody for the conference. Dr. S—Spaulding, that is—was tied up. I'm his errand boy." He took Felicity's bag and led them through the airport as he talked. "We're delighted that you can be with us for both installments of the conference. We can't expect conferees to travel from one side of this country to the other, so it seemed more practical to drag our speakers across the distance." He flashed his winning grin again. "That's after dragging you across the ocean as well, of course."

"We're delighted for the opportunity," Antony said.

"Ever been here before?"

Antony shook his head, but Felicity told about growing up in Idaho and enjoying a couple of family trips to Victoria.

"But your first time in Toronto, as well?"

"First time east of Calgary," she agreed.

"And I understand you're taking the opportunity to see the country. That's splendid." Zack led the way through sliding glass doors, across a walkway and into the parking garage. "I was lucky. Got a first row spot." He pointed to a gleaming black SUV.

Felicity climbed into the front passenger seat as Zack held the door for her. "What a great vehicle." She ran her hand over the tan leather seat.

"Fearsome winters here. Have to be prepared. This baby handles great in the snow."

Antony noticed that it handled equally well in the traffic as they rolled down the highway. "Can't see it from here, Father, but the St. George Golf Course is over that way." Zack gestured with his left hand. "You asked me for locations named for saints that you could take your students to—I'm afraid you'll be disappointed. There's nothing much left of the old saints in Toronto. A few churches and name markers, that's about it. But I'm sure your students will appreciate your on-the-scene approach."

Antony picked up the hesitation in Zack's voice that indicated he might be somewhat less than sure; still, Antony firmly believed in doing what he could to make history concrete. He would just have to work with whatever was available.

At his invitation, Felicity told their host about the plans for their train journey between the two venues of the conference. "I'm so glad the schedule was timed so we could do that. It's a great opportunity," she concluded.

"Best way in the world to see the country," Zack agreed. "And you'll be going to Saint Benoit as well—before Westminster?"

Felicity proceeded to chat about their plans to visit the monasteries on each side of the country, but refrained from talking about her work on the manuscript she held tucked in the briefcase that she had hardly let go of all the way across the Atlantic. Antony was pleased with her restraint. The fewer people who knew she was carrying a priceless document the better he would feel.

They turned to drive along the edge of an enormous body of water. "Lake Ontario," Zack explained. "Responsible for the vagaries of our weather. You've heard of lake effect snow?"

Antony hadn't, so Zack proceeded to explain how living next to one of the largest lakes in Canada could cause enormous dumps of snow any time from the first of October to late March. "Farther out they get 'creeping ice' if the wind is right."

"What?" both his passengers asked.

"Yeah. Really weird. Like a tsunami, only slower. A wave of ice just creeps up from the river—right into peoples' houses sometimes. But don't worry," he shot his passengers a smile. "The prediction is for clear and sunny all the time you're here."

They had just turned north away from the lake when Zack pointed to the right. "There's our most famous landmark. The CN Tower, for the Canadian National Railway who built it." Antony regarded the lofty spear, seemingly piercing the sky with its pointed spike. "Tallest building in the world when it was built," their host continued. "Then Dubai out-did us. Still the tallest in the western hemisphere, though."

On up University Avenue their host pointed ahead—"There, Queen's Park. That architectural gem—or anachronism—depending on how you view it—is our Provincial Parliament building. Canadian Gothic Revival, they call it. Used on most of our institutions a couple of hundred years ago. They say it's one of our signature styles." His shrug indicated that he wasn't one of the "they" who made that claim.

A few minutes later they turned into Saint George Street and stopped in front of a castle-like grey stone structure topped with a crenelated roof. "Here we are. Knox College—your home while you're in Toronto."

"Knox? I thought we were going to be at Saint George?" Antony asked.

"Ah, yes—confusing that. Knox College is part of the Saint George campus of the University of Toronto. U T has three campuses: Mississauga, to the west—where the airport is; Scarborough, to the east; Saint George, downtown here."

Antony nodded. Right. Again, nothing concrete to serve as a backdrop for his lecture. Still, there was bound to be something in the Old Toronto ward to serve as focus. He had done all the homework he could to prepare, but it still wasn't clear in his mind. Thankfully, Dr. Spaulding had promised to provide a guide for his group.

"We've put you in a guest room in one of our student residences. Hope that will be all right?" Zack pulled their cases from his vehicle and started forward, obviously assured of their affirmative replies.

They were on the ground floor of a building that looked out on a green expanse across to other university buildings. "Plenty of time to settle in. Take a nap. Meet your fellow presenters tonight at dinner. Six o'clock at the Faculty Club." He gave Antony a schedule for the conference, maps of the university campus and of the city. "Oh, and my cellphone number just in case you need anything else."

And with that he was gone.

"I suppose we should unpack," Felicity said, "but I would love to go for a walk. This looks like a gorgeous campus."

Antony had actually been thinking he wanted to sit down, study the conference schedule, and organize his notes. But after nine hours in an airplane and half an hour in Zack's SUV, a walk did sound like a good idea.

"What shall we do with the manuscript?" Felicity regarded the locked case she had dropped casually on the bed. "I don't want to carry it with me everywhere. Of course, there's no reason it shouldn't be perfectly safe in the room, but..."

Antony agreed with her discomfort at the idea. "No, it's priceless. We shouldn't just leave it lying around."

He led back to the main entrance of the college, hoping the receptionist who had greeted them when Zack brought them in would still be on duty. She was, and was happy to put the small case in their safe.

Now they could concentrate on getting orientated to the Knox buildings, which was Antony's first priority—in spite of Felicity's impatience to get outside. At the back of the entrance, two flights of wide, stone stairs led upward. He led to the one on the left that should have taken them into the library. Since they were out of term time, however, the door was securely locked. They went back down, and up the other side to what his map told him would be the chapel. Also locked. They were able, however, to look through the glass in the double doors to view unornamented grey stone walls and vaulted arches leading to a large Gothic window of clear glass. Dark wooden pews, pulpit and altar completed the furnishings.

Rather than attempting to locate the lecture hall they would be meeting in, Antony led back down the impressive stone staircase and around to a grill opening onto a classic, vaulted cloister, each pillar between the open arches supporting a hanging pot of ivy, and beyond the open arches, a green courtyard with a fountain in the center. "Make you feel you're back in Oxford?" he asked Felicity.

"Almost." She smiled, recalling her much-enjoyed undergraduate days.

At the end of the cloister walk they entered another wing of the building—probably classrooms from what Antony could make out. A bit of rambling along lengthy, deserted corridors brought them to a surprise find. They stopped in front of a classical, larger-than-life, white marble statue of a woman, naked to the waist, her head held high, flowing tresses cascading down her back. In spite of her almost triumphal pose, she was bound to a tree trunk with rough ropes.

"Margaret Wilson, Wigtown Martyr." Antony read. "Look, Felicity," He stood back, admiring the statue and smiling with the joy of recognition as if he had met an old friend. "This is one of 'the two Margarets.'"

"Um, huh?" Felicity looked blank. "Well, if that's anything to go on, she was pretty. What a surprise to find a half-clad maiden in this unadorned building." She regarded the bare walls around her. "I mean, it's really beautiful in an imposing, rather austere way, but I've seen enough grey stone... Of course, from what we learned in your class, John Knox was way beyond austere himself, so I suppose it's appropriate enough."

"Felicity," Antony pointed at the statue again in an attempt to get his beloved to focus. "Don't you know the story of the two Margarets who were martyred for their faith?"

"I must have been absent for that lecture. But I have a feeling I'm about to do a make-up lesson." She gave him a grin that he was coming to know as her *I'm submitting for the moment, but I'll reserve my own judgment* look.

He chuckled. "I do appreciate your forbearance, but I think I'll save it to inflict on my class. Here's something concrete—well, marble, actually—but something to focus a talk on, and it's a grand story for a conference on ecumenism." He paused. "At least to the extent that negative examples are a good teaching technique—it certainly demonstrates the need."

Felicity's ready acceptance told him that his decision to move on had been a wise one. Just one more turn of the corridor produced an exit that deposited them back on Saint George Street. Now Felicity took the lead, striding past a variety of university buildings, and turning along Hoskins Avenue. By the time they had covered the length of Queen's Park they agreed that the nap Zack had suggested sounded like a good idea.

Two hours later, a five minute walk took them to the ivy-covered Faculty Club. Zack was waiting by the door to usher them down a carpeted hall to the dining room. With a flourish that seemed entirely in keeping with his free, out-going manners, he opened the door on an elegant room filled with linen-draped, round tables gleaming with silver and crystal. Their host led them the length of the dark, polished-wood floor to one of the round tables set just in front of the head table at the top of the room.

Felicity looked around at the large room, admiring its Wedgewood blue walls and brass chandeliers. "I didn't realize there would be so many at the conference."

"Not all conferees tonight," Zack explained. "A lot of academic and religious leaders. Even a passel of politicians who want their name associated with what this conference stands for. Good for the image. A lot of lip service for ecumenism—sounds like tolerance, integration, consolidation, harmony..." He shrugged. "What Canada prides itself on being all about —diversity."

Felicity gasped. "Zack, you sound like a skeptic."

"No, no. It's all perfectly true. As far as it goes." He held a chair out for Felicity to sit. "All makes for good press, so can't knock it."

Zack seated himself next to Felicity and, leaning rather close to her, Antony thought, proceeded to introduce the others at their table, all of them conference presenters: a monk from Westminster Abbey out west in British Columbia, where the second part of the conference would be; a sister from the convent attached to Saint Benoit's Abbey, to the east of them, near Montreal; and the director of the Gregorian choir at Saint Patrick's Church, right there in Toronto.

Antony turned to the Westminster father, seated next to him, and asked what he would be speaking on. The black-robed monk began explaining about his topic. "Ah, yes—'A Canadian Microcosm: Cross-fertilizations of the Faith.' It's a particular pet theme of mine as a Canadian. We do rather pride ourselves on our open, welcoming policies. We haven't forgotten that this nation has been built by people from all backgrounds working together. Now, that's exactly what we need in the church—"

His enthusiastic discourse was cut short by Dr. Douglas Spaulding, the conference director, who rose from the middle of the line-up at the head table and asked for silence. He gave a brief invocation which then freed the guests to turn to the bowls of chilled melon soup before them. Antony explained to Felicity that, as well as being a lecturer on theology and Biblical archeology at Knox, Dr. Spaulding was the head of the Canadian branch of the Ecumenical Commission which Antony himself chaired in England.

Conversation around the table became general, with all but the silent musician from Saint Patrick's chatting. Antony was glad when Felicity addressed the choir director as soon as Zack's attention shifted from her.

She leaned forward to speak to the quiet man, "I'm Felicity."

"Surindar," he responded.

"I hope I'll get a chance to hear your Gregorian choir. I want to learn more about the chant." Antony held his breath. He hoped she wouldn't go on to discuss the manuscript, but he needn't have worried. "All our Offices were conducted in Anglican chant at the Community of the Transfiguration, but I don't know anything about older chants."

The dark eyes behind the metal-rimmed glasses lit up, making the musician's face appear not only thoughtful and sensitive, but also deeply intelligent. "Yes, your Father Peter is well known. I have several of his recordings."

Felicity's reaction showed that this was news to her, but Surindar continued, "As you may know, Anglican chant grew out of plainchant at the English Reformation." Felicity's raised eyebrows indicated that she wanted to know more. Surindar continued. "It is an excellent example of what I will be talking about. My topic is the ecumenical effects of music. Today Catholics, as well as Lutherans, Presbyterians—all stripes of reformed churches—use the Anglican chant."

Felicity nodded. "That's a great topic. I don't know much about chant, but I'll never forget how surprised I was when I was in a Catholic church that sang 'A Mighty Fortress is Our God.'"

Surindar smiled. "Ah, yes, exactly—what was once the battle hymn of the Reformation is now a uniting concept." He was quiet for a moment, then added, "Perhaps you would like to come to our Mass at Saint Patrick's tomorrow evening? It is entirely done in Gregorian chant."

Felicity readily agreed.

The efficient wait staff removed the soup bowls and placed colorful plates before them. Antony stole a glance at his printed menu to see what he would be eating. The roasted vegetables and rice pilaf he recognized, but roasted supreme of chicken stuffed with spinach, feta cheese, and caramelized onions, in a chardonnay cream sauce was beyond his experience. His first bite, however, suggested that perhaps he had been living in a monastery for too long.

There was little conversation while guests enjoyed their gourmet dinners. As soon as the main course platters were replaced with Belgian chocolate cups filled with mango gelato, the chairman rose again to present the head table guests. First was the Chancellor of the University, a vivacious blond in a brilliant blue suit, who gave the conference participants a warm welcome. Next was one of Toronto's Members of Parliament. While she was bringing a likewise enthusiastic welcome, Zack informed Antony and Felicity that Toronto had twenty-five MPs who serve in the House of Commons in Ottawa.

The Member of Parliament was followed by a Member of Provincial Parliament and then the Mayor of Toronto. As each expressed their delight at the guests' presence in their fair city, Zack said *sotto voce*, "See, I told you ecumenism made good press."

Finally their Master of Ceremonies could introduce the Reverend Doctor William Bruce, Senior Pastor at Saint Andrew's Church in Toronto who was to give the keynote address titled "Standing Together"—which was also the conference theme. The speaker's youthful face above his full white clerical collar beamed on his audience. An unruly lock of curling black hair fell forward onto his forehead. The slightest Scots accent softened his voice. "Aye, I'm happy to be here to bring you greetings from the auldest Presbyterian congregation in Canada. We were established in 1830 direct from the Mother Church of Scotland.

"I think you'll agree that, as pastor of Saint Andrews, I'm especially suited to be opening a conference on ecumenism when I tell you that our present church was built in 1876 on one of the busiest corners of Toronto, as it still is today. In those days Government House was across the street from us. Upper Canada College was on another corner, and on a third was a popular tavern. The four corners were known locally as 'Legislation,

Education, Damnation and Salvation.' Now, you don't get more inclusive than that."

After his audience's polite chuckle, the speaker then went on to discuss the Biblical basis for Christians coming together and the importance of standing together in an increasingly secular society. Antony agreed with every word the speaker said, but had trouble keeping his mind from wandering.

The past few days had encompassed so much: the business of term end, arrangements for their up-coming move, the arrival of Felicity's family, her ordination—and then to have it all culminated with Felicity witnessing a murder...

Antony hated to think that he agreed with Inspector Nosterfield, but it did seem that his beloved had a propensity for stumbling across disturbing incidents. Antony couldn't be more thankful than he was for the three-thousand-plus miles that separated them from the scene of that unpleasantness. Felicity hadn't been able to give the police much of an identification of the murderer. But the killer didn't know that.

Chapter Five

Following Morning Prayer in the solemnly elegant Knox College Chapel, Antony met in his assigned lecture room with the conferees who had opted to attend his lectures. He welcomed them, gave a brief overview of the subjects he would be covering, and explained his on-site approach. Then he led them along the cloister and into the main building.

At the end of a lengthy corridor he stood beside the white marble statue of Margaret Wilson, feeling dwarfed by the larger-than-life replica. For a moment he held his hands behind his back, trying to think what it would feel like to be tied to a rough-hewn stake, knowing that the damp sand beneath his bare feet would soon be washed by the rising tide that even now one could see advancing up the bay. And to know that the water would continue to rise until one was washed into Eternity.

He shook his head to bring his mind back to the here and now, and make himself focus on the present. He had always found it easy to get lost in the stirring moments of history. They said that was what made him a good storyteller, when otherwise, he so seldom indulged in flights of fancy. But the group of perhaps twelve listeners before him, comprised of students in the summer program at Knox, clergy and lay members of the ecumenical council, and simply interested lay people who had chosen, for their own reasons, to register for the conference, were far more heterogeneous than his usual audience of ordinands earning college credit in church history. He could only hope they would be receptive. And that they would see the connection he felt that the two Margarets made with the "Standing Together" theme.

How much background should he give his listeners? They would need enough to understand where and why the events took place, but he didn't want to insult their intelligence. "I take you to Wigtown, Scotland, in the year 1685. A royal decree outlawing any worship outside the official Church of England, or Episcopal form, with King James II as head of the church, had forced those loyal to the Scottish Covenant, which opposed royal control of the church, to worship in secret." He hoped he hadn't thoroughly confused his hearers in his first sentence. Mixed expressions on the faces he saw staring at him told him it would be best to get straight to the story and let the events speak for themselves:

The word went round. The preacher was come. The MacLachlan farm —down Kirkinner Lane. The house boasted a large kitchen so the preaching could be indoors, a great comfort in the February cold with snow on the mountains. A great comfort at any time, to hear preaching indoors, since mostly the conventicles were out on the open moors under the sky with lookouts posted against surprise by the king's troopers.

Dusk drew on. The aged Margaret MacLachlan pulled the shutters tight-closed over the windows, lighted her daughter-in-law's best beeswax candles on the chimney piece, and covered the table, now pushed against the wall, with the gleaming white linen cloth she had woven with her own hands just the month before. "There, all's ready, Master Martin." The grandmother nodded to the frail, stooped man in the tattered black gown and limp Geneva bands.

As the preacher took his place before the stone fireplace, the shadows from every corner of the farmyard and field took shape and seeped silently into the house. Soon the room was full to overflowing with faithful Covenanters who would not bow to any but Christ as head of the Church, sitting on benches and floorboards, standing pressed against walls, and spilling into the passageways. All had gathered to hear the Word of God. The intensity of their belief was reflected by the light in their eyes, the tightness around their mouths, the whiteness of their knuckles as they clasped their hands in prayer, and the fervor in their voices as they chanted the metrical psalms.

Their fervent belief and the danger of their meeting made the air vibrate. The king's troopers were quartered in nearby Wigtown. There had been many arrests and fines already. Those who defied the claim of the king to be head of the Presbyterian church of Scotland; those who refused to submit to the introduction of Episcopalian bishops or the use of liturgy in their services; those who would not drink the health of the new Catholic king—in short, everyone in the room—stood in danger of feeling the mailed fist of a royal trooper. And the note of defiance rang through their chanting of the metrical psalm:

O Lord, my God, thou art my trustful stay:
Oh, save me from this persecution's show'r;
Deliver me in my endangered way

Lest lion-like, he do my soul devour,
And cruelly in many pieces tear,
While I am void of any helping pow'r...

Thou, Lord, the people shalt in judgement try:
Then, Lord, my Lord, give sentence on my side
After my clearness and my equity.

Perhaps many thoughts in the room turned to the family of Gilbert Wilson, a prosperous farmer from just over the next glen. Wilson's three children—Agnes, 13, Tom, 16, and Margaret, 18—after a short imprisonment, had fled into the mountains rather than conform to vain religion. Wilson was staggering under the weight of crushing fines and worry for his children. Who in this room would be next?

Oh, let their wickedness no longer bide
From coming to the well-deservéd end:
But still be thou to just men justest guide.

It was not so much a sound as a vibration. There was a tremble of the earth that held the throat and made the room fall silent. Those nearest the front dowsed the candles. The black of the night entered with the wide-flung door. A strong hand seized Master Wills and drew the aged preacher down the passage along with many of the shadowy forms melting from the room before the first soldier's boot rang on the floorboards. But Margaret MacLachlan, true to the habits of her long lifetime, stayed on her knees. She would not be run from her own fireside or the worship of her God by any man, be he the king himself.

The sixty-three-year-old widow was imprisoned in Wigtown's tolbooth with little food, a straw pallet for a bed, and not even a light to read the Holy Scriptures.

Antony paused and surveyed his listeners. This was a long story—and not even about one of Toronto's founding saints as his course description promised. He didn't want to lose them with his first lecture. Reassured by the intent look on most of the faces, he took a breath and continued.

. . .

"I'm so cold, Meg." Agnes Wilson gripped her sister's hand and tried to keep herself from shivering by sheer force of her will. It didn't work. Her teeth would chatter no matter how fiercely she gritted them together.

"It's just a little further, dear." Margaret put her arm around her little sister whose last bout of the grippe had driven them from the cave where they had been hiding with their fellow believers. "As soon as it's dark we can slip into Goodwyfe Stuart's kitchen. She's sure to have a grand blazing fire. Remember how kind she always was to us when you were a wee bairn? If you close your eyes you can almost feel the warmth now."

Agnes relaxed a fraction at the thought. "Aye. 'Tis a fine thing. But won't it be dangerous? What if we're taken up again?"

"Nay, nay. Everyone says the persecution's nae so bad now that King Charles is dead. And we'll be meeting friends. Look, there's young Patrick now. I swear he's grown almost as tall as our Tom."

Their childhood acquaintance waved to them, and they slipped across the deserted market square. The Stuart household was a busy place. Friends and family gathered there regularly to share the latest gossip, and Goodwyfe Stuart kept her servants busy serving their guests. Delighted, Agnes held her hands out to the fire, which crackled even more warmly than she had imagined. The lights reflected in Margaret's long, blond tresses as she pushed back the dark hood of her cloak and then unbound the coarse woolen shawl from around her head.

"Ye puir wee lambs, yer that frozen!" Mistress Stuart fussed about, moving their chairs closer to the fire and urging them to eat more of her freshly baked oat bannocks.

Around the crisp, tasty mouthfuls, Margaret answered her host's questions about their travels through Carrick and Galloway with their brother and the others they had joined. Margaret was relaxed and open, assured she was among friends, and yet cautious not to give away the location of the outlawed Covenanters they had left. Agnes was dozing in her chair, the firelight turning her cheeks pink and gold, when Patrick jumped to his feet. "Och, and what am I thinking? You here gone sae long, and we no offer ye any better drink than warm milk?"

Margaret started to protest that the milk was delicious when Patrick set a pitcher of cider next to the pewter beakers on the table. The amber liquid sparkled as he filled the cups and passed them around to all the company. Seizing his he held it aloft. "The King!"

Margaret drew her hand back as if the cup had become an adder. "Patrick! I thought ye were our friend. How can you urge us to do that which is not warranted by Scripture? Such would be contrary to Christian moderation." Margaret felt Agnes tremble beside her. She clasped her sister's hand for courage. Both girls were all too aware that refusal to drink the king's health was tantamount to treason.

Patrick gave them a long, hard stare, then emptied his tankard at one gulp. He set the empty cup down with a clatter and wiped his mouth with the back of his hand. "Well, then, I see that yer time in exile has nae taught ye the error of yer Covenanter ways." Muttering about seeing to the cows he turned on his heel and ambled from the room. Although conversation continued around the fire, Margaret felt a chill in the air deeper than the mere opening of the door.

They should leave. But where could they go? They could not go home. A hundred King's Troopers had been quartered on their father's farm and their parents charged on their highest peril that they should neither house their defiant children nor give food to them, speak to them, or see them. The country people were ordered by law to pursue them. And delicate little Agnes could not endure many more nights living in caves as the outcasts had been doing. But before Margaret could form a plan the door flung open again and the heavy boots of King James' Troopers stomped across the floor.

Antony paused, aware of a small movement at the back of the group. He was surprised to see Dr. Spaulding had joined the group. Hoping the director would approve of his impromptu addition to the curriculum, he continued.

. . .

Margaret and Agnes were thrown into prison along with Margaret MacLachlan and a twenty-year-old serving maid Margaret Maxwell. There they lay until their trial on 13 April in the tolbooth.

The four women were hauled roughly before the assize court on charges of "Treason... and being present at twenty field-conventicles." They all steadfastly refused to take the Abjuration Oath forswearing their heretical opinions.

Judge Grierson of Lagg was well known as a violent persecutor of the Covenanters. He ordered that they should receive sentence on their knees. "Sir, we bow the knee to no man." Margaret MacLachlan spoke first.

"Only to God." Margaret Wilson raised her chin as she spoke in a voice that rang to the back of the crowded room.

Grierson grew red in the face. "I'll not be defied by a pack of heretical women. Kneel!" The women were thrust to their knees and held there by red-coated troopers.

"Margaret MacLachlan, widow, sixty-three years of age; to die by drowning. Margaret Maxwell, serving maid, twenty years of age, to be flogged publicly through the streets of Wigtown three days in succession, and to stand each of these days for an hour in the stocks. Agnes Wilson, thirteen years of age, her father, Gilbert Wilson, to pay one hundred pounds bond for her." The hush in the courtroom turned to the chill silence of the grave as the judge paused for breath. "Margaret Wilson, farmer's daughter, eighteen years of age, to die by drowning."

The room broke into a furor of protest. Gilbert Wilson rushed forward and grabbed his elder daughter's arm before the guard pushed him away. "Do not despair, daughter. I ride this instant to Edinburgh. I shall appeal this infamy. Trust in the Lord." Margaret was dragged from the room, her head still held high.

By the time Gilbert Wilson returned it was all over.

Margaret Maxwell's sentence was carried out first. For three days she was flogged through the streets of Wigtown. The citizens showed their sympathy for her by refusing to look on her shame. For all the time of her *punishment there was scarce one open door or window to be seen in the entire town. No leering men, laughing girls or stone-throwing boys accompanied her exposure. On the last day the hangman who had been ordered to scourge her, seeing that no one was looking on, proposed that his officers should shorten the hour of whipping. "No!" she said. "Let the clock go on." Margaret Maxwell was neither wearied nor ashamed.*

Then, on 11th May, 1685, the two Margarets—Margaret of the flaxen hair and Margaret of the grey—were taken from their prison and marched between soldiers past the stone church on the hill with its wide green graveyard, down the narrow, curving lane to the banks of the Blednoch Burn. At that hour the river was nothing more than a soggy mud flat. But all the citizenry who gathered on the grassy bank that morning knew that when the swift-running tide came in, the channel would be filled with sea water from the Solway.

Two long wooden stakes had been fixed deeply in the riverbed. Margaret the grandmother was lashed to the farther out one, nearer the oncoming waves. The other, nearer to land, was reserved for Margaret the Maid.

The tide came in. The water rose swiftly. Margaret MacLachlan never uttered a word as the waves washed over her head.

"What think ye o' that, Mistress Margaret?" A bystander prodded the bound girl with his fist. "Do ye see the auld witch's struggles?" He gave a gap-toothed cackle.

"I do see Christ, in one of his members, wrestling there. Think you that we are the sufferers? No, it is Christ in us, for he sends none a warfare upon their own charges." Then, as the water rushed toward her, Margaret Wilson began to chant:

> But Lord, remember not
> Sins brewed in Youthful glass:
> Nor my rebellions' blot,
> Since youth, and they, do pass.

But in thy kindness me record
Ev'n for thy mercy's sake, O Lord.

Of grace and righteousness
The Lord such plenty hath
That he deigns to express
To sinning men his path.
The meek he doth in Judgement lead,
And teach the humble how to tread.

One comfort had been granted Margaret Wilson. She had been allowed to carry her Bible to the stake with her. Now, as she was but loosely tied, she opened the Holy Scriptures to her favorite passage. "There is therefore now no condemnation to them which are in Christ Jesus, who walk not after the flesh, but after the Spirit. For the law of the Spirit of life in Christ Jesus hath made me free from the law of sin and death..."

She bowed her head in prayer as the water reached her neck. It would only be a few moments now. "Help me, Lord. I would see only you. Help me to keep my eyes only on you." *But the next face she saw was that of a soldier, pulling her head from the water with a handful of hair.*

"*Madam, now will ye pray for the king? Pray his health and ye'll be saved yet.*"

She blew the salty water from her lips. "I wish the salvation of all men and the damnation of none."

Goodwyfe Stuart pushed her way through the crowd of spectators and splashed into the water. "Dear Margaret, say God save the king. Say it. Say God save the king!"

Margaret answered in a voice far steadier than any around her. "God save him, if he will, for it is his salvation I desire."

Margaret's uncle stood nearby. "Sir," *he called to Major Windram,* "She hath said it. She hath said it."

The Major strode into the swelling water, holding the abjuration oath aloft. "Here. Swear it. Instantly. Otherwise return to the water."

The soldier pulled harder on Margaret's hair, keeping her above the water. "I will not. I am one of Christ's children. Let me go."

The soldier thrust her head into the water.

Antony surveyed the faces before him, most of them gazing raptly at the statue of the young woman before them. Should he say more? Be explicit about the need for all believers to work together? But, really, what could speak more loudly, down through the ages, than Margaret had spoken with her life?

Chapter Six

❧❦❧

As the conferees dispersed for lunch, Felicity stepped forward and slipped her hand into Antony's. Rather than taking her hand, he put his arm around her shoulder, and they stood side by side, gazing wordlessly at the statue.

"What did you say to them?" Zack nodded his head in the direction of the departing students. "Must have been pretty serious, judging by the expressions on their faces. Or maybe they're just hungry." He shrugged and didn't pause for an answer. "You ready for lunch? Richmond Station all right with you? It's a favorite of mine and not too far from your next venue."

Felicity blinked at their exuberant host, trying to pull herself away from the power of an event that took place well over three hundred years ago. "Um, sure. Whatever you recommend."

As they walked down the corridor she tried to answer Zack's initial question. "It was the most wonderful story. You should have heard it..." She tried to recount what had held her so spellbound, but her words paled in comparison to the shining image in her mind.

By the time they were back on Saint George Street in front of the college, the Uber Zack had summoned was arriving. A few minutes' ride toward the waterfront brought them to their destination just off a busy street. Felicity bent her neck backward as she gazed upward at the tall buildings of glass and steel all around them. Antony took her arm and moved her to the back of the sidewalk, out of the path of bustling pedestrians rushing in both directions.

"I thought you said we were going to Old Toronto?" Felicity's forehead furrowed.

"Yup. This is it. Old City Hall is back that way, Kensington Market and Chinatown to the west." He pointed in directions that meant little to Felicity.

Antony shook his head. "But there's nothing old here." His gaze followed Felicity's to the tops of the towering superstructures surrounding them.

Their guide laughed. "Therein speaks the Englishman. We think we have plenty of antiquities, but probably nothing that looks old to you. In your terms we are so young—just a baby city. Of course, a lot of our old buildings were bulldozed to make way for the modern."

"And columns of mirrors put in their place." Antony spoke almost under his breath, but Felicity heard him.

"This *is* where Old Toronto was. So yes, I'm sorry, it's the best we can do. I'm afraid today Old Toronto is simply downtown Toronto. It's one of the most densely populated areas in North America with over eight thousand people to the square mile."

Felicity, who had been expecting cobbled streets and quaint Victorian buildings, regarded the sunshine reflecting silver from every building, in every direction. "It's amazing that a city of three million people could look like a fairyland."

Her reply seemed to please their host who led them into the busy restaurant. Zack was apparently known to the staff because they were instantly led to a table, in spite of the fact that others were waiting. Felicity and Antony both agreed to Zack's suggestion of Station Burgers with rosemary fries.

While awaiting their food, Zack held forth on how apropos it was that the opening sessions of this continuing conference should be in Toronto. "It is said that if New York and Amsterdam had a love child it would be Toronto. I'm not quite sure what that means, except that Toronto prides itself on standing for the fusion that is supposed to be all of Canada. Kensington Market was predominantly a Jewish community, then you have Little Italy, then the Irish section." He looked at Felicity. "Of course, you'll be aware that a lot of escaping American slaves came here, as well as to other places in Canada. And then draft protesters from across the border in the Vietnam War era."

Zack paused for Father Antony's brief blessing when their food arrived. Felicity dipped one crisp, hot fry in the garlic aioli and savored it as their guide continued enthusiastically, "I like to think we're the most diverse city in the world. We have three Chinatowns because so many Chinese laborers came here in the 1920s to build the railroad." He paused. "Of course, at that time they lumped all Asian people together, no matter where they came from. They were denied citizenship until 1947. But then, multiculturism really began to flourish here in the l970s and 80s. So, as I said, a great place for a conference on bringing people together.

"I may be prejudiced, of course. I'm one of those rare things—a Toronto native. I love it here. All cities have flaws, and I'm sure we do, too, but there's so much great stuff here." He expanded on what was apparently his favorite subject, then added, "Only city I know that comes close to it is Montreal. I like to visit there."

Antony brought their host back to the topic by asking for an explanation of the old wards, which their host gave in between bites of his burger. At the end Antony asked Zack if he would give that introduction to his class, as it formed the reason behind the "on location" talks he would be giving over the next two days.

"Or would everyone know that already? Maybe it's just my being from across the pond that makes it all news."

"It's news to me," Felicity said.

Zack grinned. "Okay, I confess—I had to look it all up. I don't think anyone knows this stuff anymore."

Antony sighed. *Or cares?* He added internally.

A short time later, when the group assembled on the corner of Simcoe and King streets in front of the Romanesque, golden brick Saint Andrew's Church, Zackary stepped forward to give his introduction. Felicity smiled at his evident pleasure and winked at Antony for his tact in giving their guide an opportunity to display his abundant local knowledge.

"When the land that now comprises this city was purchased from the Mississaugas by the British Crown in 1787, it was called Fort York. It wasn't until 1834 that the name Toronto was applied. The name means 'meeting place' in the Huron language. Whether it was for the many indigenous tribes that lived in the area or for the major waterways that meet here is unclear. But we still like to think of ourselves as a great place to meet."

Felicity noticed several local conferees smiling and nodding their heads. Others were scribbling notes as conscientiously as if they would later be tested on it.

"Father Antony has asked me to explain about the old wards which served as administrative districts for the small population huddled around the waterfront. Four of them were named for the British saints who were patrons of the countries many of the settlers had come from: Saint Andrew of Scotland," he indicated the surrounding area with a sweep of his arm. "Saint Patrick of Ireland, the area north of us," again he pointed. "Saint George of England, south of here to the lakefront; Saint David of Wales, to the north east; and, I should add, one Roman saint, Lawrence, whose area was east of Saint George to the lakefront.

"These old wards have been replaced by twenty-five modern

wards which primarily serve as voting districts. Father Antony asked me to show you what there is of the saints in the old wards, which I will attempt to do, but the truth is, there's very little left to show."

On that somewhat deflating note, Zack stepped down for Antony to take front and center on the stone landing at the top of the steps leading up to the church. Felicity looked from Antony to the church behind him. He was standing before the center of three rounded archways surrounding the church doors under a magnificent rose window. She had to smile when she spotted the CN Tower in the background beyond the sturdy corner turret. What an appropriate symbol of this city—the old and the new.

Still, she worried, and from the furrow in Antony's brow she could tell that he was concerned as well. She knew the whole premise of his lectures was to present the qualities these saints stood for as appropriate bases for building a modern community. But there was so little concrete. She could only hope that the saints' names cropping up in subway stations, churches and schools could give Antony's stories relevance for the conference topic—and more importantly—for the conferees' lives.

He cleared his throat.

The noise of the taunting crowd behind him faded to a mere murmur in Andrew's ears. A soldier of the occupying Roman army in Patras seized his arm with a rough grip, then thrust him toward the X-shaped Greek cross. Andrew's mind flooded—not with fearful visions of the hours of agony ahead of him as he would die, slowly suffocating to death, bound on these rough beams—but rather with images of joy and peace from the years behind him: Fishing on the Sea of Galilee with his brother Simon Peter, then that moment when the simple wandering prophet, whom they came to know and love as Jesus Christ, called Andrew and his brother to follow him and become fishers of men. How strange it seemed, even now, that Andrew had immediately recognized this stranger as the Messiah for whom his people waited. Andrew had responded first, had out-run his impetuous brother to respond to the call, and so had become known as the first-called.

Those three glorious years spent following Jesus, listening to his preaching, witnessing his miracles, learning from his teaching flashed through Andrew's mind. To be followed as quickly by the vivid memory, that came like a stabbing pain, of the crucifixion. And the shameful memory of Andrew, with the other disciples, turning away, leaving their friend to suffer and die alone. And then the unspeakable joy of Easter morning, when the truth of all Jesus had taught dawned on them with the news of his resurrection.

"You shall be witnesses of me to the uttermost parts of the world," their risen Lord had told them before he ascended to heaven. And Andrew had. Even as the soldiers approached to lash him to the saltire, bursts of memory took Andrew to Scythia, Novgorod, Byzantium—all the places Andrew had been privileged to carry the Gospel in the almost thirty years after his Savior's death.

Soldiers grabbed him on each side and thrust him on the cross. "No, no!" Andrew struggled to get up. "I am not worthy. Not to die in the same position as my Lord." The soldiers stopped, even as the leather thongs descended toward Andrew's wrists. "Please, head down, I beg you. I am not worthy."

The soldiers thought it a great jest. Something to brag about in the tavern over a beaker of sour beer. Besides, it should be a more painful death. Laughing raucously, they spun Andrew around. The lashes cut deep into his wrists and ankles.

Antony paused. Around Felicity listeners shifted their positions, coughed, or took a deep breath, as if they had had forgotten to breathe. Some scribbled hurried notes on the blank pages they held.

"Today the relics of Saint Andrew remain in Patras in Greece and in Amalfi Cathedral in Italy. At least, some of the relics."

Antony gave a brief nod, indicating that his story was about to change venue.

"The story goes, though, that, in the eighth century, at a time of turmoil in the church, a monk now known as Saint Regulus, or Rule, whose job it was to guard Andrew's relics, was warned by an angel in a dream to take the saint's bones 'to the ends of the earth' to protect them from being used as a pawn in the power struggle between Rome and Constantinople. Indeed, the land that was to become Scotland fit that requirement.

"Obedient to the angel's warning, Rule took the precious remains—smuggling them in a bale of hemp, some say—and boarded a trading vessel for the west. The ship was caught in a sudden violent storm. When the vessel found safe anchorage in the harbor of a small settlement on the southeast coast of the land we now call Scotland, Rule led all aboard in a service of thanksgiving. Then, knowing with a certainty that, hitherto, the Lord had led him, he put ashore in a coracle with his sacred charge.

"Years later, about 841, Kenneth MacAlpin, King of Dalriada in the far west of Scotland, seeking a way to unite his kingdom with that of Alba in the west, arrived at the monastery of Kilrimont, which has become the city of Saint Andrews. Finguine, the head of the community of monks and hermits, met this mighty ruler from the neighboring kingdom and acquiesced to his request to see the sacred relics the community guarded."

Finguine led Kenneth not to the church, as the king had expected, but to a small wicket gate in the turf wall on the seaward side of the enclosure, where a steep path led down the rock face toward a pebbled beach. Just before they reached the level ground, Finguine indicated a small, damp-looking cave to their left.

"Saint Rule's cave, where he first placed the relics of Saint Andrew until he could build his church," the monk explained.

The cave stood empty now, save for the flicker of a single rush-light, which Finguine said one of their brothers always kept lighted. "Brother Ekeld. It is his duty to see to the precious relics of Saint Andrew, just as it was the duty of Saint Rule at Patras, and so will there always be one of our brotherhood to care so for our holy charge."

Now Finguine turned his steps back up the path. "Saint Rule ministered here for thirty years and established the greatness of Kilrimont." The abbot looked at the crumbled wall of the enclosure, at the monks' cells in need of repair. "Well, the work has fallen on bad days, but it was great —and it can be again. Kilrimont, the Church of the Royal Mount, can become a center of holy fire to shine out across all Alba and call men back to the true faith."

He turned toward the church. It, at least, had not been allowed to fall into disrepair. It stood a sturdy rectangle of pale amber, clay-daubed wattle and had a well-trimmed, thickly thatched roof above the small monks' cells, just as a king's hall house would stand above the other buildings at a royal dun.

Inside the small sanctuary, dust motes danced in the bright beam from the high window and fell on the simple altar adorned only with silver cross, chalice, and monstrance. But there was nothing simple about the carved stone casket that held the most elevated position in the room against the eastern wall.

Kenneth admired the sarcophagus from every side. The end panels were ornately engraved sun crosses, with angels kneeling over the top, and intricate boss patterns adorning the spaces on either side of each cross as if studded with jewels. The long front panel was framed at each end with interwoven, elongated animal bodies. In the center was a richly carved portrayal of scenes from the life of King David.

The king was stunned. Even in a nation renowned for its rock carving, as his Pictish hosts were, such workmanship seemed near to miraculous. "Never have I seen animals portrayed so realistically. Look—the wool on the sheep, the muscles of the lion, the delicacy of the dog's legs..." He rested his hand on the hip roof that gave the casket the appearance of a small church. "Surely such workmanship is not of Rule's time?"

"No, no. It is of this century. Ordered by King Óengus. You will be knowing that Saint Andrew appeared to Óengus before his battle against

Athelstan of the Anglians. The blessed saint told Óengus to watch for the sign of the Cross of Christ in the air. When the sign was vouchsafed, victory was the Picts'. In gratitude for winning a battle in which they had been greatly out-numbered, the Picts agreed to venerate the saint that had aided them.

"King Óengus it was who also ordered this abbatical seal struck." Finguine picked up a bronze seal from a small table and handed it to Kenneth. The seal showed Saint Andrew looking up to heaven, standing behind the tall, thin X of a saltire cross formed by two timbers lashed together in the center.

Kenneth looked long at the seal in his hand, thinking of the great wonder that such sacred objects as the bones of Saint Andrew should be brought to these shores by the very hand of God. Surely, a tremendous miracle indeed.

He thought of the journey the trading vessel would have made across the Mediterranean Sea from Greece, around the jutting land mass of Spain into the open waters of the Atlantic Ocean, then up the narrow channel between England and the Empire of the Franks—sitting late into the night, he had heard many traders entertain his court with tales of the dangers of such sailing. At what point, he wondered, did the storm capture Saint Rule's vessel? Certainly none could doubt that so perilous a journey had been guided by the hand of God.

But the next matter was not an easy one. Kenneth clung to his faith that he, too, was being guided by the hand of God in his desire to unite Dalriada and Alba into one kingdom. After his death Óengus had been followed by a string of nephews whose reigns of short duration had allowed the kingdom to become weak. Now it was time to bring these neighboring kingdoms together to stand united under one banner. But it would take more than that for a peaceable union.

Kenneth planned carefully. If the state was to unite, the church must agree. He called for Corbanac, the Dalriadan abbot of DunKeld, to join him there in Finguine's community. When all were gathered, and proper feasting enjoyed and lengthy speeches of welcome and acceptance exchanged, the king met the abbots alone in the church to present his plan.

It was several moments before Corbanac's shock at Kenneth's

announcement could find words. "Saint Andrew? Not Columba? You would make Andrew patron saint of this land?"

Kenneth's answer was gentle. "I know how great a disappointment this is to you, my brother. As it is to me, for I have loved and revered Columba of Iona from my earliest youth."

"Indeed. Columba it was who brought the faith to this land. Columba lived and worked here. Died here. Columba gave this land Christ. And Columba gave us his own life. What has Andrew done for Dalriada or for Alba?"

Here Finguine spoke up. "Can it be that you do not know the story? Know you not that it was our great Pictish king Óengus to whom Saint Andrew appeared in a shining white light. King Óengus was locked in a battle to the death, completely surrounded by the Britons who would have invaded our land, when a divine light shone from heaven and Andrew spoke to Óengus, promising him victory.

"After the victory of Óengus over the Britons, the Lord led him to Kilrimont, where he was met by Saint Rule, bearing the relics of Saint Andrew, and Óengus knew it for the fulfillment of his vision." Corbanac was silent. As was Kenneth. He had heard the story before, but it seemed Finguine related it with special power this time. It confirmed in Kenneth's heart what his head told him was right.

"But Andrew is already the patron saint of Russia," Corbanac argued still.

Finguine nodded. "Russia might have chosen Andrew for their saint, but God chose Alba to receive Andrew's relics. And Rule, who bore them hither, ministered for thirty years. Would you go against the choice of our Lord, brother?"

Corbanac looked at Kenneth. "And such is truly the choice of our king as well?"

Kenneth nodded. "Columba is Dalriada's patron saint, Andrew is Alba's. We are to be a united people. We must have one patron saint. Andrew was an apostle of our Lord himself. Our shores were honored to receive his relics. Surely, brother, you would not have us refuse so special an honor from God?"

And so was the nation of Scotland born of King Kenneth's careful weaving of strands from both traditions.

Felicity smiled at her beloved's gentle portrayal of his theme. She wondered whether he would make explicit the need for such careful weaving in today's ruptured church—in today's fractured world. As usual, though, he let the story speak for itself.

Antony was busy answering questions from his class, and it appeared that he would be similarly occupied for some time. She looked back down the bank of steep stone stairs and spotted a bench just on the edge of the grassy lawn surrounding the church. A perfect place to wait for Antony.

She turned and took one step downward. But there was nothing beneath her feet. She felt herself launch toward the cement pavement below.

She barely had time to cry out when she felt herself being lifted mid-air. "Careful. That would make for a nasty landing."

Felicity was too shaken even to thank her rescuer—apparently one of the conferees.

She was still shaking when he led her safely to sit on the bench. A fall just now could be so disastrous. It wasn't her near-calamitous mishap that caused her the strongest tremor, however.

It was the clear view she had of her rescuer as he rounded the corner beyond the church—a tall figure with a hooked nose peeping beneath the brim of a panama hat.

She took a deep breath and ordered herself to be sensible. Of course it wasn't the man she had last seen committing murder in a wood in Kirkthorpe. It was just that suddenly seeing someone who resembled him brought that awful experience flooding back.

Felicity lifted her chin and tossed her hair. She had left all that thousands of miles behind her. And nothing was going to ruin this special get-away time with Antony.

Chapter Seven

Antony held his hand up to the students surrounding him on the church steps. "Right, I'm really, really pleased with all your questions." He swallowed and forbore telling them how worried he had been that no one in this most modern, forward-looking of cities would want to hear his ancient tales. "But if you can put up with it, there is one more bit of the St. Andrew's story I'd like to tell before we adjourn to the pub." Then, realizing his reference might be too English added, "or whatever."

He looked around, hopeful of spotting a Scottish flag. That would give a perfect focus for the last part of his tale. At that moment a very cute young lady in a very short, red plaid kilt walked by, long red hair blowing in the breeze, perhaps making his point about the city's Scottish heritage, but more likely serving as something of a distraction.

Zack approached. "Need something?"

"I was hoping to spot a saltire." Antony continued in response to Zack's frown, "You know—Scottish flag?"

"Ah." Zack looked around as if expecting one to appear. "Too bad the World Cup isn't on—you'd see international flags everywhere. Um, possibly the subway station?"

Antony shook his head, thinking how difficult it could be to lose one's heritage, but Zack had warned him. "Sure, worth a try if it isn't too far."

Zack shrugged. "Five minutes." He turned to lead the way.

Then Antony spotted Felicity sitting on the bench beside the stairs. She looked strained, sitting stiffly erect, her face white and drawn. He darted down the steps to her side. "Felicity, are you all right?"

She jumped a bit at his touch, but managed a smile. "Sure."

"If you're tired, Zack can take you back to the room."

She shook her head, making her long hair shimmer in the sun. "No, of course not." She jumped to her feet and followed the group being led down the street by Zack.

Antony wasn't completely convinced there was nothing wrong, but it was clear she wasn't going to go into it right now. At the subway entrance he looked around hopefully. He hadn't really expected to find a waving blue flag with a white X-shaped cross. But there was a small badge embedded in a nearby wall. That would do as a symbolic focus. He shepherded his little group into an unoccupied wide space by a doorway, took a deep breath, and began.

Kenneth McAlpin led his followers to Scone for the final sett in the pattern. From the first it had been clear to Kenneth that the new nation must call itself by a new name and must march under a new banner. Already the mormaors and leaders of Alba were gathering for his inauguration, and the decisions must be made. And made right. He would have this new union be as strong and mutually fulfilling as his own marriage to his Pictish queen.

If the regional leaders accepted these new symbols of nationhood, if they took them back to their people with gladness, the weaving would be sound. If not, a raveling would set in at the first snag. But the choosing was a heavy matter.

With a furrowed brow that told his worry, Kenneth approached the problem with his queen Maia in the royal chamber that night. "I would not have the new banner be red or white, wolf or boar. I would not have one kingdom feel subject to the other. We need a new symbol for our new country, neither wolf nor boar. But I do not know what. The horse is Olaf's symbol, the dragon Gwynedd's. A bear, perhaps?"

Maia, in her blue nightshift—the color most beloved of her Pictish people—and with her waist-length hair falling over her shoulders, sat on the bed in the royal sleeping place in Scone and leaned against a cushion covered in softest fur. She patted the place beside her. "Have you thought that it need not be an animal at all?"

Kenneth laughed. "No, I had not thought. Always our people have used animals."

She nodded. "And ours also. Our carvers have a great love for entwined animal bodies. But we also use other symbols on our stones—crescents, mirrors, combs, rods, crosses . . ."

Kenneth was just sinking into comfort beside his wife, but now he sat up straight. "Crosses! Yes, we could have the cross of our Lord on our flag. A fine sun cross with a great wheel of light behind it, like the standing crosses that call men to prayer across our land."

Maia smiled. "Yes, perhaps that would be best."

He noted the doubt in her voice. "Did you have another idea, my heart?"

"You did a fine thing in choosing Dalriada's Andrew to be patron over all. My Pictish women say good things about you—even when they do not know I hear their gossip—and always they praise your naming of Saint Andrew. And so I was thinking, when I was a little girl Finguine would tell me often stories of Andrew, of how he worked among the people in response to the Lord Jesus' order, and how he ventured far into ancient lands taking the gospel to people who had never heard, and how he was finally crucified, but not as our Lord was crucified.

"That always captured my imagination—the picture of the dear saint lashed hand and foot to his saltire, taking days to die so, but preaching the gospel to the very end until weakness overcame him and finally his soul was freed to paradise."

As she spoke she traced the X pattern of Andrew's cross on the skirt of her blue shift, her white fingertip leaving an impression in the fabric spread over the soft furs.

Suddenly Kenneth saw it. He grabbed Maia's hand. "Yes! That shall be it. Neither wolf nor boar, not any animal with its roots deep in pagan meaning, but a cross. The cross of Saint Andrew—white on blue like your tunic." Kenneth smiled. Surely the Albans would agree if the banner was of their own device—a Saltire on a field of blue, reminiscent of the cross on which Saint Andrew died, as well as the one that their king Óengus saw in the sky—the clear azure that canopied over their own beloved land.

He paused as a tiny frown creased his forehead. "Your ladies, can they make sufficient dye? We will need a great quantity—our banners must unfurl as wide as God's blue heavens."

Maia's laughter filled their chamber. "Fear not, my lord. The woad plant grows in abundance. I shall send my ladies to gather leaves and set them a-simmering at dawn."

Kenneth was quiet for a moment, his former exuberance and worry turning to resolve. At last, a brief nod. "It is good. With this symbol Scotland will be reminded that it is called to be truly Christian." He pulled Maia into his arms and kissed her enthusiastically.

But suddenly she pushed him away. "What did you say? Scotland? Where did that come from?"

Kenneth grinned. His enthusiasm had betrayed his final step. But perhaps it was best so. "It came from my head. We must have a new name for our new country."

"Think you not that the choice might be somewhat one-sided?"

He grinned again. "I had feared you might think so. Yet it sits well on the tongue."

"Scotland, Scotia, land of the Scots..." She paused. "Yes, it sounds well..."

"It is a thread from the Dalriadan side. The saint, the flag, the high seat are all Alban. This is a balance."

And two days later when he stood on the small mound called Moot Hill in front of the chapel near the hall house of Scone Palace, so he told all gathered there. Behind him stood his faithful armor-bearer, proudly *holding the white-crossed banner that Maia had directed her women to make from the same weaving as her blue shift. And the wind fluttered it bravely against the woad-blue sky.*

"And so the saltire—the broken cross on which Saint Andrew died so nobly—shall be our official banner at Scone and at Forteviot and wherever the king of Scotia holds sway—over all Scotland. Perhaps even someday beyond that, for united in faith and purpose this Scotland will become a great nation."

Antony heaved a sigh of relief. It had been a huge load of history for these modern-minded listeners in this state-of-the-art setting. And no one had complained. Perhaps today's generation did want to get in touch with their roots more than they demonstrated outwardly. Or maybe it was just the famous Canadian courtesy. Either way, he was glad this first hurdle was over.

Now, for a quiet evening with Felicity. She had regained her normal glowing complexion, but the smile she seldom failed to greet him with still looked forced. "What do you say we go back to our room and put the kettle on?" Without waiting for her reply, he took out his phone and clicked on the Uber app. He had to admit, some modern conveniences were to be lauded.

A few minutes later, he handed her a steaming mug, then took the chair across the room from where she sat propped up on the bed. He waited until she had finished her first deep swallow. "Now, tell me."

"Just me being silly—tired—jetlagged..." Antony waited while she took another sip. "I sort of lost my footing on the steps. I guess. I mean, I don't really know what happened, but this man rescued me. Just plucked me out of mid-air. Really—I mean, there was nothing beneath my feet..."

Antony made short work of the two strides to her bedside and grasped her hand. "Felicity—"

"No, wait, that wasn't it. Well, that is, it was upsetting, but the thing is—I assumed he was a conferee. Just one of the listeners who happened to be in the right place at the right time and with really good reflexes. But then he walked away and I got a look at him. Of course, it was only a glimpse as he rounded the corner. I could be wrong. I probably am…"

"Felicity!" Antony suppressed the desire to take her by the shoulders and reset her as one would a stuck record.

"Well, it sounds so improbable, but he really did look like that man I saw in Thorpeside Wood…"

Antony gulped. "The murderer?" She was right. It certainly did sound improbable. But then his Felicity had never been short on imagination. "So he pushed—or more likely tripped—you. Then rescued you. Then disappeared. But what would he be doing here?"

"I know—it's crazy. It makes no sense. And I must be wrong. After all, if something is impossible, then it can't have happened."

Antony agreed with her readily—more from his desire for her comfort than from his belief in her conclusion. After all, something did happen. And for all her ability to jump to erroneous conclusions, she was extremely graceful and had extremely good eyesight. Which meant that she well may have been tripped and she likely did see the man correctly. After all, it wasn't entirely impossible. They had made the journey from England. There was no reason the murderer couldn't have, too. But why?

Chapter Eight

"Are you sure you want to go to that Gregorian chant Mass tonight? We could just find a nice, quiet restaurant for dinner and then have an early night." Antony tried to keep any note of pleading out of his voice. He knew Felicity would refuse his offer, however pleasant—and safe—it sounded to him. And, he had to admit, she did look better. The short nap she had after they finished their tea had obviously done its job.

Felicity stretched and smiled. "Mmm, sounds lovely. Exactly what we should do after Mass. But I can't miss this—besides promising Surindar, I need to hear the chant. It will help me on that transcription I'm supposed to be making for Father Peter's friend. I do need something of a jump-start if I'm to have it ready to deliver when we get to Westminster."

Antony shook his head, but he was smiling.

A short time later, Felicity craned her neck backward for a better view of the statue of Saint Patrick high on his niche in the tympanum between two square towers fronting the church. She was becoming accustomed to the grey stone Gothic Revival architecture, such as she had seen in Knox College and the Legislative Buildings, that was so typical of Toronto's historic structures. The distinguishing features of this building, though, besides the statue, were the four stone Celtic crosses adorning the front and the numerous gold crosses embellishing the dark wooden doors at the top of the stairs.

Inside, Antony went on into the sanctuary, but Felicity turned aside to ascend a steep, turning stairway to the organ loft, as Surindar had directed her earlier. He was seated at the organ, examining a hand-written score on the music rack. He turned in his quiet manner and welcomed her with a smile.

"I hope I'm not interrupting. If you need to prepare…" Felicity faltered.

He adjusted his gold-rimmed glasses. "No, no. You are fine. The choir will be arriving soon, but I can make a start on your questions. Then the best thing would be for you to join us for dinner after Mass. We always have dinner together on Thursdays, with choir practice afterward. Very informal, just potluck, but you'll be most welcome."

So much for the quiet dinner *au deux* Antony had planned, but this gracious invitation seemed like a golden opportunity to gain some much needed background for her project. She really felt a bit adrift at the moment. Her classics education had prepared her well to deal with just about any challenge in the way of Latin manuscripts. And she had done a little work with classical Greek. But she had never before been confronted with a work taken from Gaelic to English and asked to put it in Latin phrases appropriate for use in an art form she knew nothing about.

She felt so at sea it was almost impossible to form a question —her own lack of background made even worse by the fact that she was probably facing one of the world's experts in this rather esoteric field. She nodded at the manuscript her host had been studying when she came in. "Your own work?"

"Yes, the *Sanctus* for tonight. I do all of our music." He indicated a stack of scores on a shelf near the organ.

"That's amazing." Felicity tried to calculate. She had read that they offered a Gregorian chant Mass every day. Even if the choir repeated some settings this must require hundreds of compositions.

Because of the value of the document she was transporting and the confidentiality Father Peter had implied hung around the translation he had requested, she had been reluctant to talk about her project with anyone, but she could see no way except to plunge in if she were to learn anything. "You see, I've been asked to produce a translation from a really old document for the Gregorian Society conference." She paused. Oh, dear. Had she said too much? Well, too late now. "Have you ever chanted 'Saint Patrick's Breastplate'?"

He raised his eyebrows. "Mmm, that would be lovely—perfect for Trinity Sunday. But I've never done it."

"Has anyone?"

"Not that I know of—but there's no reason not to."

"Would it have to be in Latin? I mean, since it was originally in Gaelic, is it important to hold to the original language of a piece?"

"Ah, there's the crux of much of the controversy in our rather recondite world—some say you can't possibly do Gregorian chant in anything but Latin. The traditionalists." He removed his glasses and rubbed the bridge of his nose. "That's one reason Anglican chant is so much more popular—that and the fact that it's so much simpler."

Felicity nodded. How tactful of her instructor to bring the conversation back to something she knew a bit about. He probably sensed how overwhelmed she felt. "What do you think?"

"I'm more flexible. It's possible to do Gregorian chant in any language—of course it is. It's the flexion and the intervals that make it Gregorian. But somehow, it just works better in Latin."

"And what about accompaniment? The Irish wouldn't have

had an organ." She recalled their chanted Psalms in the monastery in Kirkthorpe—always with the organ setting the sustained note for the line, then giving the flex at the end.

A noise behind them announced the arrival of the choir.

"Again, a highly contended can of worms. The classic definition of plainchant is unaccompanied, monophonic—a single line, that is—sacred music in Latin. But the truth is, they were always innovating. There is a statue from the 1500s—about the time chants began being written down—of monks chanting while one plays the flute, so we know instruments were sometimes used. Bach was familiar with Gregorian chant; he used plainchant melodies in several organ and choral compositions." Surindar paused and looked around at his singers. "I, er—"

Felicity sprang to her feet. "Oh, yes. I mustn't keep you. Thank you so much."

She found Antony standing in front of one of the many altars that ringed the sanctuary. They found a pew in the rapidly filling church. Felicity was amazed at the number of worshippers on a midweek evening. As she tried to focus she was taken with the statue of Christ at the front, his arms spread in welcome, wearing green and orange robes—matching the vestments of St. Patrick, offering a blessing from his statue on the plinth next to the altar.

As the service progressed through its familiar parts Felicity tried to follow the music, to pick out the distinguishing features of Gregorian chant, but, perhaps because it was accompanied by the organ, it seemed to lack the characteristic simplicity of the single line she had been looking for. Lovely, but she felt more confused than ever.

She thought back to the story of the two Margarets she had heard that morning. Antony had told it in English, but surely the Scottish Covenanters would have sung their psalms in Gaelic? She had heard references to metrical psalms, but she didn't know what they were. Was this a form of chant? Maybe there would be a clue there to help her with her translating.

By the time she and Antony joined the choir in the church basement for supper she was bursting with questions. She even had her notebook and pen out and at the ready.

Their host introduced the visitors and they were warmly welcomed by the choir, most especially by Surindar's gracious mother whose pride in her son shone in her eyes. "Oh, yes, he works so hard. It is wonderful what he has accomplished."

"How did he get interested?" Felicity could understand a monk like Father Peter's interest, but this young, lay musician seemed like an anomaly.

Surindar answered for himself. "I went to the monastery at Saint Benoit-du-Lac for a visit. I thought I would stay a weekend and wound up staying for three years. Their life is centered around the chant and..."

He didn't finish, but Felicity thought she could understand. It must have been rather like falling in love. She had gone to a monastery for three years and, even though they would be moving on to a parish, it seemed she would carry the experience inside her for a lifetime. As strange as it had all seemed at first, she couldn't imagine having done anything else now, and she suspected Surindar felt the same.

The line moved ahead and Felicity turned her attention to the buffet. The variety of dishes was extensive and tasty, but she put only small portions on her plate, knowing she would rather spend her time talking than eating.

Once she was at her seat, she greeted the choir members around her and told them how much she admired their dedication to keeping an ancient art form alive, then she turned to the director, aware of the fact that the meal would be short since their rehearsal was scheduled next.

"I'm still trying to figure out where this all fits. Metrical psalms—are they a form of chant?"

Her instructor shook his head. "Just the opposite. Almost a reaction against plainsong, I would say. The psalms were to be sung in the common language of the congregation, so were rewritten to have metre and rhyme and fit hymn tunes and popular melodies."

"Oh, so if Patrick's Breastplate were to be sung in that style, one would just stay with the familiar melody."

"Exactly. You asked me about that earlier and I've been thinking that for an appropriately Celtic feel one should look to the Gaelic chant."

Too baffled to ask a question, Felicity simply looked at him, her pen poised, hoping for an explanation she could understand. Please, one that would give her a clue as to how to approach her task.

"Gallican was a plainchant that preceded Gregorian. It was used in Gaul, hence the name. The Celtic rite was closely related. Although most of the music has been lost, most scholars believe it influenced Gregorian chant. The main difference was the Gallican use of *melisma*."

Felicity's pen stopped moving and she looked up for enlightenment.

Surindar smiled. "Sorry." He spelled it for her. "That is singing a single syllable of text while moving between several notes." He gave a simple "Ah-h-h-h-h," his hand rising as each sound moved up a note. "The common name is vocal run."

Felicity nodded and resumed writing. Vocal run—that made perfect sense.

"That's opposed to *syllabic*, where each syllable of text is matched to a single note—as is more common in Gregorian, and as you would be accustomed to in Anglican chant."

"But one could have—" she looked at her notes, "*melisma* in Gregorian chant?"

"To a limited extent. But keep it uncomplicated, not over-ornamented. Keep your work simple, but don't be impeded by what the early musicians did. After all, they were innovators in their day."

The scraping of chairs around them told Felicity it was time for them to be moving as well. She thanked her host profusely, allowing her relief to show in her voice. She had started the evening too unsure of her territory even to ask an appropriate question; she was leaving with a whole new understanding, and, most importantly, a clue as to how to proceed. *Melisma*, she said the word over and over in her head. Vocal run. The word itself was so poetic. That would be the link between the flowing Gaelic and the stiff Latin. Not too many, she reminded herself, but a few extended syllables to serve as a bridge.

She was still trying to explain it all to Antony when they arrived back at their room. "I mean, I was just so completely blocked. I didn't have any idea how to go about producing a translation in a form I know nothing about. But now I see that this could help bring a whole new aspect to the chant—well, not new, really more bringing back some of the really ancient beginnings..."

Felicity continued to chatter as Antony ran the key card into their lock and preceded her into the room. "I'm just bursting to get to work on the translation. The fact that I'll be working, indirectly even, from an original manuscript—"

She almost ran into Antony who had stopped abruptly in front of her. "Antony, what—"

He silenced her with an upraised hand. "Something's wrong." He gazed around the room. "My papers. I put them in my briefcase before we left. I'm sure I did." He pointed to the littered desk. "And the closet door—I remember closing it."

A chill went down Felicity's spine. Details like that she would be unlikely to notice—or to remember the exact position of papers or doors if she did notice. But Antony—his fastidiousness was remarkable. "You think someone has been in our room? Why would anybody—" She stopped with a gasp. "The manuscript!"

"Thank goodness I had it put in the safe."

"Yes, but my copy. Would anybody steal a copy?" She lunged for the closet and pulled her briefcase from the back. If she were as careful as Antony she would be able to tell whether it had been tampered with, but since she didn't bother with a lock...

She shuffled through her papers, then gave a sigh of relief. "It's here." As was her passport and a small amount of English money she wouldn't need until they were back across the water. "It doesn't look like anything was taken."

She was relieved and yet, a small shiver lurked at the back of her neck. Antony was right. Someone had been here.

Antony finished checking the desk and his suitcase. "Nothing taken." Still, he frowned.

"So, why?" They spoke together.

Why, indeed, would anyone go through their things? It had to be someone who knew they had a precious artifact in their care. But who? Surely Father Peter would have told no one, and they had been so careful.

"I suppose we should alert the campus police." Antony sounded a bit doubtful. "Although we don't have any real evidence that anything happened."

"Still, I would feel better if they changed our lock—maybe just re-keyed it? I don't know how these things work. Do call them." Felicity surprised herself. She was never the cautious one. She had to admit though, her near fall earlier that day at St. Andrew's, then seeing that man who brought back such vivid memories of her alarming experience in Thorpeside Wood had unnerved her.

It took Antony only a few taps on his laptop to locate a number for the University of Toronto Campus Community Police Service. In a matter of minutes a young woman, her sleek blond hair pulled back in a bun, and a tall black man with a wide, comforting smile, were at their door. The two officers, in their dark blue uniforms with POLICE written in large letters across their shirt fronts, listened carefully to everything these guests of the university told them.

The male, Special Constable Adams, apologized profusely that such a thing should have happened to them, and his colleague assured them that, indeed, the lock would be changed and they would be issued new keys within the hour. "And we do recommend you keep the dead bolt and chain lock both engaged when you are in the room," she added.

Felicity nodded vigorously and wondered briefly whether or not she should tell them about the event she witnessed in England, or if she should mention the manuscript. But, really, both things seemed beyond their jurisdiction.

It wasn't until later that night, their newly keyed cards in the desk drawer and both interior locks secured, that Felicity relaxed sufficiently to think of going to bed. Only as she was pulling the covers up did she stop to consider—she had told only one person in Canada about the manuscript. But Surindar? The gentle musician? Impossible to think he could be involved in a plot to steal an ancient copy of "Saint Patrick's Breastplate." Or was his interest—support even—just a ruse to learn more?

She knew professional jealousy among musicians could be fierce, but this was unthinkable. Only when she realized Surindar would still have been leading choir rehearsal when they discovered the break-in, did she relax.

Until she asked herself who else knew?

Chapter Nine

The next morning Antony woke with a sense of relief that this would be their last day in Toronto. As interesting as it had been to see this vibrant city, and happy as he was to participate in the conference on unity, he would be happier to get a considerable distance away from whatever seemed to have been going on since they arrived here.

A look at his sleeping wife, her long blond hair tangled on the pillow, made him smile. But then his throat tightened. Such a responsibility to be accountable for the safety of another person —especially a person as likely to attract trouble as his Felicity. The sooner he could get her to a remote monastery in the Eastern Townships of Quebec, the better. But then, Kirkthorpe had been remote and she hadn't always been safe there. And the safety he thought they had secured by traveling across an ocean appeared to have been illusory.

"Mmmmmphf," Felicity stirred and opened one eye. "Why are you looking at me like that?"

"Sorry. Like what?"

"You were frowning. That's not the way a girl likes to be greeted in the morning."

Antony rearranged his features and was given a kiss as reward for his efforts.

"That's better." Felicity leaned back on the pillows. "You can make amends by making me some tea."

Felicity's smiling banter and a good cup of tea did much to set Antony's world right. By the time he stood before his group of conferees on the lawn in front of Knox College he was able to relax and enjoy the warmth of the July sun on his head. Perhaps a bit too warm, though, he decided, and suggested they move to the shade of one of the leafy trees lining St. George Street.

He ducked his head and gave a rather apologetic grin. "Well, thank you all for coming out here to stand on the Saint George Campus of the University of Toronto alongside Saint George Street to hear a talk about Saint George."

"Is there an echo here?" a wit quipped from the back of the group, and everyone tittered somewhat uneasily, perhaps fearing their guest speaker would be insulted.

Instead, Antony's smile broadened. "I think that rather helps make my point—all we seem to have is the name. The patron saint of England, undoubtedly of great significance to the early settlers from that green and pleasant land who had endowed the ward, the street and the university campus with the name, but left little to serve as a concrete focus for our subject, so I have provided my own for us."

He reached into the case at his feet and unfurled a flag of Saint George: a field of white quartered with a red cross, attached to a telescoping rod. "These days this is mostly flown in England by enthusiastic football supporters (that's soccer to you), but I like to think it can play a useful part in today's story." He pushed the shaft into the grass near him and a breeze whipped the banner gently.

"Very little is known for certain about the soldier who came to be venerated as Saint George, but it is believed that one

Georgis Nestor Anastasius was born of Greek Christian parents in Lydda in Cappadocia—which is modern day Turkey. The best accounts say that he was a member of the Praetorian Guard for the Roman emperor Diocletian. It is possible that the man we know as George protested when soldiers were ordered to burn the library of sacred scrolls at Nicomedia, causing him to be arrested for being a Christian.

"So let me take you to 23 April, in the year 303, to Nicomedia, the eastern and most senior capital city of the Roman Empire:

On the morning of the fourth day of his imprisonment and torture, guards marched into George's cell and yanked him to his feet. He prayed for the strength to stand unaided. He could stand, but his damaged muscles could not move his legs, so he was dragged from his cell. "Caesar says we're to clean you up. Seems he wants a pretty sacrifice." One of the guards laughed as he poured a bucket of water over George's head and scrubbed at him with a sponge.

The other guard dragged a coarse bone comb through George's hair, yanking chunks of hair out with the straw. Then they pulled a white tunic over his head and hauled him forward. At the door of the prison he was shoved into a litter and carried to the front of the palace. The Augustus Galerius—that fierce advocate of the old gods—sat on the highest step, surrounded by elite officers from the Guard. A large crowd had gathered in the street below. This execution was intended as a warning to all who would defy Caesar, so people had been rounded up from every corner of the city. It was not as great a spectacle as a wild beast show in the arena would be, but since a Roman citizen had a right to death by beheading, it was the best that could be done.

As George was lifted from the litter, he saw the world with a new clarity, as if by the light of a brightly burning fire that had purified the air of any smoke or dust. Lord, grant me this last favor, *he prayed.* Let me not suffer the ignominy of being dragged to the post. *He felt the strength flow into his legs. Pushing his guards firmly to the side,* he stepped unaided to the execution post. He made the six steps in triumph.

George grasped the stake in front of him and lifted his face to the warmth of the sun. A special golden light surrounded him, light not of this world, but the glory of the world to come.

In the first row of observers, Valerius, George's closest friend in the Guard, saw the aureole surrounding George. Then Valerius' attention was caught by a low, but firm voice speaking from somewhere behind him. It was Eusebius, pastor of the church that the Augustus Diocletian had ordered closed on pain of death. Eusebius spoke out with great courage, given fire by the man who stood before them with the light of heaven radiating from his face.

"And the dragon was wroth and went to make war with the saints which keep the commandments of God and have the testimony of Jesus Christ... And all that dwell upon the earth shall worship the dragon—all those whose names are not written in the book of life of the Lamb who was slain from the foundation of the world. But it shall be given to those who believe on the only begotten Son of God to trample upon serpents. If any man have an ear, let him hear.'"

In the moment of silence that followed, George cried out, "Fear not, my friends. If the spirit of Him who raised Jesus from the dead dwells in you, then He will bring your mortal bodies to life also through His Spirit dwelling in you."

Galerius jumped to his feet in anger and signaled to the executioner. The burly officer started forward, sun glinting off the sharpened edge of his gladius. But George didn't falter as he called out, "It matters nothing whether life is on earth or in heaven. Rejoice in that offering of yourselves to Him, whether for service here or above."

The executioner was in place, and the axe was swinging as George looked up to heaven and cried, "My Lord Christ, by your death on the cross you opened the gates of heaven. Admit into your kingdom one who hopes in you."

The flow of red blood made a stripe down the front of George's white tunic, and the rush of air following the return swing of the axe blew a red line across the first, forming a cross.

The gloating look left Galerius' face as Constantine, the fast-rising young legate and son of the newly appointed Augustus in Britannia, rose from his bench just below Caesar. The tall soldier knelt beside the fallen body and gently pulled off the blood-stained tunic. Holding aloft the pristine white banner bearing the red cross of George's blood, Constantine spoke so quietly that only those standing closest heard. "This shall be my banner, and someday I will raise it over the Empire."

A hush filled the silence as Antony stepped back a pace. The breeze increased, whipping the red and white banner beside him. As always, Antony pondered where to go from there. Good teaching technique would prescribe leading a discussion that let the learners make personal application: How is this instructive for a conference on ecumenism? What might the fact that so little is left of the saints say? For Andrew and Patrick he'd found churches and subway stations, for George, a street sign—was such disregard for heritage symbolic of today's society? Did it matter?

When Antony thought of the secularization of modern culture he shuddered. Christians were again—or still—persecuted in many parts of the world. Would simply making such stories known help combat that—or give strength to those who faced oppression? Antony decided not to raise that question—as much as he believed in the importance of concrete reminders, perhaps just telling the story was best. Anyway, it was all he could do.

Even if Antony's decision had been otherwise, the situation was taken out of his hands. Zack, who had been leaning against a tree on the fringe of the gathering, to all appearances bored and distracted, without warning stepped forward, seized the flag and hoisted it aloft. "For God and Saint George!" he cried.

He was answered with an echoing shout from all around him. "For God and Saint George!"

"Let's show 'em!" Holding the banner high with both hands, Zack led a parade up Saint George Street, followed closely by Felicity and the rest of the class.

Amazed, and rather embarrassed by such a reaction, and thoroughly confused as to what Zack meant by it all, Antony followed along. Wondering just how long Saint George Street was, and hoping Zack didn't mean to traverse its full length, Antony looked around. A cyclist in the pavement waved. Two students coming out of Whitney Hall cheered. A passing motorist honked. Well, Antony's goal was always to raise awareness of faithful holiness in ages past; it seemed he had accomplished that at least. Just how much that might translate into building faith for today was unclear, but perhaps he had planted a seed.

Antony pulled a white handkerchief from his pocket and wiped his forehead. The wheezing sounds made by a marcher behind him made him realize he wasn't the last in the column as he had thought. Perhaps one of the students had tired early and fallen behind, although he hadn't noticed that happening. He turned to say something encouraging to his fellow marcher, but stopped when he realized it didn't seem to be one of his class. Certainly no one he recognized. Some passer-by caught in the obstruction of marchers, perhaps? Should Antony apologize that they were holding him up?

Much to Antony's relief, Zack turned the corner at the top of the street. The stranger, however, continued in the cavalcade, rather than going his own way. Finally, their circuitous route led them, perspiring from exertion in the noonday sun, back to the dining hall for lunch, and Antony could forget the wheezing interloper.

When they had selected their meals from the buffet line and were sitting in the quietest corner Antony could spot, he turned to Felicity, "What was that all about?"

Felicity tossed her head and laughed. "I don't know, but it was fun, wasn't it? I had no idea Zack was so into the spirit of things."

"I'm not usually—really just a general factotum, me." Both Felicity and Antony jumped at Zack's sudden approach.

Felicity responded first. "Oh, you startled me. Want to join us for lunch?" She indicated an empty chair at their table.

"No thanks. Things to do. I just wanted to remind you we need to leave for the airport in an hour." He looked at his watch. "Say we meet at reception in forty-five minutes?"

"Oh, sure. Fine." Then Felicity let out a cry, "Eek, I'm not packed!" She swallowed two bites of her quinoa and kale salad as quickly as she could while Antony wrapped his turkey sandwich in a napkin for later.

In less than Zack's prescribed time Antony, Felicity and their tightly packed roller bags arrived at the Knox reception desk. Antony turned to the lady on duty to ask for their document case from the safe, but Zack stepped around the corner. "This what you're about to ask for, Father A?" He held the brown leather case at arms' length.

"Er—Yes. Um, thank you." Antony took the case and held it close. "But how did you get it? I don't mean to sound rude, but it was supposed to be in the safe."

"Oh, just trying to save time. Martha knows me well." He waved to the receptionist who smiled back. Zack took the handle of Felicity's bag and led them out the door. "Not a minute to waste. Lines at the airport can be fierce."

They were finally settled in Zack's SUV and on their way, with Antony still gripping the document case and wondering whether or not it would be rude to check its contents—not that he didn't completely trust the man who had been such a faithful guide for their visit, of course.

Before Antony could do or say anything though, Felicity,

whom Zack had ushered into the front passenger seat, spoke up. "That parade was such a great idea, Zack. It made our whole time at the conference seem like a celebration. How did you think of it?"

Zack shrugged. "Just a spur of the moment notion." He smiled at her. Antony refused to allow himself to think it was more of a leer. "Glad you liked it. Seemed to suit the whole spirit of the thing—Roman legions and all that."

Felicity laughed. "'Onward, Christian Soldiers,' you mean?"

"Something like that," Zack agreed. But Antony scowled.

"Hope you enjoy your time at Saint Benoit's," Zack changed the subject. "What are you going to do there?"

Antony held his breath. The question was directed to Felicity. He did hope she wouldn't tell this enigmatic man about her work with the manuscript.

He needn't have worried. Felicity laughed. "Pray a lot, I expect. What else does one do in a monastery?"

Zack shook his head. "Beats me. Great scenery around there, though. I hear. Couldn't be more boring than the closing speeches of the conference, anyway. I mean, don't get me wrong—Dr. Spaulding's a great guy, but he can run on a bit when he gets a bee in his bonnet about something like one of his archeological digs or this ecumenical gig." He chuckled. "Oops—sorry, not very tactful of me to be saying that to you, is it? Guess I'm just kinda tired."

Antony was more than happy when they finally pulled to the curb in front of the gleaming crescent-shaped terminal of the Toronto airport. He was even able to manage a smile and a "Thank you for everything," when Zack waved them off with a jaunty wave.

"See you at the other end," Zack called out.

Antony hadn't realized they would have Zack at the second session of the conference as well, but, of course, he was Dr. Spaulding's assistant. At least they would have the weekend at

Saint Benoit, and then five glorious days on the train, to recover from their hosts' exuberance.

A while later, as efficiently as modern air travel allowed, Antony sank down gratefully in his seat on the Air Canada plane. Felicity, sitting by the window, had already pulled out her book. He looked questioningly at the cover.

She read his query and held up the volume. "A contemporary murder mystery set in a monastery in northern Quebec." She grinned. "Coincidentally, they specialize in Gregorian chant."

"Maybe you'll learn something."

"I just might." She returned to her reading and Antony was thinking how good it would feel to sit back and doze when a prickle at the back of his neck made him shiver. Without stopping to analyze why, he leaned into the aisle to peer around.

Was it possible? Was that heavily breathing man from this morning's impromptu parade actually in the seat behind him?

Chapter Ten

Felicity had little patience for the nuisance of renting a car. And she had even less patience for the tangle of Montreal traffic as she maneuvered the little gray Datsun eastward past mile after mile of construction sites, each one marked by two or three towering cranes. Even with the congestion, though, it felt good to be driving. Antony always drove on the few occasions they took a car in England, but here in North America, it was her territory. Well, not exactly the French road signs, maybe, but the feel of being behind the wheel. Antony had readily handed the keys over to her—she was sure he was as afraid of winding up on wrong side of road as she would have been in England.

Once they were across the magnificent Champlain Bridge with its soaring, wing-like suspension structure, however, the *Autoroute* soon led them through picturesque farmland, then a long, straight stretch with tall, arrow-erect trees lining the way on each side. Felicity gave a sigh, feeling her shoulders relax. Then a sign pointing them to *Cantons-de-l'Est*. "This is wonderful! I feel like I'm in France," she said.

"I didn't realize you had been there," Antony spoke for the first time in many miles.

"No, I haven't. But I've seen lots of movies filmed in France." She grinned. "You can take me someday. Some place quaint and romantic with lots of rich food."

Before he could reply she directed Antony to rootle in her bag. "If you get out my phone and USB cord, we can listen to the Gregorian Chant I downloaded. I thought it would help get us in the mood."

"For romance or for the monastery?"

"Do I have to choose?" She shot him a saucy glance.

Smiling, Antony followed her instructions and the car filled with celestial sounds.

Soon their way became increasingly tree-covered and hilly, the farms further apart. After about an hour they left the main road and wound through a thick wood. Antony turned from gazing out the window and lowered the volume on the music. "And I thought the Community of the Transfiguration was secluded."

Felicity laughed. "It was far enough off the beaten path for me. When I first arrived I thought I'd landed on another planet." After more than three years there, she still couldn't quite take in the change that had come over her. "Other-worldly" still seemed the best word for such places. And when they returned to England they would be leaving their—their—what *was* the right word for it? Sanctuary? Fortress? Hideaway? Womb?

In the bustle of seeing the dynamic city of Toronto and participating in the conference, she had put her personal quandary aside, but now, here in the seclusion of these great pines, the question returned to her. What *was* she going to do?

Before she could bring the topic up to Antony, however, the lane swept to the top of a gentle hill and the magnificent stone towers of the monastery rose before them. Felicity followed the curve of the drive and came to a stop before a wing of a rambling structure that sported one of the lower towers. A small sign identified it as the *hôtellerie*. Before they were out of the car, bells began ringing from the tallest tower in the center of the building.

They reached the *porterie* beside the door inside the foyer just as the porter was pulling the shutters of his window together. "Uh, Father and Mrs. Sherwood," Antony said, stepping forward and stopping the closure movement with little more than an inch gap left to speak through. "We have reservations."

"*Oui.* Yes." The monk gave a jerky nod, opening the aperture a few inches. "But now is Vespers." The portal shut with a snap.

A moment later he appeared through the door beside the shuttered hatch. He turned with a swish of his robe and locked the door with an iron key. "Vespers." He pointed down a long corridor toward the church. "Then supper. Come back after supper. Leave your luggage here."

There was little to do but obey and follow along, while maintaining her firm grip on the manuscript case, of course. Felicity would have loved to take time to absorb the amazing architecture. The floor was tiled in an intricate pattern of white, gold, black and terracotta squares—a colorful, but hard surface that made their footsteps echo in the deserted corridor. On each side a series of pale gold, angular brick arches rose to a decorated, vaulted ceiling. Evening light flooded in the windows that lined the western wall giving the whole scene a luminous glow.

At the end of the corridor they turned left into a starkly art nouveau church. Nuns, visiting monks, and other guests sat in silence. Felicity slid into a black oak pew near the back, with Antony following her. She felt strangely disoriented by the unusual architecture—so unlike anything she had seen in any monastery she had visited in these past years—which she still thought of as being since she had, like Alice, fallen down the rabbit hole.

Although she could identify her surroundings as art deco, and she knew that, appropriately, it was a style that originated in France, she had never before experienced such a precisely rectangular room with such sharply squared arches. Being accustomed to the rounded Roman arches of early English design, or the pointed gothic arches so beloved of Victorian architects, she had to keep reminding herself she was in a church.

After a few minutes a bell rang and the congregation stood. With only the softest susurration, black-robed monks filed in from a side door near the altar and took their places in the triple rows of pews facing each other across the chancel. The black of robes and stalls contrasted sharply with the pale gold of the brick walls. A single note sounded from the organ pipes encased in a design of repeating triangles, and the monks began chanting the psalm antiphonally as the precentor began each verse, with the succentor completing it.

When they bowed deeply from the waist at the "Glory Be" Felicity stared. So few monks today still took the tonsure. Or could they just all be bald? Not the younger ones, surely.

At the second psalm Felicity managed to focus on the Office book in her hand. *Psalme 139, "Eripe ne, Dómine aba hómine malo,* *"* after a pause at the caesura, the other side continued: *"a viro vioéntiæ serva me."*

As Felicity translated she relaxed and picked up the rhythm. *Deliver me, Lord from the bad man,* * *against the violent man defend me.* At last, Felicity felt the rightness of the design around her. It was as if the precise, geometric lines of the room provided a clean slate for the purity of the chant line as the tones rose and fell just like the geometric angles surrounding them.

Felicity knew from seeing Surindar's manuscripts that even the notes of a Gregorian manuscript were square. And as she listened, she could see the long fingers of the choir master at St. Patrick's pointing upward for a rising pitch, followed by each finger extending sideways in stair steps as the scale descended. Then back up again, rising and falling as if borne on a zephyr.

The Office book before her laid out the psalms in double columns: on the left, the Latin that was being sung, on the right, French for the benefit of the francophone Quebecois visitors.

Choir and worshippers alike remained seated through the psalm, then stood and bowed at "*Glória Patri, et Fílio,* *et Spirítui Sancto*."

Felicity examined the French page, hoping her one year of high school French—before she discovered her love of Latin—would come back enough to allow her to follow along. It was obvious that a fluency in French would be an advantage while being deep in the province of Quebec. Unfortunately, any skill she had honed with that language, from using it through her years of intense ballet training, was dulled beyond recall. She quickly switched to the Latin side where she was fully comfortable. By the time they were on the third psalm Felicity began to feel at home. Perhaps this wasn't a rabbit hole, but rather a mountain top.

At the end of the brief service the congregation remained seated as the monks filed out the side exit. When the door closed with a soft click, Felicity and Antony stood with the other guests and turned to the back. Now Felicity could appreciate the design at the rear. Looking up, beneath the apex of a steeply angled, dark wood roof, she was greeted with an enormous round window lighting the space like a rising moon behind the small balcony. The lower wall was a series of precise, dark-framed rectangles of glass. But there was no time to absorb it all, for the line was moving briskly down the corridor with a monk standing by a door urging everyone forward.

It was just as well that the line moved in precision to the emphatic direction, because Felicity knew she would never have found her way on her own down the series of stairways and passages that led to the busy dining hall. At the buffet line they were served a simple meal of soup, *ragu* and *crudites*. Felicity and Antony carried their trays to a long, central table.

After only a few bites Felicity was assured that the cooking, like apparently everything else here, was done with care and lack of fuss: fresh ingredients, perfectly seasoned; no frills, but very satisfying. Felicity finished her tomato bisque and bit into a celery stick. The resounding crunch made her look around the silent dining room. How had the others mastered the art of eating fresh vegetables in silence? She had always been thankful that meals at Kirkthorpe allowed talking, but now she regretted not having had the opportunity to acquire the skill. Maybe if she cut her carrot stick into small pieces first...?

She was still pondering when she became aware of the heavy breathing of the man seated behind her. The poor fellow, he was probably asthmatic. Still, the sound made her nervous. Apparently Antony had the same reaction because he turned around sharply and frowned at the rasping sound. Odd, because Antony was usually so much more patient with such things than she was.

The sound of a wooden chair scraping on tile and footsteps behind her told Felicity the bothersome guest had left. After a few more bites of their excellent beef and vegetable *ragu* she and Antony finished as well. After depositing their dishes and utensils in the appropriate bins they made their way back through the maze to the *portiere*, with Felicity feeling thankful, not for the first time, for Antony's excellent sense of direction.

The porter explained that Antony would be housed there in the main building. "Room sixteen. At the end of the hall, a stairway up. You are on the second floor." He pointed vaguely down the hall and handed Antony a key.

"Mrs. Sherwood will be in the *Villa Sainte-Scholastique*. At the back of the parking lot, take the path down." He pointed to the door.

Felicity hoped his abrupt instructions indicated a discomfort with speaking English, rather than a dislike of visitors. And they were to be housed separately? Not just separate rooms, but in entirely different communities? Since they were here as emissaries of Father Peter, he had made the reservations. It had apparently slipped his mind to mention the separate accommodation rule—or he hadn't thought it important.

Felicity took a deep breath. What difference did it make? She was a big girl. She could take care of herself. She was good on her own. She just wished she had known what to expect. She took a grip on her roller bag and turned to the door.

"I'll walk you down." Antony took the bag from her and held the door open.

She gave him a grateful smile. And she was even more grateful after the car, which they had left by the front door, was safely parked in the lot and they headed along the dark, steep path to the nun's house. Antony had the presence of mind to turn on the flashlight on his mobile, which was a particular help in preventing stumbles when they came to a wooden bridge and then a stairway down the last steep incline of the hill.

Felicity breathed a sigh of relief when she spotted a light shining through the trees ahead of them. She was almost embarrassed to admit to herself how comforting this small sign of welcome was in what felt like a very alien universe, even to one as acquainted with religious communities as she was.

Any lingering sense of alienation disappeared completely, however, as soon as her ring was answered by a smiling nun. "Welcome. I am Sister Bernadette. Do come in. You must be Felicity. We're expecting you." She even smiled at Antony when Felicity introduced him. "We are happy to have you here. Perhaps you would like to leave the bag over there." It was spoken kindly, but the message was clear: *I'll take care of things from here.*

When the door clicked shut behind Antony after a brief exchange of "Good night; sleep well," Felicity realized there hadn't even been opportunity for a quick good-night kiss. Surely that was a first in their married life.

She must have still been looking a little lost when Sister Bernadette called her back to the present. "Mother Anne-Marie will want to see you in the morning, but for now, let me give you a quick tour."

Felicity looked at the briefcase tightly gripped in her hand. It seemed unlikely the nuns would provide a safe for their guests' use. "Um, is there some place..." She didn't want to say secure—surely the whole villa was secure?

Fortunately, Sister Bernadette didn't require explanations. "Would you like me to lock that in Mother Anne-Marie's office? We are the only ones with keys."

With the click of the lock Felicity felt an easing of the tension she had known ever since Father Peter had placed the precious document in her hands.

It turned out that the tour was very thorough as Sister Bernadette showed Felicity the bathroom, toilets, conference room, library, chapel and, down the stairs, the breakfast room. "Breakfast at eight o'clock, but tea and coffee and snacks are always available." The sister indicated a long table against the wall. Back up in the foyer, she pointed to a bowl of rosy red apples. "And do help yourself any time. We grow them ourselves."

Finally, Sister Bernadette ushered her charge down a narrow, dimly lit hall, lined with doors, to a small room, gave Felicity a key, and departed with a final, "Sleep well." With that, Felicity was alone in her small, plain, yet cozy room. She opened her bag, which the nun had left in the middle of her floor, arranged a few items on the narrow bedside table, then sat down to think over the evening.

She wished she had been able to get a better look at Father Peter's friend she was to meet tomorrow, but the choir had been too far away for her to get a clear view of Père Denis, the precentor. She was anxious to talk to him to add to her understanding of chant, but most of all to have at least half of their commission with the manuscript completed. She had not expected couriering a document to be such a heavy responsibility. It had seemed such a simple request.

Simple, indeed, until their room at the university was searched and she had developed an inexplicable wary feeling. Probably just produced from an awareness of the value of the ancient artifact. She thought of the case she had asked Sister

Bernadette to lock away, and hoped the guest sister had bolted all the doors on their cozy little white villa securely.

She sighed. It had been a long day. And Antony was up the hill locked in his own male-only bastion. She anticipated being with him again with an intensity that could hardly be explained by the few hours and perhaps quarter of a mile that separated them. And there was certainly nothing to worry about. Antony couldn't possibly be in a safer place. After all, he was locked behind solid brick walls and heavy oak doors that seemed as much like a fortress as a monastery.

Still, she slept fitfully.

Chapter Eleven

The next morning the smell of fresh muffins hurried Felicity down the stairs to breakfast even more effectively than the distant sound of ringing bells from up the hill. A few other retreatants were there ahead of her, sitting together at various small tables around the room. The sisters' gift of hospitality was displayed in the colorful cloths and small bunches of flowers in the center of each table.

Felicity helped herself to a warm cinnamon muffin and a likewise still warm boiled egg. A bowl of fresh fruit and mug of tea from the sideboard completed her breakfast, but had she been a heartier eater, there was plenty more to choose from. The array of homemade preserves, undoubtedly from the monastery's own orchards, looked particularly tempting.

As she ate, the homey atmosphere, which she had always experienced when visiting nuns, drove any niggling uneasiness of the night before from her mind. She turned her thoughts to more practical matters and attempted to form a plan for the day. Delivering the document to Père Denis was certainly the most pressing item on her agenda, but she couldn't expect him to be available until after midday Mass—where she would also meet Antony, since his abrupt departure last night had precluded making any more specific plan. The thought of basking in his smile brought an answering smile to her face. Besides, she told herself, all that meant she could spend a quiet morning in the villa. After all, this was meant to be something of a mini retreat as well.

After the brief prayer service of Terce celebrated in the nun's small chapel, Felicity was pleased to find the door of Mother Anne-Marie's office open. She welcomed Felicity readily and invited her to sit down. The way Sister Bernadette had told Felicity that the superior wanted to meet her, she had expected Mother Anne-Marie to have an agenda, but after soliciting assurances that the new retreatant was settling in fine and had everything she needed, the room fell silent.

And yet, Felicity didn't feel she was being dismissed. It was almost as if the mother superior was nervous about bringing something up. In an attempt to put her hostess at ease, which seemed like an odd role reversal, Felicity asked her about the work of Saint Scholastica's.

"Besides serving as a house of prayer and offering accommodation to female visitors to Saint Benoit, we maintain our own program as a retreat center for women and offer spiritual direction."

Ah, that was a subject Felicity had long been interested in since she first experienced it personally during her short-lived period of discernment when she was considering becoming a nun herself. As she had more recently been considering—and discarding—a variety of possibilities for her own future, the role of spiritual director had more than once flitted through her mind. Although she greatly doubted her own suitability for the role. "It must be a very challenging job?" She offered her observation in a tone of query, hoping it would encourage Mother Anne-Marie to elaborate.

"Yes, challenging for us personally and as a community. We try to offer an oasis of peace to our troubled world—a place of spiritual refreshment where the women who come to us from all walks of life, all backgrounds, and with all sorts of beliefs, can find the space and be pointed the way to reconnect to the Divine."

Mother Anne-Marie settled easily into her topic and continued to talk about the challenges and joys of spiritual direction, but Felicity's mind wandered as she thought back over her own journey of "reconnecting to the Divine" during the past three years. She had always been so self-assured, but these years had taught her so much—so much about herself—far more than the theology, history, and scripture she had learned. The most startling realization of all had been how little she really knew.

The very idea made her blanch at the presumption of considering taking on the role of spiritual director herself. How could she possibly presume to attempt guiding others in the all-important matter of their souls? The weight of the mere thought of it made her want to fall to her knees. The words of the ordination service came back to her: *that each in their vocation and ministry may be an instrument of your love, and give your servants now to be ordained the needful gifts of grace...*

The thought of how much grace she would need for such an undertaking filled her mind with an image of an old-fashioned steam engine being fed shovelfuls of coal. The idea made her smile, since they would be taking a train journey so soon.

"If you are interested in the topic, I suggest you call on Mother Mary Joy at the House of Bread. She's an outstanding spiritual director. Since you're going out west it would definitely be worth your time to talk to her. I'll make an appointment for you, shall I?"

Mother Anne-Marie's words made Felicity startle and the seemingly abrupt change of topic made her wonder what she had missed in the nun's soliloquy. How long had she been maundering, she wondered. "What? How did you know..."

"Dr. Spaulding's wife recently led a retreat here for us on Praying Together. She shared quite a bit about the plans her husband was involved in."

Felicity nodded as if that explained it all—and yet she still wondered how the mother superior connected her to that. Perhaps Father Peter had mentioned it when he made the arrangements for their stay? But she had no time to mull that possibility over as the nun hurried on.

"That was when the idea first occurred to me—when I learned that a group would be traveling from Toronto to western Canada, I thought perhaps someone could help me out—and then when it occurred that you would actually be staying with us... Well, you can see that it appeared rather like a divine opportunity."

"Mmm." Not having a clue what to say, Felicity took refuge in that ubiquitous, enigmatic English response.

The mother superior rushed on, "You see, that is—I have a younger sister who wants to become a nun. At least, she thinks she does." Her sigh spoke volumes. "Well, she is much younger than I and very, um—shall we say resolute? It all seems very sudden to me—

"That is, I never thought..." She shrugged and gave a small smile that looked a bit forced. "But after all, who am I to know God's will? And she's quite determined to test her vocation on the other side of the country."

"Oh, yes!" At last Felicity found a subject she knew something about. "That's exactly the right thing. I did that three years ago and learned precisely what I needed to know."

"Did you, my dear? Excellent. Then that gives me courage to ask—you see, she wants to go to the House of Bread in Nanaimo."

She said it as if that made everything clear, rather than speaking what was actually a foreign language to her hearer. "Silly, really, when she could do the same thing right here. Well, actually, she has been here for a few months, but it isn't working very well." Anne-Marie sighed. "I suppose she didn't want to be under my wing so to speak. She's only eighteen, and never been farther from home than Montreal. And, of course, the young do like adventures." The nun paused for a deep breath before continuing. "I think you should know, my sister was a bit of a tearaway. The last person you'd ever think would be testing a vocation—apart from the fact that she does love to sing. But, all of a sudden..." She spread her hands. "It does take some people that way, of course."

"St. Paul?" Felicity asked, hoping it was a helpful analogy.

"A Damascus Road experience—I suppose so. I hope so. That's the point of the discernment process, isn't it?"

Now Felicity's smile was genuine. How well she remembered her own testing. She had been so sure she was going to be a nun —for about the three months of exploration. A picture of Antony filled her mind. How thankful she was that she had made the right choice.

"This will be a real test for her," the nun continued, then hesitated. "I wonder... I do hate to ask, but if you could possibly just keep a bit of an eye on her?"

It took a moment for the intent of the question to sink in. "Do you mean you want us to, um—take her with us?" Felicity stopped just short of saying babysit.

"I'm afraid that is what I'm asking. As I said, she's never been west of Montreal. If you could just see that she arrives at the House of Bread safely and settles in..." The mother superior laughed at herself. "I know—I said I agree she needs to get out from under my wing, but you see I can't entirely let go. Our parents died when she was ten years old. I was already professed, but I've still been responsible for her from afar. The aunt and uncle she lived with did their best, of course..."

Felicity's head was reeling. She had so been looking forward to that second honeymoon time with Antony. A whole five days with absolutely no responsibility—just sit in their luxury cabin and let the whole of Canada roll by outside their window. And now, take on... Well, who knew what they'd be taking on? A hyper-scrupulous convert? A teenage scamp? Or worse...?

"I'll have to talk it over with my husband." And then a

thought occurred to her, surely Mother Anne-Marie was only thinking of their chaperoning duties as involving a few hours on an airplane. "You see, we're going by train. We have a cabin. It was a gift—"

"Oh, that's perfect. Of course, Cerise would only have a ticket for coach—she wouldn't be actually staying with you. I think just the journey will be good for her—give her time to think—get her away from her old friends."

Unsavory friends? This was sounding worse and worse. And yet, Felicity could see her point. "A decompression chamber?"

"That's it exactly. Thank you so much, my dear. I can't tell you how grateful I am." She glanced at her wristwatch. "Oh, my dear, I've kept you far too long. We'll work out the details later."

Felicity glanced at the clock on the side wall and jumped to her feet. How could the morning have gone that fast? "Yes, time to get up the hill to Mass." The words sounded so familiar to her own ears. She had spent three years running up the hill at Kirkthorpe to midday Office—almost always in danger of being late.

"I'll let you know, Mother," she called over her shoulder as she darted out with an enormous sense of having escaped.

The sun was bright, the air warm and humid. She had just reached the top of the stairs they had come down in the dark last night, when she realized that Mother Anne-Marie's words had sounded like she thought Felicity had accepted. Had she? What had she said? What on earth would Antony think?

Chapter Twelve

Felicity took a deep breath and slowed her steps. Suddenly, the coziness of Saint Scholastica's had become claustrophobic to her. But the thought of being with Antony in a few moments, combined with the fresh air and warm July sunshine on her head, made her relax. It would be all right. Antony would know what to do.

Now she was aware of a general movement toward the Abbey as retreatants, workers from the fields, day guests and monks and nuns all responded to the summons of the bells. Walking down the long, colorful corridor that had seemed so desolate last night, Felicity noted that the wall across from the windows was lined with an account of the abbey's history. She took time to pause briefly to note one board telling of the drowning of a monk—their first abbot—in the lake below the abbey. Antony would love the history. They could peruse the display together after Mass. Then take a long ramble over the extensive grounds. Last night she and Antony had inspected a map posted on the wall across from the Porter's lodge and noted an old chapel, a *fromagerie*, a *cidrerie* and other buildings with fields, orchards and woods beyond, running down to the body of water that surrounded them on two sides.

But for now, she stood outside the chapel, looking for Antony as others filed past her. Light from the long, louvered windows behind her flooded across the shadowed tile floor and made the amber pyramid, sitting in the middle of an elevated basin of water by the chapel entrance, glow as if lit from within. Then someone dipped a finger in the water and she realized that was their font. At first it puzzled her, then she understood the triangle symbolized the Holy Spirit. The streamlined design around her took readjusting to after the soft warmth of the villa.

In the chapel ahead of her the congregation stood as the monks filed into the choir. "In the Name of the Father, and of the Son, and of the Holy Ghost." The celebrant blessed the worshippers in French, but Felicity's mind translated the familiar words. "I will go unto the altar of God."

"Even unto the God of my joy and gladness." Felicity mouthed the response automatically, but her mind wasn't on the service. Where was Antony?

She moved into the chapel and took a seat in the back row. She scanned each pew carefully. Had he gone in before she arrived? Was he sitting near the front, undoubtedly wondering where she was? She had been certain she could recognize her husband from any angle, at almost any distance. But now she was uncertain. She spotted a sleek black head halfway up the aisle. Yes, he was wearing a clerical collar. That must be Antony. Or was that man too tall? What about the figure further up on the right?

Well, wherever he was sitting, it was certain he was in the chapel somewhere. Antony wouldn't miss Mass. And if he didn't care enough to wait for her, she could just sit by herself. She attempted for a time to focus on the liturgy—especially on the parts being chanted by the choir. After all, she reminded herself, the chant was what she was here for. Still, she felt her attention drifting to looking around for Antony, and, as last night, at the architecture.

Now she focused on the statues to the right of the chancel of

Saint Benedict, for whom the abbey was named, and his sister, Saint Scholastica. The statues were elongated in a stylized design that matched their surroundings, but one thing was very clear—the adoring look with which Scholastica gazed up at her twin brother, clutching her hands to her breast, as he held forth, undoubtedly propounding some great truth.

Felicity rolled her eyes. She couldn't imagine any sister in the world behaving like that. Not that brothers weren't great—she thought of her own with a smile—but she was certain it was far more likely that Scholastica was thinking, *All right, already, stop showing off and let me tell you about my great idea to found a house for women.* Then determining, *And it will be bigger and better-run than anything you can come up with.*

Reining in her irreverent imagination, Felicity reminded herself that tradition said Scholastica founded her house to run according to the Rule of Saint Benedict. And once a year, she visited her brother at a place near his abbey where they spent the day worshiping together and discussing sacred texts and issues. So, Felicity internally apologized to the sculptor—perhaps he did know more about his subject than she did. Felicity made a mental note to work on the virtue of humility. Someday.

She smiled. Benedict's famous Rule, under which Felicity herself had lived during her years studying at Kirkthorpe, and by which the majority of monasteries and convents were run to this day, had endured since the fifth century primarily because of its simplicity and humanity—it's understanding of human frailty and its patience with beginners—the very virtues Felicity struggled with the most. Perhaps if she could use this time at the monastery...

Felicity was suddenly aware that the congregation was standing and moving forward to receive communion. Now, if she watched carefully she should be able to spot Antony, and at least sit by him for the post-communion prayers. But it didn't work.

Wondering how she could possibly have missed him, she joined the inexorable line moving to the dining hall after the midday service. It took only a quick scan of those already seated to determine that Antony hadn't begun eating without her, so she stepped aside and surveyed each face as they entered. Antony wasn't there. Now she was alarmed. He hadn't contacted her this morning, he hadn't been at Mass, he wasn't at *dîner*, as the posted schedule pronounced the meal to be.

Fear clutched at her. All her old assurance and independence fled. Something was wrong with Antony. Her mind flooded with images of him lying ill in his bed—too sick to call for help. Or having gone for a stroll in the woods this morning and tripped over the underbrush—lying unconscious, or in pain with a broken leg. Or worse. The story of the monk who had drowned in the lake many years ago came back to her. What if Antony had walked to the lakeshore and fallen...

The line came to an end and with it, her last hope of finding Antony in the dining hall. Felicity fled up the stairs, looking every direction, down every empty corridor she passed as she hurried back to the chapel. Perhaps Antony had become engrossed in conversation with a monk. Or stopped to pray or— But the chapel was as deserted as the rest of the monastery seemed to be.

She turned and rushed back down the passageway to the porter's lodge. Firmly bolted. Where did one go for help? She was certain she could stand there and scream at the top of her lungs, and no one would hear her.

What should she do? The grounds were vast. She would have no idea where to begin searching. Staring at the shuttered cubicle, she remembered the porter's words last night: *Room sixteen, end of the hall, stairway up.* She turned the direction he had pointed. Her pounding footsteps echoed on the tiles. She was breathing heavily when she came to the *dortoir*. A solid, dark oak door marked *Entrée Interdite* halted her rush. Even if she hadn't realized that meant No Entry, the firmly closed door would have told her that.

Still, it seemed worth a try. She seized the black iron handle, pushed the latch, and pulled. To her astonishment, it opened. *Up a stairway, second floor,* he had said. When she reached the long hall at the top of the stairs she darted forward, noting the numbers on the doors. Sixteen. She knocked so hard her knuckles felt bruised. "Antony!" she cried.

No answer, so she repeated; crying his name and pounding, over and over. Pause to listen for a response; then repeat.

She raised her fist for the third time when her wrist was grabbed from behind. She gave an involuntary scream and spun around. The stern face of a tonsured, black-robed monk was inches from her face.

She gave him no chance to reprimand her. "Antony! My husband—he wasn't at Mass. Or at lunch. He must be sick." To her horror, she started to cry.

Her tears undoubtedly did more than her frenzied words. The monk pushed her aside. "I am the guest brother." He produced a ring of keys and opened the door. Felicity rushed in ahead of him. Then stopped abruptly with her hand to her mouth. The small room was in a mess her tidy Antony would never have created. But he was not there.

She spun toward the door, but her way was blocked. "The bathroom! We need to—"

"*Non, Madame.* I have just come from the *toilette.*" With a firm grasp on her arm, he was already walking her toward the stairway. "I suggest you speak with *Père Abbé* after *None.*"

Wait until midafternoon prayer was over? Not likely. Felicity opened her mouth to tell the guest brother just what she thought of such dilly-dallying, but the words that came out of her mouth startled even herself. "Yes. Good idea. Please, you report to him. I'll—I'll..." *What was she going to do?* "I'll go pray."

"*Bon.*" With a jerky nod the monk locked the door to the *dortoir* behind them. Felicity was aware of his eyes following her as she forced herself to walk calmly down the passage toward the outside.

As she passed the porter's lodge she glimpsed the map she

and Antony had studied last night. She remembered Antony taking special interest in the old chapel of *Saint-Benoît* pictured on the map at the very edge of the property beyond Saint Scholastica's. Yes, if Antony had gone for a morning ramble around the grounds that was surely where he would have gone. She was just sorry she hadn't been with him, rather than unintentionally making wild promises to Mother Anne-Marie. Her heart soared. Dear Antony, how like him to get carried away praying in an old chapel and lose all sense of time.

She all but skipped out the front door. By the time she had crossed the parking lot and found a path that wound down the hill to the west of the villa, however, her euphoria began to evaporate. She knew Antony. He would make his bed and hang up his clothes before leaving his room. He might get lost in meditation—but not to the extent of missing Mass—and lunch. No, something was wrong.

She began to run, trying to take care not to stumble on the narrow dirt path. She could only hope she had chosen the right way; there were no signposts, and she had only her memory of the map. The woods on every side of her made it impossible to see what lay ahead.

At last she rounded a turn in the path and saw before her a small hillock with a little, grey stone chapel perched atop. A stairway of wide, worn stones with heavy iron railings on each side, led to the firmly closed black double doors. Felicity didn't hesitate as she bounded upward, shouting Antony's name. For the second time that day she found herself pounding on a locked door.

Her heart beating in her ears made louder thuds than the blow of her fists. So loud that at first she wasn't sure she actually heard answering thumps from the other side of the door. "Antony?" Her voice came out on a sob.

"Felicity, is that you?"

She had to put her ear against the door to hear him, but that was no barrier to her elation. "Antony! Oh, I'm so relieved! Are you all right? What happened? Can you—"

Her words were cut off by muffled laughter. "Felicity, stop. I'm fine, but can you open the door?"

"I don't have a key." And she certainly didn't want to wait until after *None* to summon help. Felicity stood back and regarded the door. Now she saw what she hadn't seen before— the door hadn't been locked by a key. One of the black iron posts from the stair railing had been inserted between the handles of the double doors, securing them as tightly as a beam across a fortified castle gateway.

"Yes!" she shouted and began tugging at the iron bar. It refused to move, so she changed strategy and attempted to shove it out. Putting all her weight into the push she thrust her body forward. Unfortunately, her force was counter-productive as her hand slipped and the iron bar cut a gash in her wrist.

A trickle of blood oozed into her hand, but thankfully not so much as to require bandaging, since she had nothing to wrap it with. Placing her left thumb firmly over the wound, she pushed while surveying her options. Legs were stronger than arms, but she was a long way from her ballet training—even from the exercises she had kept up so faithfully for her first years at Kirkthorpe. She filed a mental note to get back to them. She would need good muscle tone if—when...

She brought her attention back to the job before her. Yes, she was out of practice, still...

Standing level with the door she raised her leg and gave a hefty kick at the bar. She told herself she felt a slight movement, but it was obvious it would take more force than that to finish the job.

She surveyed the broad landing she was standing on. Yes, there should be enough room—just. But the stone was uneven. And she was wearing trainers, not pointe shoes. Still, if she could accomplish it, the momentum from a *pirouette* should give a well-aimed kick the propulsion she needed. If she didn't trip and sprain an ankle—or worse...

"Hold on, Antony, I've just about got it!" Her shout was accompanied by a fervent prayer that it would be true.

She measured the distance from the door with an extended leg, then tried a few tentative turns to get the feel and rhythm. Finally, taking a deep breath, she spotted on the end of the bar, whirled around, and ended with the strongest *battement* she could manage.

Perfect! Except that she kicked the stone wall instead of the end of the bar. She must have made a mighty thud because Antony called, "Are you all right?"

"Yes. Sure—just practicing. Hang on."

It took two more attempts, but on her third *pirouette, battement* combination she felt the bar shift several inches. Now she could finish the job by pushing with her uninjured hand. The bar fell onto the stone with a resounding clatter.

In the next second she was in Antony's arms. "Antony, you're sure you're all right? How did this happen? Were you attacked? How long—" As so many times during their marriage, Antony simply cut off her flow of words with an extended kiss.

After they had both caught their breath, he held her at arms' length. "What a woman! I can't—" then he saw her hand. "Felicity, you're bleeding!"

"It's nothing. Just a scratch, really."

He pulled a clean, white handkerchief from his pocket and bound her wrist gently, finishing with a kiss.

Felicity laughed. "What a man! Who else in the world would be so well equipped at a time like this?"

They were both trembling a bit as he led her back into the fresh air. They sat side by side on the top step. "Now—" she began, but Antony put a finger to her lips.

"Once again, I'm fine. Nothing happened. I went to the villa to call for you, but the sister said you were with the mother superior, so I just strolled around the grounds. I was in the chapel when the door banged shut and apparently locked itself. Wind, I suppose."

Felicity shook her head. "No wind storm lodged that iron bar behind the door handles." She explained the process required to open the door. "You were definitely locked in on purpose." They were both silent for a moment. "Antony, did you go out before straightening your room this morning?"

"What an odd question. Of course I didn't. What would make you think that?"

She told him about seeing his room and the condition she found it in.

His reaction was one of amusement, rather than alarm. "Felicity, tell me you didn't? You invaded that sacrosanct male territory? And the guest brother actually opened the door for you?" He put back his head and laughed. "Oh, what a prize you are!"

Felicity wasn't sure whether to be happy at his sense of humor or insulted because he seemed to be laughing at her. Or maybe she should be alarmed at his failure to take the situation seriously enough. It was usually the reverse with them—Antony warning her to be more cautious and she failing to see any danger.

"But don't you see? Someone must have followed you this morning, waiting for a chance to get you out of the way so they could go through your room. Thank goodness all they did was bar the doors. What if I hadn't found you? What if you'd decided to walk by the lake?" She shuddered as her earlier vision of the drowned monk came back to her.

Antony held her tight. "Well, you did. And I didn't." After a moment he added, "But you're definitely right. Something is going on."

"It must be the manuscript. That's the second time someone has gone through one of our rooms—and we certainly don't have anything else of value." She pulled away from his embrace to be able to think more clearly. "Antony, have you noticed anything odd? Anyone suspicious?"

Antony grinned. "We're in a whole new country. Almost everything seems odd to me." Then he became serious. "Well, I didn't mention it—it was such a small thing—but there was a rather odd hanger-on that last day at my Saint George lecture. Then I thought maybe I heard him again later on the plane to Montreal. Of course, it was probably someone else with asthma or something."

A chill went through Felicity and she grabbed Antony's arm with both hands. "No! I think he sat behind me in the chapel last night. At least, someone with some sort of raspy breathing."

"Yes. I heard that, too, but when I turned around the only one behind us was a nun." He was silent, as if struggling to recall. "I remember what an unusual habit she wore—her veil was more like a hood, stiff, halfway to her waist. Did you see anyone like that at Saint Scholastica's?"

Felicity shook her head. "What shall we do?" She would have been happier with herself if her voice hadn't come out with a waver.

"Get that manuscript to Père Denis as quickly as we can. Then get on our way as quickly as we can. We should be safe enough on the train. And..." He paused with a self-deprecating grin. "I'd rather like to see if there's any food left in the dining hall. All I had for breakfast was corn flakes and weak tea."

Felicity was shocked, but wisely forbore telling him what a satisfying breakfast she had enjoyed, "Yes, I missed lunch, too."

The porter was in his lodge when they returned to the monastery, so Felicity was able to make an appointment to see the Precentor in an hour. That gave them time to make a quick lunch of the smooth garlic *tourin*, tangy, hard cheese and still warm baguette available in the dining hall.

"I'll see you after my appointment," Felicity said to Antony after they had collected the manuscript from Saint Scholastica's.

"Not on your life. You don't think I'm going to let you

saunter around these premises carrying that document alone after the things that have been happening, do you?"

"Wait—I'm not the one who got themself locked in the chapel, am I?" She gave him a saucy look. "But you're right. You'd best stick with me so I can protect you."

They were halfway along the corridor when a swishing sound behind them made them both turn. A tall, broad-shouldered nun swept past them, her heavily starched wimple falling almost to her waist over her black habit. A rope of large, brown wooden beads clanked at her side. She strode past them, eyes straight ahead. "Wow, if she's a mother superior, you can bet she doesn't stand for any nonsense. Is she the one you saw last night?"

"Maybe. Probably."

Felicity considered the straight back disappearing ahead of them. "Well, I didn't notice any heavy breathing as she swished past us, but she certainly looked capable of shoving a loose iron bar into that door." *And considerably more than that*, Felicity thought with a sudden chill.

Chapter Thirteen

※

Père Denis met Antony and Felicity in the foyer next to the monastery shop, as the porter had directed them. He was accompanied by a short, sandy-haired man with a small mustache and heavy horn-rimmed glasses. "I have invited Monsieur Laurent—he is a friend of our librarian and an expert in antiquities."

"*Bonjour*," the little man waved a white handkerchief and offered a jerky nod, almost in the form of a bow.

"Yes, hello," Antony responded.

With the instant transition of all Quebecois, Monsieur Laurent switched to English. "I am honored. I am most anxious to view your remarkable document."

The precentor led them down another flight of stairs and along a narrow hall, not to an office, as Antony had assumed, but rather to what their guide called his harpsichord room. "This is my most private space. We won't be interrupted here," he said, pointing to chairs his guests should take.

"Now," he sat across from them on a straight, wooden chair like theirs, with Monsieur Laurent standing behind him. "I am most anxious to see what my colleague has sent me."

Antony glanced down at his hand clasping the leather case

which Felicity, with an unaccustomed lack of reluctance, had put in his charge. He hadn't realized his grip was so tight until he saw that his knuckles were white—even though no one had shown any untoward interest in their doings as he carried it up from the villa and through the halls of the monastery.

Antony's vague reluctance to part with his charge must have shown because the monk held out his hand. "The presentation of this remarkable find—along with the chant to accompany it—promises to be the highlight of the colloquium next year. It is most kind of Father Peter to allow us this opportunity to prepare by studying it ahead. There is really nothing like working from the original—things often show up that would be missed even in a high quality photograph."

Antony placed the case in the outstretched hands and Père Denis carried it to his desk. Felicity jumped up. "Oh, photograph. I almost forgot, Father Peter asked me to send him some of the occasion. If you wouldn't mind?" She arranged the three men, Père Denis sitting at his desk with Antony standing beside him. Monsieur Laurent sneezed, then took the other side.

She took a couple of shots, then waited while the precentor snapped open the lock, pulled on a pair of white gloves, apparently placed there in readiness for this moment, and placed the sheet of vellum on the desk. "Another picture, Felicity?" Antony suggested.

"Please. Just a couple with the manuscript. Antony, if you could step a little closer." He did. "Now you and Monsieur Laurent lean forward." They did. "A little more."

Both men obeyed—a bit too quickly, and bumped heads just as Felicity snapped the picture. Only after he stood up did Antony realize he had knocked Monsieur Laurent's glasses off.

He started to apologize, but was stopped by Felicity's startled look. "Monsieur..." She murmured his name in a startled gasp, then seemed to recover. "Do you have, er—have—that is, did you have a brother in England?"

He hastily replaced his spectacles. "*Non, Madame.* I have nine sisters." He smiled. "It was a great disappointment to *mon père*—until they all took up Gaelic football. Three of them now play for St. Pat's."

"This is remarkable, indeed." Attention shifted back to Père Denis who had been studying the manuscript while the others were distracted. He waved his hand over the document in an action resembling a blessing. "I was prepared to encounter a most interesting text, but the illumination—I have never seen finer."

Felicity and Antony both leaned toward the precious artifact that had been entrusted to their keeping. Antony could see the intricate ornamentation of the initial I, scrolling down the left side of the page in rich tones of ochre, umber and red madder—all highlighted with dots of gold leaf.

Felicity spoke first. "I had no idea. I mean, I hadn't realized it would be so decorated. I have a black and white photographic copy—but none of the real beauty shows up. This looks like the *Lindisfarne Gospel* we saw on Holy Isle—only different. Not so..."

The antiquities expert nodded. "Yes, this is in the style of the *Book of Kells*, which was made some two hundred years later. Still in insular majuscule script, but the decoration is more lavish, with greater range of color and refinement."

Looking for some clue that might explain the misadventures they had encountered, Antony asked. "Do you think this might be as old as the *Book of Kells*? As valuable?"

"Could it actually be from the *Book of Kells*?" Felicity's question came out on an awed gasp.

Père Denis considered. "Ninth century? Perhaps."

Monsieur Laurent sniffed. "Most certainly not before. *Considerably* later, I would have thought."

"Could it have been made by the same monks?" Felicity's awestruck tone indicated she paid no heed to Monsieur Laurent, if she heard at all.

"Or simply someone copying their style," the expert replied.

Felicity turned to Père Denis. "I think Father Peter told you that I'm doing the translation to be used for your colloquium. It's been suggested to me that using the style of the Gaelic chant might be appropriate. Seeing this gives me more of a feel for the whole time period. What do you think?"

Père Denis considered for a moment. "Certainly more appropriate for the Irish sense, although Patrick would have spoken Latin as well, of course. And for the time period? Well, yes, this may have been produced before Gregorian chant was developed." He glanced at Monsieur Laurent and added hastily, "Or not."

"But what do you think the original chant might have been? Surely it was sung—or chanted—just as we sing 'Saint Patrick's Breastplate' today."

"An original chant? That's an impossible question. There has always been chant: priests in the Old Testament times, Romans in their temples, various ones through the liturgy of the early church. It didn't just all start with Pope Gregory. I would suggest you focus more on the feeling of the words than worrying about a specific time period."

Felicity nodded. She wouldn't argue. She got his point. Still, seeing the illumination did conjure up a sense of the time period for her.

Père Denis paused, as if considering whether or not to continue, then said rather haltingly, "I do wish you success. It may be more important than you know. It has been very strange, but I have received some rather, er—worrying correspondence. Maybe simple queries, but with something of an underlying threat, I suppose you could say, about using this manuscript for the meeting."

Felicity frowned. "Really? How could anyone possibly object? How does anyone even know?"

"Oh, we have told about it in our advance notices—to encourage attendance. But as to reasons for objection—" The monk shook his head. "That's what I can't make out. Its primary interest is to a few obscure scholars."

"Not money?" Felicity asked.

Monsieur Laurent waved a dismissive hand. "Perhaps—there's always the possibility of an obsessive collector. Museums and libraries would be very happy to have it, but their budgets are tightly controlled."

"Still," Père Denis smiled at Felicity, "we'll take very good care of this. I really can't thank Father Peter enough. It's so valuable to be able to study the original—there are often obscure markings or even scratchings-out that don't show up on any copy. You say you are working from a copy?"

Felicity explained about her translation. "I've been trying to learn more about the chant so I can, hopefully, get the rhythms right and make the best possible choices for cognitive words."

After his somewhat deflating pronouncements, the manuscript expert had withdrawn to a chair in the far corner and sat with his handkerchief to his nose as if there were an unpleasant odor in the room. Antony, however, had not stopped staring at the manuscript. The design was a fascinating enrichment to the document. Some ancient monk, toiling away in a scriptorium, must have cared deeply about this work to invest so much effort in it. It was almost as if he wanted to convey something to the viewer beyond what the text itself had to tell.

He stared at it until the inter-looping figures began to twirl as if alive. Antony blinked and pulled back, rubbing his eyes. It must be the stuffiness of this basement room. He was not given to an over-heated imagination.

Then as his vision sharpened, the spots of gold leaf seemed to stand out and become the foreground, rather than the background as at first appeared. It was almost as if the manuscript were dotted with gold coins—coins spilling from what now looked to Antony like an over-flowing cauldron in the upper right corner of the illustration. Was it possible that the ancient illustrator meant for his work to take on such an image? But if so, why?

"Well, thank you so much, Père Denis," Felicity's words

broke in on Antony's rumination. "You've given me a very helpful perspective on my work. I hope it will all come together in something meaningful for your conference."

"I'm very glad I could be of help. I understand you are going on after Mass tomorrow. I'll have this ready for you to collect to take on to my colleague at Westminster. I know he will find it as engrossing as I do."

Antony followed Felicity's lead, thanked the father and left the room with her. Only after the door clicked shut did Antony realize they had failed to bid Monsieur Laurent farewell.

"Felicity, what was that about asking Monsieur Laurent if he had a brother in England? He didn't look like anyone I know."

She seemed reluctant to answer. "Felicity? What's the matter?"

"I'm not sure. That is—I am, but it sounds so paranoid. I mean, after thinking I saw that murderer at Saint Andrews..."

Antony stopped walking and pulled her into an alcove by a closed door. She took a deep breath. "Well, without his glasses, Monsieur Laurent looked like the victim."

Antony couldn't help frowning. "That antiquities expert looked like the murdered man in Thorpeside Wood?"

"I told you you'd think I'm bonkers. I didn't say it *was* him—just looked like him. That's why I thought maybe he had a brother. A twin or something."

"You're sure?"

Before answering she took out her phone and scrolled though her pictures. "Oh dear, Père Denis turned his head just as I took the picture."

Antony looked. "Hmm, a little blurry, but he does have a distinctive profile. But what about, uh—the other?"

Felicity looked again. Her nod was more of a shiver.

They were both silent all the way back up the stairs and out of the building. Without thinking, Felicity began walking in the direction of the villa, but Antony took her arm and turned to walk across the wide green lawn toward the woods. She began chattering about Père Denis' perspective on the chant and her delight in seeing the sumptuous illumination. "I really had no idea we were carrying anything so absolutely lovely. It seems to me it should be in a museum..."

She floundered to a halt when she realized Antony was completely lost in his own thoughts. "Antony! You haven't heard a word I said. I—"

He pointed to a bench at the back of the monastery building, on the edge of the grass near the woods.

She sat obediently. "Now. What on earth has you so enraptured?"

"I wish I knew. Maybe just my imagination, but..." He shook his head as if to clear it and told her about his experience looking at the illumination. "It was almost as if the artist wasn't showing the viewer the letter 'I' at all, but just using it as background for his pot of gold."

"Oh, you mean like he was trying to say that Patrick's words were what was of real value? That's a beautiful thought. I'll try to hold to that in my translation. Makes one think of Saint Chrysostom, the golden-tongued. Maybe he wanted Saint Patrick to be seen in the same light. I wonder if—"

"Felicity."

The impatient tone in Antony's voice made her stop.

"That's not at all what I'm trying to say."

"Oh. Sorry."

He ignored her interruption. "It was more as if the illustrator was pointing away from the text, pointing to something else he wanted the viewer to see."

"A pot of gold, you say?" Felicity struggled to suppress a giggle. She could see that Antony was entirely serious and rather disturbed by what he had seen. Still, she couldn't help asking, "Was there a rainbow?"

"No. And there weren't any leprechauns, either, should you

ask." His asperity made her catch her breath. Sarcasm wasn't like Antony at all.

"I'm sorry. Really—I am. I'm just trying to make sense of it all."

"And what do you think I'm doing?" He stood abruptly. "Look, I'm sorry, too. I didn't mean to snap at you, but my bed was hard, breakfast was dismal and you tell me my room was ransacked. Then I have some sort of hallucination that doesn't make any sense at all. Is it any wonder I'm in little mood to be laughed at?"

"I wasn't..." Felicity stopped. Defending herself was hardly the point of this conversation. "Look, it's at least two hours until Vespers. Why don't you go straighten you room and try to have a nap? I'll have a go at getting some more translating done. I really do want to try to convey some of Père Denis' spirit in my word choice. And if there's some opposition to the project it's more important than ever that I get this right. Let's meet at the church at five o'clock."

"Yes, good." Antony nodded and began walking across the lawn as if she weren't even there.

"Right. Yes, and you have a good afternoon, too," she said to his departing back before turning toward Saint Scholastica's.

Once inside the snug villa, however, she decided not to go straight to her room. Instead, she went to the library, thinking that perhaps they would have a volume on Saint Patrick, or the *Book of Kells*, or chant, or illumination... Her mind was groping for possible subjects that could apply to her work as she surveyed the rows of books. The sisters had an excellent collection of works by the mystics—which made Felicity think of the television series Antony had hosted just before their wedding. Her thoughts drifted and she smiled at the success that project had become in spite of all the difficulties they encountered.

A volume titled *Sacred Places of Ireland* brought her mind back to her present search. Yes, here were three books on Saint Patrick. And another on Saint Brigit. And Irish saints in general.

She almost passed over the slim black tome stuck between Saint Brendan and Saint Mary of the Gael. She wouldn't have noticed it at all if the light hadn't caught the gold-embossed title, *Treasures of Ancient Ireland*.

It seemed unlikely that a story here could have any connection to whatever might have been in an ancient illuminator's mind—or to anything Antony might have dreamt while looking at the manuscript. A dream—that must explain it; after all, he said he was tired, and the room was dimly lighted and so stuffy Monsieur Laurent seemed to have trouble getting his breath. Dreaming explained it, but she wouldn't be saying that to Antony who seemed to be unaccountably touchy on the subject.

She returned to the book in her hand. The stories might help her get a feeling for the time period she was trying to get hold of. She had always been aware that a translator's job was as much, maybe even more, a matter of translating the feeling than the actual words. But this was surely far more important when working with a piece of poetry. Especially poetry to be chanted in a method somewhat unfamiliar to her.

She turned on a light behind a comfy chair, picked an apple from a bowl on a table in the center of the room, and within a few minutes was happily reading and chomping and smiling at the charm of the Irish imagination. The work was a compendium of legends from various parts of Ireland, most of them from an unknown date lost in the mists of time, but some seeming to have originated as recently as the twentieth century.

And all had the same centerpiece—a hoard of treasure, hidden away for centuries, each with a guard one would not wish to encounter: a galloping horseman, a large black dog, a shade with blood leaking from his slit throat, an abomination with cloven hooves... Some were quite specific as to who would be able to claim the treasure: a man named Michael, someone bearing the name Foley, one who stabbed the dog on his white spot...

The thing Felicity found of most interest, though, was those stories that explained how the gold (it seemed it was always gold) got there: hidden by a smuggler, left by Viking raiders, treasure crocks buried in wartime. At least these seemed logical. Felicity leaned back in her chair, chewing thoughtfully on her apple. The thing to consider about these legends was that by its very definition, a legend had its roots in fact—an actual event that grew to mythic proportions.

So there actually could be a hoard of gold from, say, Vikings or smugglers, hidden somewhere in Ireland. One didn't have to believe in leprechauns or ghostly specters to give credence to such an idea. And if such a hoard had been hidden—in time of war, say—surely one doing the hiding would leave a key to its location.

She groped for more specific ideas, but finally decided there was nothing to be learned from that book. She returned it to the shelf and selected one on the *Book of Kells*. Perhaps knowing more about that great work would help her understand the illumination on their document.

The scale and ambition of the work is incredible. Written on vellum, it is estimated that the skins of 185 calves were needed for the project. Practically all of the 680 pages are decorated in some way. On some pages every corner is filled with the most ornate and delicate Celtic designs, the detail and beauty almost beyond imagining...

She turned the page, hoping for something that might provide some kind of clue or lead to an understanding of what she and Antony seemed to have become embroiled in. *Remarkably, considering the book's age and history of rough handling, the majority of the pages have been passed down through the generations with only sixty pages missing. Viking raids in 806 forced the monks on Iona, who produced the book, to take refuge at Kells in County Meath, bearing their precious manuscript with them. Medieval sources record that an illuminated manuscript, most certainly* The Book of Kells, *was stolen from the church of Kells in 1006. The Annals of Ulster report that it was found 'two months and twenty days' later 'under a sod.' Cromwellian troops left the church at Kells in ruins—the book most* likely buried under rubble, and in 1653 the book was sent to Dublin by the governor of Kells for safekeeping. A few years later it reached Trinity College where it remains today.

Sixty pages missing, Felicity pondered, recalling Père Denis mentioning wanting to examine the manuscript for possible rubbings out in the text. Was it possible that an older text had been scraped away to put Patrick's words on a much older illuminated sheet? One of the missing sheets from *The Book of Kells?*

Still considering, she read on to the words of Gerald of Wales who examined the volume in the twelfth century. He described the varied designs and colors and summarized, *Here you may see the face of majesty, divinely drawn, here the mystic symbols of the Evangelists, each with wings, now six, now four, now two; here the eagle, there the calf, here the man and there the lion, and other forms almost infinite.*

It was Gerald's next paragraph that caught her attention: *Fine craftsmanship is all about you, but you might not notice it. Look more keenly at it and you will penetrate to the very shrine of art. You will make out intricacies, so delicate and so subtle, so full of knots and links, with colours so fresh and vivid, that you might say that all this were the work of an angel, and not of a man. Look at them superficially with the ordinary glance, and you would think it is an erasure, and not tracery.*

There it was again, the idea of an erasure. And certainly, Felicity herself was aware of the common practice of scraping off writings and reusing precious sheets of calfskin. With some reluctance, she set the book aside and went once more up the path to the imposing monastery.

Thankfully, vespers proved to be the calming service it was intended to be, and *souper* the light, perfectly prepared meal she had come to expect in this French-influenced domain. Accordingly, the walk with Antony back to the villa was a pleasant stroll with none of the discord they had experienced earlier. Thank goodness the day ended more peacefully than it had begun. Felicity snuggled under her covers, confident that tomorrow all the alarms would be behind them and they could begin the next part of their great Canadian adventure in peace.

She was just about to drift off to sleep when she remembered —she hadn't told Antony about Cerise. Nor had she made any progress on her translation. And how comforting was it really that the stories of hidden pots of gold in Ireland might be true? What if Antony's vision had been, not a dream, but some sort of warning?

When Felicity finally fell asleep her dreams were full of bloody ogres, slavering dogs and marauding Vikings—all protecting vast stores of treasure hidden just out of her reach.

Chapter Fourteen

Sunday morning, Felicity awoke to the sound of bells calling worshippers to Mass. At first the familiar sound made her smile, in spite of her slight headache, as she rushed to dress, but then the clanging irritated her. This wasn't the carefully patterned change-ringing she was accustomed to in England, but rather the cacophony of bells rung in the continental style, each one clanging in her head.

The sound made Felicity think of the time in Oxford when she encountered muffled bells. Today's were muffled simply by the walls of her room. Even so, she shivered, recalling the deaths Oxford's muffled bells had heralded.

Still, the bright sunshine, birdsong and July flowers raised her spirits and helped clear her head as she dashed up the hill. The congregation was already standing when she slipped into a back pew beside Antony. Even though she stood on tip-toe and craned her neck, she couldn't spot Père Denis among the monks in the choir. But then, they all looked pretty much alike from this distance.

Felicity was soon caught up in the familiar rhythms of the service, although her mind wandered occasionally to worries over the fact that she had slept too late to have her packing done, and that she hadn't told Antony about their added responsibility of Cerise for the journey. At least, she managed to banish any of the disturbing images from the night before that threatened to cloud her worship.

After Mass, Felicity joined readily in the queue progressing toward the dining hall. At the foot of the stairs, however, Antony took her arm to direct their turning aside toward the bookstore and, beyond that, the lobby to the monks' offices. "Père Denis said he'd meet us after Mass, remember?"

The reminder drove away all thoughts of food. "Yes. I can't wait to find out if he's learned anything."

They sat on a bench and while they waited, Felicity told Antony about her reading on buried treasure the night before and her thoughts about the possibility of their document having been written on an older sheet. As they talked, the other retreatants and day guests filed into *dîner*, drawn by the delicious smells that were now making Felicity's stomach growl.

When the line came to an end and their host still failed to appear, Felicity stood and looked down the small hallway he had led them along the day before. "He should be here by now. Do you suppose he meant for us to go directly to his room?"

"We might as well check." Antony joined her.

A few moments later Felicity knocked on the door. When there was no answer she called, "Père Denis?" and knocked again, harder this time.

To her surprise, the door swung open. She led the way into the room. "Père Denis, you said to meet..."

She stopped so suddenly Antony stepped on her heel. She retreated hastily, one hand over her mouth, the other pointing to the dark-robed figure slumped over his desk.

Antony pushed Felicity aside and strode to the figure. "Père?" He touched the sagging shoulder, then felt below his throat for a pulse.

Antony stepped back, his face ashen white. "We need to find the abbot."

Felicity looked around as if he might suddenly appear. "He must be eating. Do you know where the monks' refectory is?"

"No idea. Well, in their private wing somewhere…"

Felicity was already heading back to the dining hall. The first person she found was a hefty, white-aproned man carrying a large tray of dirty dishes toward the kitchen. "The abbot! We must find him. It's an emergency!"

Her urgency seemed to translate better than her words. "*Père Abbé? Oui.* In the *réfectoire.*" He turned to a worker coming out of the kitchen and spoke rapidly in French. The young man nodded and scampered toward the stairs.

"He will fetch the Father." His English was heavily accented, but communicated flawlessly.

"Thank you!" All of Felicity's instincts would have her fly back to Antony for whatever assistance she could be. At least to join him in the prayers she knew he would be saying over the dead monk. But the most practical thing was to wait where she was. In her mind she traced the hurrying figure of the young man up the stairs, down the corridor past the church and into the *monastère* wing she had seen only on the map. Then approaching the abbot, explaining the best he could, followed by the return journey. Felicity shifted from one foot to another, trying to calculate what progress her messenger could have made as the minutes seemed to drag like hours.

At last she heard rapid footsteps on the tile stairs and a tall, thin, black-robed monk came around the corner. Felicity rushed to him. "Father, thank you for coming! It's Père Denis. He's… he's—" She simply turned and fled down the hall to the harpsichord room.

The next moments passed in a blur as the abbot repeated Antony's act of feeling for a pulse, then crossing himself, murmuring a prayer. He sent the kitchen boy scampering back to the monks' wing again to fetch the *infirmarrière*. Felicity stood as closely as she could to Antony who had given his place beside the body to the abbot and retreated to a far corner of the room.

Perhaps it was irreverent of her at such a moment, but as Father Abbot's prayers continued, Felicity couldn't repress the thought uppermost in her mind. "The manuscript. Did you find it?" She whispered in Antony's ear.

Her heart sank as he shook his head.

Now she inched closer to the corpse. Had Père Denis been murdered because he possessed their document? She strained as near as she dared without being obtrusive. As carefully as she could observe, however, she could spot no sign of foul play. The papers on the desk seemed undisturbed except for where the body had fallen over them. There was no pool of blood suggesting he had been attacked with a heavy object. No small black hole in what she could see of his forehead. Still, there was so much she couldn't see.

Likewise, there was no brown leather case in view. No corner of ancient vellum protruding from under the precentor's head or from beneath any of the papers on the desk.

At last the infirmarian arrived. With calm efficiency he directed the abbot to help him lay the body on the floor. He took a stethoscope from the small bag he carried. Then a thermometer as he completed his examination. Still, Felicity could see no untoward signs of violence. Nor, apparently, could the medical monk.

At last he stood and spoke to the abbot in French. The Abbot nodded, then turned to his guests. "Père Luc believes it was a heart attack. It was common knowledge that childhood rheumatic fever had left our brother with a weak heart. It was *inévitable*. Still, we prayed that he would be spared to us for longer. His ministry in the choir was invaluable..." The abbot's words failed him as he seemed overcome by the loss this would mean to the community.

When he recovered himself Felicity gathered her courage to ask, "Can Father Luc tell how long he's been dead?"

The abbot consulted the infirmarian, then turned back to

Felicity. "Sometime between *Laudes* and *Terce*, is his best estimate."

Between seven thirty and ten o'clock, Felicity translated mentally.

"He was not at *déjéuner*, but that was not unusual."

"Père Abbé," Antony stepped forward. "We have plans to go on today. Is there any reason we would need to delay?"

Felicity held her breath at Antony's words. If they missed their plane to Toronto they would likely miss their train the next day. Could they drive the distance in time? She didn't know, but it was a feat she didn't want to have to attempt. She felt guilty when she realized that the thought of that disappointment seemed more devastating than the monk's death. But all their plans...

The abbot shook his head. "No, not at all. It would be best. We will ask all guests to depart. We will mourn our brother in seclusion."

Felicity was still trying to decide whether or not they should mention the manuscript to the abbot when Antony spoke. "There is one other thing you should know, Père Abbé. Père Denis was studying a rare manuscript we had brought to him from his colleague Father Peter in Kirkthorpe—in preparation for its presentation at the Gregorian chant colloquium next year. We were to take it on to Westminster, but it seems to have disappeared."

"Yes, I know of the matter. Père Denis was most enthusiastic. But—disappeared, you say?"

"Yes, we were to collect it after Mass—"

"Is this what you seek?" Everyone turned as the porter strode into the room holding out a brown leather case. "Père Denis asked me to lock it in the *coffre* last night and return it to him this morning. I was delayed—" He stopped abruptly when he saw the prone form on the floor with the infirmarian still bending over him "Père Denis—he is taken ill? He told me he wasn't feeling well."

Before the abbot could explain, Antony took the case from the porter's slack hand, murmured repeated thank yous to the room in general and signaled Felicity to follow him.

"We've got to hurry." He made a dash for the stairs that even the long-legged Felicity had trouble keeping up with. "I'll get my case and meet you at Saint Scholastica's. Twenty minutes?"

Felicity gulped. "Sure." As soon as she was out of the monastery she broke into a run, going over in her head how quickly she could throw her belongings into her suitcase.

Antony was knocking on the door of the villa in just over fifteen minutes, but Felicity was ready. As was the mother superior, holding a small bag that apparently contained everything her little sister would need—or be allowed—for her time at the House of Bread.

Felicity caught her breath when their charge walked out of the office behind Mother Anne-Marie. She hadn't known what to expect from the nun's terse and rather garbled explanation of the prospective nun—whether they would be faced with a poe-faced, pious saint-in-the-making or a spike-haired, pierced and tattooed tearaway.

The young girl the mother superior brought forward was neither. She appeared startlingly stylish in an almost 1920s look with bobbed black hair framing her round face. Her full lips were painted cherry red, in keeping with her name. Only her jeans and tee shirt attire proclaimed her to be a modern teenager. "This is Cerise." It was clear that Mother Anne-Marie would have said more, but Antony had grabbed Felicity's case and was already halfway to the path to the parking lot.

"We have to hurry!" Felicity likewise turned and fled. Unsure which of her jumbled thoughts she should voice, she took refuge in action.

Felicity had the engine started before Antony slammed the boot closed on their luggage and got in the passenger seat beside her. Felicity jerked her head toward the back seat as she headed the little car down the hill. "This is Cerise. We're giving her a lift." That would have to do until they could talk in private.

The girl acknowledged the gesture with a giggle, although Felicity could see no humor in the situation. And goodness knew when there would be time to talk to Antony in private. If they missed their plane that could be all it would come to. A lift to the airport—and then what? She remembered that they had chosen the last flight on a Sunday, and she was pretty sure the first one the next morning wouldn't get there in time. The only option would be to drive it. In the dark. That was something Felicity decidedly did not want to have to attempt.

She gripped the steering wheel so tightly it made her gashed wrist ache and her hands felt stiff as she took the winding, mountainous road as fast as she dared. She couldn't begin to think what it would mean if they missed their connection to the train. She knew the *Canadian* compartments were routinely sold out months ahead. Jeff had told her how lucky he had been to secure the upgrade for them. There would be little chance of simply catching the next train headed west—at least, not with the luxury accommodation she had been so looking forward to.

The thought of her family's amazing gift of this once-in-a-lifetime incredible, all-frills-included journey across the bulk of Canada, her so longed-for second honeymoon with Antony—all rolling away down the silver tracks out of Toronto without them aboard made her stomach clench. She overtook the car ahead of them and pushed harder on the gas pedal.

Chapter Fifteen

Afterward, Felicity couldn't have given a coherent account of their mad dash through the Quebec countryside, across the Champlain Bridge and through Montreal traffic to the Trudeau airport. She only knew, because Antony told her, that they accomplished the normally hour and a half journey in just under sixty minutes.

She drove straight to the departures unloading zone, thrust the keys, rental contract and two large Canadian bills into the hands of a startled porter. "Return it to Avis for me. Keep the change." She was already halfway across the gleaming lobby before he had time to react. Felicity took one glance over her shoulder to make certain Cerise was keeping pace, then plunged on after Antony, leaving other hurrying passengers to see to their own safety in avoiding the roller bag she trailed behind her.

Security was another nightmare. She could only hope Cerise had packed to travel carry-on. Apparently she had, because after a frustrating delay, they were all three once again charging head-long down the concourse to their gate. And then, blessedly, down the jet-way as the last passengers to board before the gate closed.

Felicity sank into her window seat, too breathless even to

thank the attendant who stowed her bag for her. They were in the air and well into their flight, Felicity having gulped the glass of water the attendant brought her, when Felicity jolted as upright as her seatbelt would allow. All her senses focusing on the disturbing sound behind her, sounding so close in the small commuter plane. She twisted to peer through the crack between seat backs. She could see nothing and the lighted seatbelt sign overhead prevented her standing up for a clear view. Still, the sound of the hoarse breathing of the passenger behind her made every nerve in her body come alive. It wasn't possible they were being followed. Was it?

But surely there wasn't anything to worry about. If someone wished them harm there would have been plenty of opportunities in the past few days. She wasn't sure how comforting that thought was, though—especially when she considered Antony's having been locked in the chapel. If only she could get a look at the passengers in the row behind her.

Beside her, Antony was deep in his reading of a theological tome. She nudged him and pointed behind them. "Do you hear that?" she said in his ear.

Antony listened, then nodded, frowning.

"Could it be the same person? Can you get a look at him?"

Antony twisted out into the aisle and craned his neck, but apparently had as little success as Felicity did. "Wait till we disembark. We can look then."

Sensible advice. Felicity tried to turn to her own reading, but found it hard to concentrate as the wheezing continued behind her.

Some time later Felicity looked out her window and saw the blue waters which the pilot identified as Lake Ontario beneath them. As the attendant instructed them to prepare for landing, Felicity watched Toronto come into view with the long shadows of a summer evening stretching across the landscape.

The plane had barely quit moving when Felicity poised to jump to her feet and look the stranger behind her in the eye. She snapped off her seatbelt a second before the light was extinguished, and was on her feet.

She started to turn, but Cerise, in the seat in front of Antony, had been even quicker on her feet. The girl pushed up the door on the overhead bin with great energy, then gave a startled cry, followed by a giggle, when her bag tumbled out, landing at her feet with her belongings scattered.

Felicity and Antony both sprang forward as best they could in the crowded space and began helping retrieve the contents strewn under seats and down the aisle. With the help of others everything was soon retrieved, but in the confusion Felicity lost her focus on the passengers behind her. When she finally looked back, she didn't recognize anyone.

Felicity kept going over everything in her mind. All her senses were on alert now and she couldn't accept as coincidence everything that had happened to them. But there would be no chance to talk to Antony until they were finally settled in their hotel room near the train station.

And that apparently wouldn't be until after dinner. They had just achieved the concourse when Cerise began an insistent "I'm hungry" complaint. These were almost the first words they had heard from their tag-along as she had been blessedly silent on that harrowing journey to the airport and there had been no opportunity to talk on the plane.

"We're all hungry," Felicity snapped, realizing the truth of the words. "But you'll have to wait." Cerise clamped her pouty lips shut, but her dark eyes shot darts from under her straight black fringe—an attitude she maintained throughout the half hour taxi ride to their hotel.

They all made quick work of dumping their bags in their room, although Antony took time to stow the document case in the safe in the back of their closet. The hotel coffee shop was crowded, but they found a table near the door and ordered hamburgers all around. Both Felicity and Cerise chose fries as well, but Antony hesitated. "What's *poutine*?" He pointed to the menu item.

The waitress smiled. "Almost our national dish. French fries with fresh cheese curd and brown gravy."

Antony hesitated, but the waitress didn't. "I'll bring you some. You'll love it—it's the ultimate comfort food."

In a few minutes the waitress set a plate of golden fries and cheese covered with a thick brown gravy before him with an encouraging smile. "Enjoy."

He had his fork almost to his mouth when a familiar voice behind him made him jump. "Ah, thought I'd find you here when you didn't answer my call to your room."

"Zack!" Felicity cried. "What a surprise. How did you know we were here? Sit down. You look different. Oh, you cut your beard. This is Cerise, we're taking her to a convent near Victoria for her sister who is Mother Superior at Saint Scholastica's. How are you?"

Zack sat, gave Cerise a cursory nod, and waved the hovering waitress away all in one maneuver. "Thanks. Right. I'm fine." He grinned as he seemed to sort through Felicity's run-on speech. "What did I miss? Oh, yeah, the beard." He ran his hand across the short, dark stubble on his chin and shrugged. "Just a trim-up. What else did you ask?"

"How did you find us?"

He looked from Felicity to Antony. "Dr. Spaulding has your schedule—he asked me to check if there was anything you need since we won't see you until you get to Westminster."

Antony managed to swallow a bit of the tasty dish in front of him before answering. "Very thoughtful of you both, but I think the schedule is perfectly straightforward. We'll get into Vancouver Thursday evening. Someone will meet us at the train station and drive us to Westminster. That should give us—"

He stopped abruptly as he realized what Felicity had said to Zack. "Wait. We're taking her," he nodded toward Cerise, "to a convent in *Victoria*? You said we were giving her a lift to the airport." He tried to keep his voice level. No need to let the whole restaurant know the dismay he felt—and his exasperation with his wife.

Cerise made the situation worse by giving the giggle that seemed to be the girl's standard response to most circumstances.

"I meant to explain but there wasn't time. I thought—when we were on the plane—but then there was that—"

"Yes. Quite." He cut her off. That was another topic there was no need to inform the world of. He had already noticed heads turning their direction from the next table. He had to be satisfied with muttering *Victoria* and shaking his head.

Now Antony saw that, while he and Felicity had been distracted, Zack had wasted no time getting acquainted with Cerise. Little wonder she was being sent to a convent if the smile on the girl's definitely unpouty lips was any indication of her susceptibility to young men. He wished Zack would leave.

Apparently the newcomer was aware of Antony's eyes on him because he turned back to Felicity and Antony. "Good time at Saint Benoit, was it?"

Zack grinned at their non-committal answers and shrugged. "Yeah, I could have told you so—quiet place in the sticks. I was there once. Didn't see the point, really."

Antony blinked, taken aback by his attitude. Since Zack was so involved in the conference he had thought he shared an interest in matters of theology and faith. It was just a job, apparently. "Good to see you, Zack." Antony stood. "Thanks for stopping by. We have an early start tomorrow."

"I haven't eaten!" The intractable look was back in Cerise's eyes.

Antony motioned to the waitress for to-go boxes to take the unfinished dinners to their rooms. He did not resume his seat.

. . .

Antony strode to the elevator, then down the hall, leaving the women to follow. He turned the corner just in time to see a maid approach their room from the other direction. "What are you doing?"

"Turndown service, sir."

"No thank you."

She backed off and skittered down the hall.

Antony stood stonily beside Cerise's door until it clicked shut and he heard her engage the chain lock. At last, they were alone. The door had barely clicked shut on their room before he turned to Felicity. "Right. Now, talk."

Felicity flopped on the bed, opened her box and took a big bite of her barely touched burger. After a few moments of chewing she smiled. "Oh, that's delicious. Yes, I've been dying to tell you, but things just kept happening..." She paused and sighed. "Well, all right. I wasn't really dying to tell you—I was rather worried, actually. You see, I was afraid you'd be mad at me —as I can see you are. But, really, it wasn't my fault. I don't even know how it happened, really. Mother Anne-Marie just seemed to assume I had agreed..."

Antony crossed to the bathroom. Drew a glass of cold water and brought it back to Felicity. "There. Drink. And catch your breath. Then tell me from the first." He didn't actually say *sensibly*, but his meaning was clear.

After a drink, another bite of her supper and another drink, Felicity explained about the mother superior being responsible for her orphaned sister who had never been away from home and wanted to test her call to become a nun at a convent near Victoria. "Well, not Victoria exactly, it's at a place called Nanaimo. I looked it up. Apparently they make a really scrumptious chocolate bar there—kind of like a brownie. It's become famous all over Canada. I'm sure you'd love it and we could get some while we're there..."

"Felicity!" Antony almost choked on an unfinished bite of

poutine. He normally found Felicity's rattling charming, but he was in no mood at the moment.

"Oops—sorry. Really, I am." And she did sound it. "Actually, the important thing I found out was that there's a direct ferry line to Nanaimo from Victoria. We can easily get Cerise there Friday morning and be back in time for the start of the conference that evening. Or you could go on and I could take her—after all, I got us into this."

The idea of sending Felicity off by herself held no appeal to Antony. Not after all the strange things that had been happening. He shot her a look meant to convey his skepticism at the thought of letting her out of his sight, but he bit his tongue.

Felicity didn't wait for his reply anyway. "And I did think I would like to talk to one of the sisters there if I could. I had a really good talk with Mother Anne-Marie about spiritual direction and I'm thinking that might be a really good course for me. Apparently the sisters at the House of Bread—"

Antony pushed the last few bits of his food away. He knew all too well when it was useless to argue with his wife. Besides, they were too far into this now. It was obvious they couldn't abandon the girl. He sighed. "Never mind. I'm sure it will all work out." He reached for Felicity's hand beside him on the bed. "I didn't mean to bark at you. It's just that I thought we had come to Canada to get away from interruptions, and it seems like that's all we've had since we arrived."

Felicity squeezed his hand. "Before we arrived, even, if you count that scene in Thorpeside Woods." Antony felt her tremble at the remembrance.

He sat up straighter. "Yes, that's exactly what I mean. So many things—most of them really little—hardly enough to notice until you put them all together."

Felicity reached for the pad and pen beside the phone on her bedside stand. "Everything seems so random—entirely disconnected—but maybe if we make a list we'll see a pattern."

Antony's reaction was that he would rather *not* see a pattern.

He would rather dismiss the whole thing. But he knew that would be foolhardy—maybe even disastrous if anything were going on. "Right. Start with the scene in the woods—but just list it. Don't relive it. This is purely objective."

Felicity nodded and wrote. "There was that odd man that showed up at your lecture at Knox."

"Yes, but that was our last day there. Before that there was our room being disturbed."

"Oh, right." Felicity wrote. "And that other man at Saint Andrews—the one that caught me when I stumbled on the steps."

Antony nodded. He had been talking to students and missed the incident, but he remembered Felicity being visibly shaken afterward. "Tell me about that again."

"I was on the top of the church steps, not paying enough attention. I started to fall and this man caught me. I thought he was a conferee, but then I saw him walking away." She closed her eyes as if seeing it again. "That was what really shook me. It was spooky—but he looked like the man I had seen in the woods. The murderer."

Antony took the list from Felicity and made a note.

"And then there was that wheezy breather again at Saint Benoit and on the plane. Well, that one, or others. Maybe there's a lot of asthma in the area."

"Or maybe it is the same person every time," Antony noted.

Felicity nodded. "And then your room at the monastery was messed up and you got locked in the chapel."

A brief quiet time for thought, then Felicity asked, "Is that stuff I read about buried treasure too far-fetched to bother listing?"

Antony recalled his daydream of golden coins tumbling from the illumination on the manuscript. He recorded the incident and Felicity's research. "Are we forgetting anything?"

"Monsieur Laurent's resemblance to the victim—maybe?" Felicity suggested.

Antony wrote. "Anything else?"

"I don't think so." They were both quiet for a moment, then she went on, "Well, there was that odd-looking nun, but that—Oh!" Her hand flew to her mouth. "How could we forget? Père Denis!"

Indeed, how could they have forgotten that? No matter that everyone insisted it was natural causes from a weak heart, Père Denis' death certainly deserved a place on their list. Antony looked back at the assorted jottings. What a random list. Surely only someone very paranoid or someone with a very vivid imagination could make a pattern of all that.

"Have we missed anything?" Felicity broke in on his thoughts.

Antony shook his head. "I don't know—once you start thinking that way everything seems suspicious—even Zack turning up so unexpectedly tonight."

"And Cerise, I suppose."

"What about Cerise?"

"Nothing, I'm sure. But you've got to admit, she seems a little—well, different? Different from what you would expect in someone thinking of becoming a nun, I mean."

Antony gave her an amused smile. "Well, you would know best about that."

She grinned. "Yes, that's exactly what I mean. When I went off to test my ill-conceived vocation, I didn't take a bag stuffed with make-up and jewelry and—well, when her case spilled in the plane—there was a packet of pills that had fallen under the seat near me..."

"Drugs, you mean?" Antony was truly alarmed.

"No, prescription. That is, I could be wrong, but they looked like the kind I'm not taking any more."

His blank face must have shown his complete lack of understanding because she went on. "Since I graduated. And we decided to start a family...?"

The penny dropped. "Oh, you mean Cerise is taking contraceptives to a convent?"

Felicity nodded. "I didn't say anything to her. Do you think I should have?"

Antony considered. "Yes. I do. If we're going to be responsible to ferry her the breadth of Canada, I think we need to know more about what we're dealing with."

Felicity gulped, then reached for the phone. "No time like the present. I don't want to wait till morning—it'll be on my mind all night. I'll ask her now."

She started to dial the room next, then stopped. "On second thought, I'm not sure that's a topic I want to discuss on the phone. I'll be back." She pushed off the bed and strode to the door, then paused. "She's probably asleep."

"Are you havering?"

"Yeah. Okay." She grinned. "I'll knock on her door—not hard enough to wake her if she's very sound asleep."

Felicity rapped lightly on the door, then held her breath. She really did hope the girl was asleep. For all her brave words, what was she going to say? It wasn't as if she were the girl's mother—or even any kind of a friend.

Trying to decide whether to knock again, she put her ear to the door. A female giggle penetrated the heavy barrier. Followed by a male voice. Now Felicity knocked with determined energy. If Cerise was entertaining a male friend—

"Just a minute." A muffled response from inside.

A moment later Cerise answered the door in a hastily donned robe, her normally sleek hair askew. She looked at Felicity sleepily.

"Sorry to bother you—" Felicity began.

"Oh, no problem, I was just watching TV." Cerise stood back and gestured toward the wide screen where a frantic car chase was in progress. "Did you want to come in?" It was a flat question; not a warm invitation.

"Er—no thanks. I just had a quick question." She was still fumbling for the right words when Cerise yawned. "Never mind. It'll wait till morning." Felicity fled.

"She was almost asleep." Felicity explained her speedy return. Antony looked up from the list he was still studying. "Are you brooding over that?" She took the paper from his hand, thinking to lay it aside, but instead, she read through it herself.

Then she wished she hadn't. It gave her chills—whether because there was so much there, or so little, she wasn't sure.

Well, never mind. Their door was firmly locked and in the morning they would be speeding across Canada—far away from whatever it might, or might not, be.

Chapter Sixteen

❧

"Cerise, Cerise!" Felicity was pounding on the girl's door once again the next morning. "We have to go. We can't be late!" Felicity's own urgency was fueled by the fact that she had overslept a bit herself.

"You calling me?" Cerise sauntered along the hall toward the door.

"Where were you?" Felicity didn't mean to sound quite so accusatory.

Cerise shrugged. "Breakfast." She smiled and stretched. "I'll just get my bag."

Outside, Antony led the way down the block and across the street to Toronto's grand Union Station, a marvel of 1920's architecture. As Felicity rushed to keep pace with Antony the sounds of their luggage wheels and pounding feet mingled with scores of others reverberating from the arching, coffered ceiling and pillars of the massive hall lined with flags of each Canadian province. They had been instructed to arrive half an hour before departure, but that deadline was well gone when they reached their platform and were whisked aboard by a waiting official. They were standing in the aisle of the next to last car when Felicity looked out the window and realized they were moving. The train left the station three minutes behind schedule.

The steward looked at their tickets and called an attendant to show Cerise to her seat near the front of the train. Felicity wondered whether she should go with her, but settled for calling out, "I'll see you later, Cerise."

"Don't bother," the girl called over her shoulder. "I'll be fine." Her signature giggle floated back over her shoulder.

Felicity wasn't sure whether she felt stung or relieved at the abrupt dismissal, but turned to follow the steward to their accommodation. She drew in her breath at the understated elegance of their room and sank down on the nearest leather-covered banquette that ran along two of the walls, while the steward pointed out the bathroom, dry bar, and various features. She watched, fascinated, as the city of Toronto, complete with the CN Tower, slid past the window that ran the width of the compartment.

"Champagne?" the steward, who had identified himself as Yoan, asked.

"Tea. Black and strong, please," Felicity replied. "Oh, and would it be possible to get a muffin or something? We missed breakfast."

"But of course. I would be happy to bring it to you, or perhaps you would like to see the club car? There are snacks and drinks available there all day."

Antony nodded his approval of the plan and Felicity happily followed along to the end of the train where more staff awaited them behind a counter set with muffins, croissants, pitchers of fruit juice and bowls of fresh fruit. Along the side wall were urns of coffee and various flavors of tea. "Thank you. This will do very well." Felicity tried to strike a middle ground between gushing and sounding gob-smacked. In her head all she could think of was *Thank you, Jeff. Thank you.* She couldn't imagine what her family must have paid for this fabulous getaway. She had no idea they cared this much for her.

She selected a chocolate croissant and banana to accompany her tea and sank into a comfortable chair. Now the relaxing could start. She sat back and sipped her tea and let the world roll by.

She had barely finished her tea, however, when Antony stood and held out his hand to her. "Let's go up to the dome car. I'm anxious to take in the view." He led to the stairway at the front of the club car.

They settled in seats offering a spectacular panorama of forest punctuated with massive rock formations and lakes of all sizes. Felicity was just thinking of going back to their room to get the *Trainscapes* book, which the steward explained gave the details of their journey, when the voice of the concierge greeted them over the PA system. "Welcome aboard. Today we journey through the immense Saint Lawrence Forest which extends over 71 million hectares of Ontario. That is equal to the land mass of the Netherlands, Germany and Italy combined. You are guaranteed to see billions of trees by the time the *Canadian* crosses the Ontario-Manitoba border." The speaker signed off with a challenge to passengers to start counting.

"I wouldn't even be able to count the lakes," Antony commented without taking his eyes off the view. "And look at all those tiny islands."

Felicity was equally mesmerized by the scene. "Each one seems to have a house on it. Can you imagine living there?"

The public address system came on again and the pleasant female voice informed them that they were traveling through what was known as the Muskoka cottage country. "This is a favorite family retreat for more than two million people each year."

Oh, summer homes. That explained it. How idyllic. And even more idyllic, the steward came up the stairs to announce to all in the dome car that lunch was now being served. Felicity jumped to her feet. Never mind that she had just eaten—that was really only a snack anyway.

The steward had recommended that they hold to the railing while walking along the aisles, but Felicity already felt quite at home with the sway of the train as she strode the few cars forward to the dining room. The host welcomed them and directed them to a table where they became acquainted with a retired couple from New Zealand seated across from them. "Oh, yes, our first time to Canada," the lady who introduced herself as Essie said. "We both just retired from school teaching this spring, so this is a big celebration for us."

Felicity chose lobster ravioli and Antony the French dip sandwich, as they continued chatting with their table mates. Outside the windows, the train seemed to be plunging deeper and deeper into the wilderness. Any sign of towns or vacation homes disappeared. Immense rock formations beside the tracks were overshadowed by heavy timberland.

Felicity was trying to decide between a chocolate bar and a vanilla slice for desert when she felt the train slowing. "Are we stopping?" She looked around and saw only boulders and trees. "There's nothing here. Is something wrong?"

The waiter passing their table explained. "Probably hitch-hikers—most likely sports enthusiasts—fishers, backpackers. We get lots of hunters in the fall. Have to stop—Canadian law. It's a valuable service for the small communities along the route, too, and in our harsh winters it's not merely a service, it can be a life-or-death rescue."

They were on their way in a matter of minutes and Felicity saw the now-empty wooden platform built over the trackside boulders which must have been where their hitch-hikers had hailed their ride. An impressive service.

As much as she enjoyed looking at the view and chatting with fellow passengers, Felicity was finding the motion of the train soporific. Back in their room she selected one of the novels she had chosen especially for train reading. She had been surprised and delighted to discover that Graham Greene, one of her favorite authors, had set a novel on the Orient

Express a year before Agatha Christie wrote her famous mystery.

Now she curled up on the padded bench. She positioned her ereader so she could still peek over the top for glimpses of the view out the window, and opened *Stamboul Train*. Greene's characters left the Ostend ferry and settled into their accommodations on the train, discussing the relative merits of first and second class and agreeing that the important thing was to have a sleeper.

That made Felicity think, with a bit of guilt, of Cerise up front in coach. Could the girl really survive three nights without a bed? And how well supervised were those carriages? For all her veneer of sophistication, she was little more than a child. She had declared she would be fine, but Felicity felt her responsibility as a chaperone.

Not so much, however, that it overcame the sedative effect of a cozy cabin and a rhythmically swaying carriage.

A knock on their door wakened Felicity some time later. Antony opened the door to the steward bearing a tray of afternoon tea with a selection of cheese and salami with seeded crackers and tangy olives. "Oh, heaven." Felicity gave a euphoric sigh and pushed herself to a sitting position, just enough to be able to take the steaming cup Antony held out to her.

Maybe the tea would energize her and she could get some work done on her translation. Or maybe she would go check on —no, visit—Cerise. Or maybe she would read and doze again.

Which was pretty much what she did until the second call to dinner took them to a well-appointed table, a 4-course dinner, and a get-acquainted visit with a couple from France. The couple described the world tour they were undertaking—all part of his photojournalism career. It sounded immensely glamorous, especially as Basile recounted some of their adventures in his charmingly accented English. His wife, who spoke little English, smiled and nodded at the names of places she understood.

When the conversation turned to Felicity and Antony's

careers their companion was fascinated with Felicity's description of trying to reflect the Gaelic chant in a translation, although he declared he knew nothing about the topic.

After dinner, Antony wanted to go up to the dome car again and Felicity readily assented. Talking about her project, however, had made her feel rather guilty for lounging away her afternoon. Now she was anxious to get back to work. "Yes, I'd love to go up, but I'll take my papers with me. Maybe looking out over this amazing sweep of creation will inspire me to an appropriately Gaelic poetic phrase."

They were just settled near the front of the dome when the speaker over their heads informed that they were passing through the Canadian Shield—a region of billion-year-old rock that lies between the Great Lakes and Hudson Bay. "Here, ancient glaciers scoured thousands of lakes with rocky, granite shores. This is rock country, so be on the lookout for places where the rock towers over the track."

Felicity did watch for a while before turning to her work, but the sun was sinking rapidly ahead of them and it would soon be too dark to spot the looming structures the concierge described. It took her a while to get back into the rhythm of her work since she had been away from it for several days. Really, she scolded herself, this wasn't a lengthy document. And she did need to finish it before they returned to England and took up all that their new life there would hold—whatever that might be.

Soft, nighttime lighting came on in the dome, enough to see by, but not harsh enough to blot out the effect of moonlight on the landscape—all the better to make the impressive stone ribs jutting from the earth even more dramatic. Felicity was looking down at her paper when the first flash of bright green light swirled across the page. Alarmed, she jerked her head up, wide-eyed, to see a chartreuse band of light curl in an undulating wave from the horizon and sweep upward to the east. Others in the dome gave a chorus of "Oooooohs"

"Northern lights!" she squealed. "I've wanted to see them all my life!"

At that moment their informative concierge came on the speaker to alert any passengers that might have closed their window shades for the night. "It looks like we're in for a good display. We hope for this all year round—but you never know. They're entirely unpredictable. They're often harder to see in the summer because of longer daylight hours, so we're extra lucky tonight. Enjoy."

"My camera! I want pictures of this." Felicity nudged Antony, equally glued to the sky, to vacate his aisle seat.

"I'll get it for you. Stay here and enjoy."

She didn't argue with him as streaks of iridescent blue joined the green aura. How wonderful that she had just been working on that part of Patrick's great song:

"I bind unto myself today
The virtues of the starlit heaven,
The glorious sun's life-giving ray,
The whiteness of the moon at even,
The flashing of the lightning free,"

She looked down occasionally to fill in the words she might have lost in the shadows between the intermittent illuminations.

Antony was by her side again quickly, holding out her phone. "I took a few pictures from the club car, too."

"Great. Thanks." She gathered her papers and the manuscript copy from the small tray table, to rescue them from their imminent danger of being scattered, and stuffed them in the folder which she thrust at Antony. "Here, will you hold these for me?"

Clasping the file, Antony took a seat to enjoy the heavenly

show in quiet contemplation, but Felicity was far too excited. She hurried to the very front of the dome which offered the most panoramic view and set her camera to video. And none too soon, because now hot pink flares fired through the green band arcing above the horizon.

The heavenly illumination continued and Felicity breathlessly continued her photography, now taking stills from many angles, from various places in the car, some next to the window, some from angles across the car showing silhouettes of other passengers as enrapt as she was. At last the show faded to darkness. "Oh, is it over?" she said, lowering her camera and turning to the passenger who happened to be beside her.

"Seems to be. Brilliant, wasn't it?" His English voice made her turn more directly to him.

She clapped her hand over her mouth to keep from screaming and stumbled backward. He held out his hand to steady her. "Whoa, careful."

She looked at him again, blinked to be sure, looked again, and gave a strangled reply as she looked wildly around for Antony. He must have gone back to their room when she was engrossed in her photography. She stumbled down the stairs and sped along the hall to their compartment. She was too shaken to unlock the door, so she merely pounded on it.

When Antony flung it open she all but fell into his arms. "Felicity! What's the matter? You look like you've seen a ghost."

"I have. It's the murder victim..."

Chapter Seventeen

Antony was more alarmed for Felicity than for anything she might have seen. There was obviously some mistake. The idea was patently absurd. She was obviously seeing things. First the murderer in Toronto, now...well, his beloved had always had an over-active imagination. "Felicity, I realize you've had a bad experience, but..."

She pulled away from him and drew herself up stiffly. "I am not being an hysterical female."

He bit his tongue to keep from replying.

"Well, okay. Just a little bit. But I have good reason. Wait—" She looked at the camera still in her hand. "I can show you. I didn't get a very clear look at that man at Saint Andrews who looked like the murderer—really just more of an impression, but this is different. Maybe—" She scrolled through her pictures. "I got the passengers in some of my shots..."

She stopped scrolling and held the camera out. "Yes! See!"

"Well, it's only a silhouette." Antony struggled to be conciliatory. "And I didn't see the victim. I suppose he does look a little like that antiquities expert did without his glasses—and you said he looked like the victim."

"More than a little. Without the glasses and mustache. Here,

I'll show you." She began scrolling back through her photos. Then she stopped and scrolled forward. "Antony, those pictures I took in Père Denis' office—they're not here."

"Did you delete them after sending them to Father Peter?"

"No. I wanted to keep them. Thank goodness I sent them on to Father Peter before we got on the train. I can get copies from him." She sighed. "I must have hit the wrong button somehow. Technology drives me crazy."

"Let me take a look." Antony held out his hand. After several moments of clicking he shook his head. "Those pictures are gone from your cloud storage and the recycle bin as well."

Felicity shivered. And Antony sympathized. She couldn't have done all that by accident. Someone had been very thorough. But how could anyone have got hold of her phone? As he recalled, she hadn't taken her phone with her to dinner, but their compartment was always locked. Of course crew could get in. He looked at their bed which had been so beautifully folded out during their absence—complete with chocolates on the pillow.

Following Yoan's instructions, they had hung the yellow "Please make up my room" card on their door when they went to dinner. A signal to any steward or porter that their cabin was empty. But what motive could any steward or porter possibly have to interfere with Felicity's pictures?

Antony put his arm around her. "Come to bed. We can't do anything tonight. There will be a stop tomorrow sometime. We can get off and send the photos from last night to Inspector Nosterfield. Maybe he can apply facial recognition; see if his corpse has a twin or something."

Felicity nodded. "Good idea. And suggest he ask Father Peter for a copy of the photos I sent earlier."

Antony grinned. "And ask him if his corpse has recovered. He'll love that."

. . .

A few minutes later Felicity snuggled into their crisp, white bed next to Antony, determined to forget all alarms and imaginings. They were alone in their tiny, rhythmically jiggling world. Safe. She told herself.

In spite of the coziness, however, sleep did not come. Perhaps it was the effort of not permitting herself to worry about what she had—or preferably hadn't—seen.

She scrunched her pillow up to raise her head a few inches so she could gaze out the window which they had left unshaded. Mesmerized, she watched the silhouettes of that other world streaking past outside. Inside, they were in their own world, as if sliding through a long, dark tube. She played dreamily with her metaphor. Perhaps they were inside a big, black bubble. Or maybe a spacecraft hurtling among those stars she could see in the sky.

She recalled the sense of being in a cocoon that so drew her when she first went to the Community of the Transfiguration. The sense of being in a secret, hushed world. And yet that world had so often been interrupted by violence.

The next thing she knew was Yoan knocking at their door with morning tea and a reminder that breakfast would be served in an hour. After thanking him profusely, she asked, "Did we stop in the night?"

She had finally been lulled into slumber, but had drifted into consciousness enough to sense—or had dreamed—that all was quiet and still. She had the impression that they had been stopped for some time, but nothing had been certain in her drowsy state.

"Yes, we were side-railed for quite a while. Via Rail doesn't own the tracks. Freight trains have right-of-way." He set the tray on the foot of the bed, then turned back to the door. "That can amount to some serious delays, but we usually make it up."

Felicity scooted up in bed and sipped her tea, just the thing to settle her slightly queasy stomach—she hadn't slept on a train since childhood. She smiled, enjoying the clear, morning sunlight flooding in their window as the Canadian landscape rolled outside. She was just about to ask Antony if he had any idea where they were when the concierge's voice came on the overhead speaker to inform passengers that they were approaching Capreol. "You will see the landscape becoming increasingly rugged and angular as we cross the thousand-mile area of the Canadian Shield. Watch out for exposed bedrock which was formed between 500 million and five billion years ago, creating a hard blanket for half of Canada and parts of the northern United States. You will see dense forests where it is covered with soil, but elsewhere you'll note countless lakes and streams, alongside treacherous bogs called *muskeg*, a Cree word meaning wet, unstable soil. Manitoba is known as 'The Land of 100,000 Lakes.'"

Felicity laughed. "Well, that's us outdone—Americans know Minnesota as Land of 10,000 Lakes."

As if he had heard her, the concierge added, "Canada has the most lake area in the world. Historically the area provided a canoe route for European fur traders. Today it is a center for fly-in hunting and fishing camps."

The massive boulders, birch trees and interspersed pines blurred outside the window. That must mean that the train had sped up, trying to make up the time lost during the night. Antony seemed to notice the same thing because he said, "I read in some of the information that came with our tickets that passengers shouldn't book onward passage from Vancouver because arrival times are approximate."

Felicity hoped they wouldn't be too far behind schedule. She was rather vague on how much time it would take to see Cerise to her convent. But at least they could be flexible. She had glanced at ferry schedules and saw that walk-on passengers didn't need reservations, so no worries there.

Thinking of Cerise, however, reminded her that she really should give her charge a visit today.

They ate breakfast while parked on a siding, awaiting another freight train. Bright yellow wildflowers grew along the track just outside their window; beyond that a wide expanse, covered with tall grasses blowing in the breeze, ran down to a blue lake rimmed with dark green pines. Overhead, a cloudless blue sky promised sunshine all the way.

Eventually, the seemingly miles-long freight train rumbled by and they resumed their progress. Felicity put her fork down, too full to finish the last bites of her smoked salmon and spinach omelet. "Fancy a walk through the train? I thought I should visit Cerise."

Antony grinned. "She won't thank you for it. That one is fighting hard for her independence, if you ask me."

"Which is precisely why I should check on her."

"That's probably right. Just don't let her know you're checking up."

"Well, I can hardly say I was just passing."

Antony chuckled as he rose and held out his hand to help Felicity stand. "Well, good luck to you. I need to spend some time with my lecture notes. Westminster won't offer the location tie-ins that Toronto did—such as they were—so I've got to rework my material a bit."

"I know what I'll do. I didn't eat the chocolates the steward left on my pillow last night—unlike some I know." She gave Antony a saucy grin. "I'll take them to Cerise. Tell her I wanted to stretch my legs."

Yoan was just leaving their cabin as they approached from the dining car. "Good timing. Just got your room made up. Is there anything you need?"

Felicity and Antony agreed that they didn't need anything—

everything was great. "How many compartments do you have to do?" Felicity asked.

"There are two porters for every three cars."

"And how many cars?"

"It varies. I think there are about sixty on this run."

"I want to visit my friend in coach. There's no problem about that is there?" Felicity suddenly wondered if there might be rules about passengers wandering through the train.

"No problem at all. Actually, I'm going on break, so I'm headed forward now. Would you like a tour?"

"Yes, thank you. Can you wait just a minute?" Felicity darted in, tucked the tiny box of chocolates in a pocket and waved good-bye to Antony.

Yoan led the way forward, talking over his shoulder. "Your friend will be in one of the front cars. I think we have two or three coaches this time."

"How many classes are there?" Felicity wasn't sure which category they had been up-graded from, but she was interested in seeing the other accommodations.

"Three, basically." Her guide pushed the pad to open the door at the front of their carriage. They stepped into the noisy connecting space, and through the door into the next carriage with a long aisle on the left and doors to compartments like theirs on the right. "There's Prestige, like these," Yoan continued his lecture. "Then sleeper plus, and coach."

They passed through another carriage of compartments, then the dining room Felicity was familiar with. "Each section has their own dining car. And each dining car has its own kitchen—with chef and cooks." The kitchen exuded intense heat as they passed it.

The car past the dining room, however, was open and sunny with tables on each side of the aisle. Some had table games and jigsaw puzzles set out on them. A few were in use by passengers playing card games or chess. "Occasionally they have live entertainment in here—talks, music and such—sometimes. You'll hear the announcements."

Another dome car signaled that they were entering the sleeper accommodation. "There are actually four tiers within sleeper class: Cabin for one, Cabin for two, upper berth and lower berth."

They went through another decompression chamber, as Felicity thought of the connecting hatches between cars, and walked down an aisle with heavy grey fabric serving as doors for the seats on each side of them. Felicity heard muffled conversations through the hangings over some of the roomettes. A few had their drape open and Felicity viewed the grey seats which would transform into bunks at night.

Was that what their accommodation would have been if Jeff and her family hadn't come forward with their largesse, she wondered? Or would it have been in the less private rows of seats that were likewise made up into bunks for sleeping, which they went through next?

After the dining car for that group, and passing the heat of their kitchen, Yoan pointed out another carriage of grey-curtained compartments. "Staff accommodation," he explained. They were just at the front of that car when the train jerked, throwing her against one of the curtained enclosures.

Yoan, barely a step ahead of her, shot out an arm and caught her. "Whoa, you almost landed in my room." He held her arm until she had her feet firmly under her.

She gave a nervous laugh. "Good catch thank you. So that's your room?"

"For what it's worth. I don't see much of it, but the bunk is all right. We're usually tired enough after a shift that accommodation doesn't make much difference."

Felicity had also noted the shower rooms and toilets at the ends of the carriages that didn't offer private conveniences. Another thing to thank Jeff for.

Again, the heat in the aisle told Felicity they were passing a kitchen. This, for coach. Not a sit-down dining room like the others, but a counter where one could order hot dogs, hamburgers or pizza. And, she noted, the popular *poutine*. Since these cars accommodated many families with young children, Felicity was sure these were passenger-friendly choices.

Beyond that was a carriage of reclining seats, much like those one encountered on an airplane, although, thankfully offering slightly more space. "There are two more coaches in front of this. I'm sure you'll find your friend in one of them. All there is in front of that is the baggage car and the engine."

Felicity realized her guide was leaving her at this point. She understood—he had finished making up the rooms, now he had come up to his bunk for a rest. "Oh, thank you so much. I hope I haven't kept you too long. I'll be fine now." She wondered fleetingly if she should offer him a tip, but she was pretty sure she had read somewhere that wasn't done on the train. She hoped so, because she hadn't brought her purse. "Thank you again," she called to his retreating back.

Now she turned to survey the busy car in front of her. Children played in the aisle; a mother was struggling to change a diaper on a squirming baby laid out on the seat beside her; a large lady in the next row attempted to sleep with a folded cloth over her eyes, while the children next to her devoured a pizza with sauce-covered hands and faces.

She spotted a young woman with sleek dark hair near the front of the car, but when the girl turned around Felicity saw that her brown face was not Cerise's.

The next carriage was equally busy with passengers passing the time reading, playing games, or attempting to doze. But no Cerise.

Felicity hurried on to the last coach car. She was so certain she would find her charge in the next carriage that for a moment she was completely flummoxed when her second walk up and down the length of the car failed to reveal a young woman with shining black hair and vibrant, if moody, countenance. But then Felicity relaxed as she realized how many places she hadn't checked—the games car, dome car, washroom. Cerise might even have been in one of the shower rooms when they walked through her car.

Felicity only began to panic when all those locations failed to yield results. Where could the girl have possibly hidden herself? Was she purposely trying to avoid her chaperone? But if so, where could she hide? The luggage room was locked—Felicity had checked. What had she missed?

Then she spotted a porter. "Please, can you help me? I'm looking for my friend." She described Cerise's distinctive appearance.

"Oh, yeah. Cherry—why didn't you say so?" A broad smile covered his face "A right corker, that one. She had half the car laughing most of the night. She can't half sing."

Felicity frowned. Could they be talking about the same girl? If so, little wonder Mother Anne-Marie wanted her to be overseen on her journey. But a future nun?

Before Felicity could form a reply, the porter jerked his head toward the rear. "Tucked up back there. She'll probably be around this afternoon."

Felicity frowned. "But I don't understand..."

The porter smiled again. "Too pretty a missy to sit up all this way, especially after keeping our spirits up so. She earned herself a nap."

"Cerise got a sleeper?"

The porter shrugged. "It wasn't in use. Not hurting anything. I'll see that it's all put back right. Can I give her a message?"

"No thanks, I'll probably be back later. Actually, don't say anything. I wanted to surprise her." She thought about holding out the box of chocolates to lend credibility to her story, but instead, simply turned and left.

Felicity was walking back through one of the sleeper carriages when she heard a distinctive giggle.

"Cerise!" Felicity's confusion showed in her voice. Should she reprimand the girl who was supposed to be sleeping, or be relieved to have found her? She started to yank the curtain aside, but the girl was apparently holding it tightly. "What's going on in there?"

A tousled, dark head peeked around the edge of the drape from the upper bunk. "I'm reading a funny book. Any objections?" As proof she withdrew her head and stuck a book out, displaying its comic, if rather lurid, cover.

It didn't make much sense to Felicity, but then, nothing about Cerise did. She sighed. "Try to get some sleep. I'll see you later."

"Yeah." The curtain jerked shut.

Felicity turned back toward her cabin, trying to convince herself that she hadn't heard a low, male chuckle from Cerise's bunk.

Felicity arrived back at their compartment breathless. "Antony, the most awful thing! Well, that is, maybe—the thing is, I don't know for sure. And I don't know—what can we do about it?"

Antony set aside the notes he had been working on, stood, and crossed the small space to put his hand on Felicity's shoulders. "Whoa. Sit down and tell me what happened." He turned her toward the banquette and sat beside her. "Now. Take a breath and tell me all about it."

She did, as clearly as she could, although she had to admit that even to her own ears it didn't sound as earth-shattering as she at first thought. Had three years in a monastery really made her so unrealistic? Still—"We have to do something..." She faltered to a stop.

Antony considered in his quiet way. "Well, I suppose it might help in her discernment process."

"Antony!" Felicity gaped at him. "I didn't expect you to be so flippant."

He grinned. "Well, maybe it is. But really—if she's thinking of being a nun and this is actually what she wants, it's better to find it out now, rather than later."

"But..."

"Besides, what can we do? I can hardly storm up there and pull her out physically. I don't know Canadian law, but she's probably an adult. And, in reality, we aren't here in *loco parentis*."

Felicity frowned, but couldn't think of a reply.

"Would it make you feel better if I had a word with her? When she's likely to be in a more, er—receptive mood?"

Felicity readily agreed. And really, she understood the common sense of what he said. Still, she spent the rest of the day worrying. She couldn't put the girl out of her mind—especially when she returned to her Graham Greene novel and read the part where Coral Musker, the showgirl who couldn't afford a sleeper and was given a bed in a first class compartment by the kindly Myatt, appeared to be coming to a bad end.

Chapter Eighteen

The next morning at breakfast, Antony observed the dark circles under Felicity's usually bright eyes, a sharp contrast to the brilliant morning sunlight highlighting the thick spruce forest rolling by outside their window. "Trouble sleeping last night?"

Felicity sighed and dropped her generously buttered and marmaladed English muffin back on her plate. "What are we going to do about that girl?"

Antony merely shook his head as Felicity repeated the question she had asked countless times. There was really only one possible answer to that—get her to her convent as soon as possible, inform her sister that the deed was accomplished, and wash their hands of the whole bothersome job.

The thing that was worrying Antony at the moment, however, was the first part of that plan. They had spent almost three hours sitting on a siding during and after dinner last night, waiting for the freight train that had broken down in front of them to move. That, added to the innumerable shorter delays, must have put them many hours behind their scheduled arrival time. According to the map in their room, Winnipeg was the halfway point, which they should have reached this morning.

Yoan had mentioned that city as where the crew changed, but they hadn't even reached Sioux Lookout yet. The steward said there would be a brief stop there where they could get out and walk about a bit—something Antony was much looking forward to.

Besides feeling a need for fresh air, Antony would breathe easier when they could send Felicity's photos to the Yorkshire police. The internet connection had been too weak during both of their brief stops yesterday. He wasn't sure whether it was just concern for Felicity, or whether her alarms were arousing his own fears, but he knew that the sooner they could hand their information on to the authorities—even in the likelihood of being laughed at—the better he would feel. And hopefully some of Felicity's apprehension would be alleviated.

They were just finishing breakfast when the announcement came that they would soon be stopping in Sioux Lookout, known as "'the Hub of the North' because it connects twenty-nine remote First Nations communities who live deep in this forested region."

The announcement was barely over when he felt the train slowing. Antony dropped his napkin beside his plate and stood. "A walk will feel great. Don't forget your phone. You should be able to send those photos to Nosterfield here."

From the little stool outside the open door of their carriage, they stepped out onto the graveled right of way. Across the street a few trees punctuated a row of timber store fronts, including an A-frame outdoor adventure supplier and a legion hall adorned profusely with bright maple-leaf flags.

Felicity pulled her phone from her pocket. "Ah, three bars, this should do the trick." After a few moments of tapping keys, a soft whoosh sound told them they had done their duty to inform the authorities, even though Antony doubted that Felicity's email would receive a warm welcome.

Felicity started to return her phone to her pocket, then said, "Just a minute. I want to see…" She pushed the calendar button, then counted on her fingers. It was so easy to lose track of time when traveling. Then she smiled and slipped her phone away. "Done. Let's get some exercise."

Antony strode off toward the front of the train, with Felicity keeping pace. They paused for a moment to look at a carriage on a side track promoting Expedition Churchill, painted with a panoramic waterscape featuring the polar bears and beluga whales visitors could see in that far northern outpost, then continued crunching along the stony path.

They were nearing the middle of the train when Felicity grabbed his arm and pointed forward. "There's Cerise."

He looked up just in time to see the young man she appeared to be walking with turn around sharply. Antony considered as the broad back disappeared behind a group of other strolling passengers. Something about the man's gait seemed familiar. Would this be a good time to have his promised chat with their charge?

Before he could puzzle more, however, the stewards standing by open doors along the *Canadian* began ushering passengers back on. With a sense of relief, he turned toward their carriage after only the sketchiest wave to Cerise before she also turned.

"Did you see him?" Felicity demanded as soon as they were back in the privacy of their cabin. "That man with Cerise? See— I told you there was something going on. Oh, why didn't I think to take a picture?" Then she clapped a hand to her forehead, "And I didn't text Mother Anne-Marie, either."

Antony consulted the map in the *Trainscapes* guidebook. "Well, if we aren't held up too much by all that rolling stock keeping the Canadian economy vigorous, we should be in Winnipeg by midafternoon. You should have a chance then."

The book also informed him that in the 230 miles between Sioux Lookout and Winnipeg the *Canadian* would rarely be interrupted by settlements. Their morning in the dome car proved that to be true, although they were interrupted by numerous freight trains. Each delay increased Antony's concern over arriving in Vancouver in time to see Cerise safely to her convent, then allow him to get on to Westminster Abbey before the conference began.

At last they reached the Ontario-Manitoba border where their informative concierge reminded passengers they were now in Central Daylight time. The voice over their heads also informed them they were approaching the western edge of the Canadian Shield and were traveling through a Precambrian park known for canoeing, fishing and wildlife including moose, caribou, eagles, beaver, and deer.

Setting his watch back helped Antony relax, as he realized there would be two more such adjustments, each one increasing their chance of fulfilling their obligation.

Shortly before midafternoon they rolled into the Winnipeg station. As the train slowed, the announcer came on again, "Winnipeg is at the junction of three rivers, which inspired the Cree to call this place 'Wini-nipi,' meaning muddy water. This cosmopolitan center is often called 'the Chicago of the North.'"

Felicity smiled at the reference, until the speaker added, "It is also sometimes called 'Murderpeg' because it has the highest murder rate of all Canadian cities." Then he turned to a more positive note. "Winnipeg is typically Canadian in its multicultural population, being home to more than two hundred ethnic groups speaking over one hundred-thirty languages."

A few minutes later they were walking under the vast Beaux-Arts dome of the Winnipeg Union Station, admiring the elegant blue and white expanse, all accented with gold. Outside the front door, they stood at the edge of the bustling sidewalk and admired the wide, tree-lined streets with modern towers and heritage buildings spread before them.

"I love the way the sunshine makes all the buildings look golden," Felicity remarked as she snapped several pictures. "And that French fairytale looking one." She pointed to a building with pyramid-shaped towers and multiple pinnacles that was probably a hotel. "Do we have time to walk over there?"

Antony looked at his watch. "Half an hour, they said. I think so, but better send that message first."

Felicity typed her text to Mother Anne-Marie, then frowned. "I hope she gets it. They didn't have very reliable internet service at Saint Benoit."

Felicity tucked her phone away and they crossed the busy street. They were just leaving the gleaming, marble lobby of the hotel a few minutes later when her phone pinged. "Oh, that must be Mother Anne-Marie. My message must have sent. What a relief!"

Her elation faded when she looked at the screen. "It's from Nosterfield." She read out. "'How can you be meddling from 3000 miles away? Corpse definitely dead.' Typical." She snapped her phone off.

Antony smiled. "Well, really, what did you expect? He was hardly going to be pleased with you questioning his competence and complicating his case."

They had only been back in their room a short time when a knock at their door announced the arrival of a new steward, this one a woman in a smart navy blue uniform with her long dark hair pulled back in a ponytail. "Hello, I'm Lynda. I'll be with you to Vancouver." She set a tray of fruit-topped warm Brie, crackers, and tea on their coffee table. "That's Saskatoon berry chutney." She pointed to the dark purple preserve on the cheese.

"Saskatoon berries? I've never heard of them," Felicity said.

"Not many people have—they're native to the Canadian Prairies. The trees grow wild, but they've started growing them commercially recently."

The door had barely closed before Felicity was topping the seeded crackers with wedges of oozing cheese spread with their new culinary adventure. "Oh, this is amazing!"

After his first bite, Antony agreed with her pronouncement, but his mouth was too full to reply, so he settled for nodding.

Outside their window the scenery underwent a radical change. After three days of massive rock structures, dense forests and thousands of lakes and waterways, they were now traveling through a wide, green, flat terrain that stretched as far as the eye could see.

They had devoured the last morsel and washed it down with final sips of tea when the concierge, this time a male voice, announced that there would soon be a talk on archeology in the club car at the rear of the train.

"Want to go?" Antony asked.

Felicity shrugged. "I was going to try to get some work done this afternoon." She grinned. "Or maybe take a nap to sleep off that decadent treat. I really shouldn't have followed it all up with those chocolates."

Antony chuckled and, likewise sated, pulled himself to a standing position. "Right, then, a walk is just what you need. We can always come back and nap if the speaker is boring."

"Or nap right there," Felicity suggested.

In the lounge they recognized several of the people they had met at mealtime. They nodded to the ladies from Tokyo they sat with at lunch and took seats between the New Zealanders they first met and the French couple they dined with the first night. Antony was concentrating to catch the details of the Winnipeg art gallery's collection of Inuit art and sculpture, which the Frenchman had read about and regretted not having time to see, when Felicity grabbed his arm insistently.

"Look, Antony—it's the man in my picture," she hissed in his ear.

The concierge introduced Professor Ewan McKinnon from the archeology department of the University of Glasgow who was in Canada to lead a team exploring Viking activity in Canada.

With heightened interest, Antony listened to their lecturer's soft Scottish voice, but watched Felicity for her reaction. Now that she saw him in daylight, would she be as certain as earlier about his likeness to the man she saw in the woods? Felicity seemed to be riveted to his words, but as far as Antony could tell, not upset by his appearance. Nosterfield's snide message must have set her mind at rest on that score, at least.

Antony mentally tried putting glasses on him and darkening his hair and mustache, but couldn't conjure up a striking resemblance to the documents expert at Saint Benoit, other than their both probably not being above five feet, ten inches tall.

"The Norse colonization of North America began in the late 10th century. About the year 1000 Leif Eriksson sailed to what is now North America from Iceland. He called this new country Vinland. It wasn't until the 1960s, however, that the remains of Nordic buildings were found at *L'Anse aux Meadows* near the northern tip of Newfoundland.

"It represents the farthest-known extent of European exploration and settlement of the New World before the voyages of Christopher Columbus almost 500 years later. Historians have speculated that there were other Norse sites, or at least Norse-Native American trade contacts, in the Canadian Arctic..."

The professor went on to describe the archeological findings in more detail—including a bronze cloak pin, a soapstone spindle piece, iron nails and rivets. He accompanied each item with a photograph which he passed around as he named it. Antony observed Felicity remaining relaxed until Professor McKinnon began expounding his theories that led to his team's current work. "Historians have speculated that there were Norse trade routes to the indigenous peoples of the Canadian Arctic long before the Viking settlements here. Undoubtedly similar to the routes established somewhat earlier to Ireland. Archeological activities in this century have uncovered evidence of a layer of civilization beneath the Norse settlement which would support this theory."

He went on to detail the findings, again, accompanied by

photographs, but it wasn't until he explained his own theories behind the explorations of his team that Felicity leaned forward intently. "So all that ancient commercial activity leads me to conclude that there is far more waiting to be found in the peaty soil of Newfoundland than a few bronze and soapstone artifacts."

Polite applause followed and the concierge, who had introduced himself earlier as Liam, invited questions from the audience.

"I thought the Vikings were Danish," an Australian lady at the far end of the car asked.

"Ah, a common misunderstanding." The professor nodded. "Since Victorian times, all Scandinavian seafaring traders, settlers and warriors have commonly been lumped together under the term Vikings—no matter whether they came from Sweden, Denmark, or Norway."

"Can you be more precise about what you hope to find?" This question from their French acquaintance.

Professor McKinnon smiled enigmatically. "I guess I'll have to say that we'll know when we find it." He paused. "It isn't difficult to speculate, however, that commerce leads to wealth, and there is no reason to believe that there couldn't be similar findings to those made from that same period in Great Britain."

"Are you talking about treasure troves?" the questioner persisted.

The guest speaker gave another inscrutable smile that made his reddish mustache twitch. "Certainly there have been some in Great Britain. As to Canada—well, as I said before—we'll know when we find it."

The door to their room had barely clicked shut when Felicity turned to Antony with an eager look. "See! I was right! I knew it. I mean, okay—he's not the murder victim. But I'll bet he's a brother—or cousin or something. It can't be a coincidence that he's hunting a treasure trove, and you had a vision of treasure on the manuscript, and I read all that about Viking treasure in Ireland, and McKinnon is Scottish, and didn't Father Peter say Brother Finbar came from Nova Scotia, and people seem to be following us and—"

There didn't seem to be any likelihood of Felicity running out of breath—or wild speculation—so Antony resorted to his usually successful method of calming her torrent of words by kissing her. When she was calm he would point out that it was all quite likely sheer coincidence.

Unfortunately, this time his ploy didn't work. She pulled away. "Not now, Antony. We've got to think. Nosterfield will never follow up on that—even if he were here to do so."

Antony's amusement turned to chilling fear. "Felicity—you aren't thinking of taking on detective work?" He was truly frightened at the prospect of her plunging into danger.

"No, of course not." Her words would have been more reassuring if she hadn't gone on. "But it wouldn't hurt to ask a few questions. Archeology, wasn't that Dr. Spaulding's expertise? We should talk to him—he might have some ideas. He could even have met one of McKinnon's team through some archeologists' association. Maybe he even knows him."

Antony was too concerned for Felicity to voice his objections, fearing it might make her even more determined. His only comfort was the fact that it all seemed much too far-fetched.

Chapter Nineteen

The next morning Felicity awoke to a scene very similar to the one before it got dark outside their window the night before. In every direction an expanse of green prairie swept to the horizon to be met by a dome of blue sky. Between sips of her morning tea she observed, "You know, my dad's brother lived in Nebraska—Uncle Henry—we went to visit him a couple of times when I was a child. I was pretty amazed by that prairie, but I've got to admit we've been well and truly outdone. The Canadian prairie is wider, broader and flatter than ours."

As if in reply to her remark, the melodious male voice from the speaker informed them that they were crossing Saskatchewan and would be entering Alberta before evening. Felicity smiled; realizing that they were nearing the border of her native Idaho she felt almost as if she were home. The voice continued, "We are truly traveling through a breadbasket for the world as these plains produce almost forty million metric tons of grain a year, including wheat, barley and oats."

At breakfast Felicity seemed more aware of the motion of the train than she had before. And she noticed the waiter taking extra care as he filled their glasses with their morning orange juice. He grinned when she asked him about it. "We're trying to make up time, but it's harder across the prairie. We don't have the rock foundation of the shield under the track, so it's less stable." He moved his hand from side to side to indicate shifting ground.

"Something else I've noticed," Felicity continued. "On trains in the States," she jerked her head to the south, "there's a constant clickety-clack. I haven't heard that on this trip."

"No, no. Different rails." The waiter spoke with pride. "Canadian rails are continuous—no plates joining rails like you have in the States."

The waiter moved on and the conversation became general with the couple from Connecticut sitting across the table from them. They were interested in how Felicity and Antony met and how living in England worked for Felicity, since their daughter was seriously dating a young man from England she met at Yale.

Back in their cabin Felicity and Antony agreed that, since they were scheduled to arrive at their destination the next day, they really should settle down to some serious concentration on their work. Felicity pulled the manuscript copy, its Latin translation, and her English notes from the zipper pouch in her suitcase which travelled under the banquette that made into their bed at night. She relaxed into one corner of the padded bench, her long legs stretched out in front of her, using their coffee table as a footstool, and her stiff folder as a writing desk.

She looked back, counting. Ah, she was ready to start on the sixth stanza. More than halfway, then—there would be four more stanzas to do after this one, and the last stanza echoed the first one. Still, as slow as her progress was on this, it would take some serious concentration to have it finished to leave with the monk in Westminster. She needed to be free of it before they went back to England and the busy life that awaited them there— whatever shape hers would take.

She struggled to get the rhythm of the chanted lines she had heard at Saint Patrick's and at Saint Benoit-du-Lac, allowing the sway of the train to help her. Eventually the cadence took over and Latin words began to flow from the English that would give scope for the melisma—the extended syllables—that would give the piece the Gaelic feeling she was striving for.

Against the demon snares of sin,
The vice that gives temptation force,
The natural lusts that war within,
The hostile men that mar my course;
Be they few or many, far or nigh,
In every place and in all hours,
Against their fierce hostility
I bind to me these holy powers.

As much as she wanted to concentrate on the poetry and the metre of her work, it wouldn't be an honest—or successful—job if she didn't get inside the meaning. It was known that Patrick had committed some great sin in his youth, of which he heartily repented later in life. Was that what he was thinking of when he wrote of "the vice that gives temptation force" and "the natural lusts that war within"? Whatever he was thinking, it was certain he knew a lot about human nature.

And the hostile men that marred his course with their fierce hostility—was this a reference to the raiders that snatched him from his home and sold him into slavery? Or the murderous Irish king he confronted? Or was it a more general reference to the pervasiveness of evil in the world? She would have liked to ask Antony his opinion, but she could see he was concentrating on his lecture notes, so she returned to focusing on the pages before her, and to the pulse of the swaying train carriage for a feel of the vocalized sequences she hoped to create.

'*I bind to me these holy powers.*' She wasn't choosing the melody this would be chanted in, but in her mind she heard it in sounds more appropriate to an oratorio than a chant—loud, triumphant, with a real sense of standing against evil.

The banging at their door broke in so suddenly that Felicity knocked her papers to the floor. She swooped them up and opened the door, expecting the steward.

"Cerise!" She stepped back to allow the girl to enter, shocked by her stricken face. "What's the matter?"

"Nothing!" She began with her usual defiance, then her shoulders slumped. "I don't know. I just... well, I guess I just needed somebody to talk to. I didn't sleep very well last night. The train kept stopping and starting and I don't like the swaying... and then, I have this eerie feeling that someone is watching me. I think they went through my bag when I was in the washroom."

Felicity blinked. Was this the contrary, obstreperous young woman who had marched off telling Felicity not to visit her? What could she say to her? She could hardly assure her that there was no possibility of any ill-doing on the train, since she had been wrestling with similar worries herself.

Thankfully, Antony put his papers aside and leaned forward. "I'm so glad you came to us, Cerise. Sit down." It was as much a command as an invitation. Cerise sat. "Now, do you have any idea who might be bothering you? Or why?"

Cerise shook her head vehemently. "What could I have that anyone would be interested in?" Antony's concern and his taking her fears seriously seemed to make her relax.

"There's nothing missing from your pack?" he persisted.

"What's to miss? They don't let you take anything to that convent."

A ring of the old Cerise was back in her tone. For the first time, it occurred to Felicity to wonder whether the convent idea was really Cerise's, or whether she was being pushed into it by her sister.

"This is a long trip to take on your own," Antony continued. "It's especially hard if you aren't sleeping."

"Didn't you have that bunk again last night?" Felicity cut in.

Cerise made a face. "I tried with the new porter that got on at Winnipeg, but he wasn't as inclined to be helpful as Joe-Joe was."

So someone was impervious to her wiles, Felicity thought. Probably a good lesson for her to learn. Still...

"Antony, why don't you find our steward and see if you can buy Cerise an upgrade for tonight? I know she doesn't want to arrive at the House of Bread exhausted tomorrow."

"Oh, no!" Cerise resumed her worried look. "Don't do that. Couldn't I stay here with you?"

Antony looked as taken aback by the suggestion as Felicity felt. He stood. "I'm sorry, but there isn't room." He moved toward the door. "I'll try to find Lynda, our steward, and see what arrangements can be made. Surely there's a spare bunk somewhere on the train." He paused at the door. "Have you eaten? Do you have any money with you?"

Felicity smiled. Leave it to Antony to be practical; he must have remembered Felicity telling him about the pay-as-you-go system she noticed at the fast food kitchen in coach class.

Cerise shrugged; whether it was reluctance to admit that she did have money or that she didn't, Felicity wasn't certain. It occurred to her to try asking Cerise if she couldn't get her young man to buy her a meal—it might have been interesting to see how she would react—but probably not helpful at this moment.

"I'll see if I can make some sleeping arrangements for you, and Felicity can buy you some lunch." Antony exited.

In spite of the promise of food, however, Cerise seemed to be in no hurry to leave. Instead of jumping to her feet, as Felicity expected, the girl eyed the papers lying beside Felicity on the bench. "What are you working on?"

Felicity told her in a few sentences.

"Hmm, interesting." Felicity doubted that Cerise found it so. Still, she persisted. "Can you show me?"

The girl's giggle seemed nervous. Could someone have put

her up to asking this? "Wouldn't you rather get something to eat?"

"Please show me."

It was unlike Cerise to beg—even to say please—so Felicity complied. She sifted through her papers, knowing her guest would have no interest in her random notes on Gregorian and Gaelic chant and other such bits in her folder. "This is a copy of the original document..."

"Only a copy?" Cerise sounded disappointed.

"Of course. I could hardly be wandering around with a valuable document in my pack." She held out another sheet of paper. "This is my translation—as far as I've got on it." She held it out. "You're welcome to read it if you want to."

Not surprisingly, Cerise yawned. She seemed to have lost interest in Felicity's project. "I think I'll take you up on that lunch."

Felicity checked that she had her billfold with her, then led the way toward the front of the train, staying well to the right, as several people were in the aisles since the first call to lunch had been announced. They were leaving the last car of compartment accommodations when the door of the final cabin swung open so abruptly it almost hit Felicity. Professor McKinnon left the room and strode toward the dining car. Oh, if he was in first seating that explained why they hadn't met him at a meal. Pity, it would be interesting to chat with him about his archeological experiences. Felicity made a mental note to look out for him in the club car. She might learn something important if she could engage him in conversation.

For the moment, however, she needed to concentrate on getting her charge fed and settled. Thank goodness, only one more day of this responsibility.

Felicity was barely back in her own room before the second call to lunch was announced. Antony, after reporting his successful arrangement of accommodation for Cerise, led the way to the dining car. They had just introduced themselves to the mother and daughter from California sitting across from them when the concierge's voice broke in to explain that the bobbing pumpjacks dotting the fields outside their windows, like some kind of prehistoric birds, were among hundreds of oil and natural gas wells scattered between Saskatoon and Edmonton.

After lunch, Felicity readily agreed with Antony that a change of scenery—or at least of perspective on the view—might aid their work, so they gathered their papers and went to the dome car. The rolling grasslands, with their numerous oil wells and an occasional cattle ranch, appeared even more endless from that prospect. Felicity admired the view for a few moments, then disciplined herself to return to work. She really needed to finish the next stanza—and hopefully, get onto another. She sighed; she had been doing so well before Cerise interrupted her—it was always hard to pick up the tempo again once it was lost.

Felicity was just turning inward when a passenger came from the back of the carriage to take photos in the front of the dome. Ah, Professor McKinnon. Felicity considered attempting to get into a conversation with him, but he was involved with his photography and she really did need to work. Maybe he would still be available when she finished…

Against false words of heresy…
The choking wave…

Felicity thought briefly of Antony's story of the two Margarets, accused of heresy, tied to a stake in Galloway Bay as the choking wave washed over their heads. She shuddered.

Protect me, Christ, till thy returning.

The image of Margaret, especially the younger one, filled her mind and the final line became a prayer in the writing.

With a real sense of accomplishment at having finished a stanza, she looked up to take in the country around them. Oh, they were approaching a bridge, the first she had noticed since they crossed the wide Saskatoon River, but it had been dark then. She pulled out her phone and went to the front of the car for a clear view. The train rumbled onto the bridge, vibrating in response to the flexibility of the framework. The voice of their guide informed them of the height and length of the impressive steel trestle they were crossing. Since the distances were given in metres Felicity didn't find the data particularly helpful, but her eyes told her the structure was remarkable.

When the scene returned to grassland, interestingly dotted with ponds that seemed to be home to a multitude of wildlife, Felicity disciplined herself to return to work. *Christ be with me, Christ within me...* She was already mentally working on the next stanza when she reached her seat.

And gasped. The motion of the train traversing the trestle had shaken her papers from the tray table. The sheets were flung along the aisle and under seats for the distance of two rows. She dropped to her knees and picked them up before an unwary passenger could step on them. Antony had returned to their room well before they reached the bridge and now she understood the wisdom of that, if one hoped to accomplish serious work. What a shame, though, to have to be so type A in the middle of all this natural beauty.

Felicity stopped in the club car, thinking she might be able to catch the professor in a loquacious mood. Several passengers had congregated there and were chatting with one another, but no archeological lecturer. She waved to the mother and daughter they had shared breakfast with and turned to make cups of tea to take back to the room for herself and Antony. She disciplined herself to take only one package of shortbread—they could divide it.

Back in their compartment she sipped her tea and turned to organizing her papers so she could continue her work. She sorted through the stack three times, each time with more frenzied attention, before she spoke. "Antony, it's gone. The manuscript is missing."

His head jerked up. "*The manuscript?* You had it with you?"

"Oh, no—I mean, just the copy. The papers fell—" Without waiting to explain more she turned to the door. "I was so sure I got them all..."

Back in the dome she searched on and under every seat near where she had been sitting. A porter came up to bring a guest a drink and she asked him if he had picked up any scrap paper. He hadn't. Nor had any of the passengers Felicity quizzed. She went down to the lounge, but none of the other stewards could be of any help either.

Back in their room she found Antony on his hands and knees, returning the locked case to its storage place. "The original is fine." His relief was apparent.

Felicity sank onto a seat. "So why would anyone take a copy? Père Denis said the value in seeing the original was that it would show things not otherwise apparent. I mean, the style of the lettering showed in the copy, and the outline of the illumination, but none of the color or the depth—certainly no evidence of erasure or the sort of thing Père Denis suggested."

Antony shrugged. "I don't suppose a would-be criminal would know that until they looked, though. And it would hardly be of importance to a passing guest who might have picked it up to make a note on—or just to tidy the car."

"Yes. I did ask those who were there. No one noticed anything, but people do come and go. Still..."

Felicity was unconvinced by any simple explanation. Too

much had happened to brush this off. She tucked her folder of work securely away and sat down to consider. McKinnon was the logical suspect. He had admitted being interested in discovering Viking treasure—and everything seemed to point to their manuscript having ties to that era. Saint Patrick himself had been kidnapped as a youth by Irish raiders—and the Vikings were the next wave of such marauders... Her thoughts got lost in the tangle of history. Antony would be able to sort it all out for her, but she didn't want to alert him to what she was thinking.

He would be certain to forbid her—and she was determined to get to the bottom of this.

Chapter Twenty

Felicity waited until the first call to dinner, then told Antony she was going to check on Cerise. "I want to be sure Lynda got the arrangements made for Cerise to sleep tonight—and communicated them to her."

She barely waited for him to reply before she was out the door and down the hall. She lingered at the far end of the next carriage and waited until the door of the cabin at the other end opened and the professor came out. He hung the yellow "Please make up my room" card on the door and headed forward toward the dining car. Even then, she hesitated. What if he came back for a forgotten item?

It was only minutes, however, until Lynda entered the carriage to take care of the rooms with similar signs on their door. Felicity turned to her. "Oh, Lynda, just the person I wanted. I loaned a book to Professor McKinnon after his lecture and I find I need it back. Could you open his door for me?"

The steward hesitated. Felicity gave her a friendly smile. "It's just that I was hoping to finish up a bit of work and there's an item in the book I need to consult."

Lynda nodded and took out her passkey. "I'll be in the next cabin."

Whether that was to reassure Felicity or to prevent her rifling the professor's belongings, she wasn't sure. Either way, however, Felicity thanked Lynda and nipped inside the room before the attendant could change her mind. McKinnon had only a small bag and his briefcase under the banquette. Expecting her paper to be in the briefcase she looked there first, but was disappointed. His bag held only a few personal items and bits of clothing. She turned to the tiny closet on the wall next to the bathroom. And there it was, in a folder on the top shelf.

Felicity started to grab the document, then hesitated. If she took it he would know someone had been there. And suspect her. He could hardly complain that she had stolen the document he had stolen, but he could make up a story—like declaring that someone had taken money from his room. At a minimum, Lynda could get in trouble.

Felicity pulled out her phone and snapped a photo of the document. She only had two stanzas to go, and she could do those from the picture. Things were back as if untouched in a moment.

She pulled out the paperback she had tucked in her pocket and waved it at Lynda as she passed the compartment the steward was preparing. "Got it. Thanks so much." Felicity skittered down the aisle.

Antony looked up as the door to their cabin clicked shut behind her. "How was Cerise? All settled?"

Felicity hesitated—she had completely forgotten that her excuse had been that she was checking on the girl. "Oh, um—I didn't find her. Probably in the shower or something. We can look her up after dinner if you think we should."

Antony shrugged. "I'm sure the steward took care of her. After all, I paid for her upgrade."

At dinner they were seated once more with the couple from France. Felicity was pleased because she enjoyed Camille's shy smiles and Basile's courtly manners and interesting observations on cultural differences, such as the fact that Americans ate with their left hand in their lap and the French always kept two hands on the table.

Felicity looked down at her left hand in her lap and laughed. Then returned to eating—one-handedly—her succulent herb-crusted salmon. It seemed that no matter how often they ate, she was always ready for more.

"It is convenient for you?"

It took Felicity a moment to realize Basile referred to her entree, not her manner of eating it. "Oh, yes, it is delicious."

They were enjoying their desserts: white chocolate cake for Felicity and berry cobbler for Antony, when the concierge announced that, although they had been doing their best to make up time, they were currently running eleven hours behind schedule. "We will continue to do our best to make our arrival at Vancouver as timely as possibly, but as we will soon be traveling through the Rocky Mountains, I can't promise a major improvement."

A passenger at the next table groaned, but their French companions shrugged in the best Gallic, *c'est la vie* style.

Antony agreed with the groaning passenger. Of course, they understood that delays were to be expected—and he had certainly been aware of the multitude of times they had waited on sidings as seemingly mile-long freight trains thundered by—but he had no idea they could be that far behind. Already he could feel the train beginning to climb and realized it would be increasingly difficult to gain speed as their way became steeper and more winding.

Would he make it in time for the opening session of the conference? Of course, Dr. Spaulding would understand. And his only obligation Friday night was to give an overview introduction to his class to help attendees choose the lectures they wished to hear...

Important as that might be, however, his real conflict was over getting Cerise delivered to her convent. Felicity had been nonchalant about the possibility of taking on the responsibility by herself. Even then, though, he had been skeptical. And that was before all the other complications had arisen. Still...

His mind sorted through possibilities, as soon as they were back in their compartment. He picked up the map and perched on the edge of the bed, which had been efficiently readied for the night while they ate. If the train stopped at Mission and he got off there, rather than going all the way into Vancouver to be ferried back by Zack, and left Felicity to go on alone with Cerise... As little as the idea appealed to him, that way he just might make it in time for the session.

Felicity emerged from the bathroom in her Canadian "pajamoose" sleep shirt adorned with sleeping moose. She curled up on the bed. "What are you frowning about?"

He sighed. Should he even mention the possibility to her? "Well, with our late arrival, I've been wrestling with the idea of arranging to get off at Mission."

He held the map out to her.

"Mission? I thought we were going to Westminster."

"Ah, yes—Mission is the town. Westminster Abbey is the monastery just outside."

"Yeah, looks like a good idea. I can see it would save you several hours." She passed the map back to him.

"Yes—but it would mean you going on with Cerise on your own."

Felicity shrugged. "I told you way back when we started that I'd be happy to."

"Yes—" Her impetuosity to plunge into such challenges was exactly what worried him. "But that was before she had started playing up. And before your paper was—um, lost."

"That makes it better, doesn't it?"

Antony gaped at his beloved.

"I mean, if someone wanted to steal that copy of the document—well—they have it. So they won't be bothering me for it. And if they want the original—and you take it with you—they won't be bothering me for that either." She snuggled down in the bed and pulled the duvet up to her chin.

Just then the concierge came on the speaker to inform them that they would be reaching Jasper, the gateway to the Rocky Mountains in a short time. The *Canadian* would be stopping there for necessary supplies and maintenance, so passengers who wanted a night-time stroll before bed, could get off.

Felicity sat up, threw off the duvet, and reached for her jeans in one smooth movement. "That sounds perfect!"

Antony smiled and shook his head, but he had to agree that the idea of a walk in the fresh air before bed sounded like a good idea.

"Don't stray too far. This will be a quick stop," Lynda reminded the passengers as they left the train. "We'll only be here about half an hour."

Hand-in-hand Antony and Felicity crossed the street from the station, breathing deeply of the cool, fresh, mountain air. "Oh, it does feel good to move." Felicity dropped his hand and strode ahead. "Isn't it beautiful!"

Antony agreed. There was still a tinge of pink to the west in the darkening sky, highlighting the rugged mountains with an attractive village clustered at their feet. Lamp posts lining the walkway shed golden light on wide, green lawns bordered with trees. Many of the passengers from the *Canadian* were milling around the stone and timber tourist information center, viewing the posters displayed on the porch, but Felicity made a beeline for a statue of a loveable-looking Jasper Bear. She hugged the town's tall, black and white mascot, then skipped on toward the swinging town center where brightly lit bars and cafes welcomed their many tourists.

At the end of the block Antony suggested they cross to the other side of the street and make their way back to the train. Felicity readily agreed and fell into step beside him. A club in the middle of the block drew their attention because it emitted louder music and brighter lights than any other on the street. They were almost past it when the door flew open and a tall, broad figure stepped out, almost tripping Felicity.

"Oh, pardon m—" he began, then gave a cry of surprise when he saw Antony, "Father!"

"Zack?" Antony blinked, unsure of his eyes in the dim light, but the black beard was distinctive.

The intruder held out a hand to Felicity. "Sorry about almost running you down. You all right?"

She assured him she was. "But what are you doing here? Aren't you supposed to be at the monastery?" Blasting music from the bar almost drowned her words.

Zack strode on down the street, leading them away from the noise. "Looking for you, actually. Dr. S. checked on the train— knew it was notorious for delays—and found you're running almost a day late, so he suggested I catch up with you here and take you off at Mission."

And you thought you'd find us in the loudest bar in town? Antony resisted voicing his skepticism of Zack's explanation as a blast from the *Canadian*'s whistle told them they needed to hurry back.

Once on the train Antony led the way to the club car where he hoped he could get a sensible answer from Zack.

As if purposely avoiding questions about their awkward meeting, Zack plunged straight into explaining how important Dr. Spaulding felt it was that Antony attend the opening session. With internet connections being so spotty for the train, this seemed the best way to connect since the stop at Jasper was the only scheduled one before Vancouver. Dr. S. had already arranged for them to get off at Mission. Zack had the grace to duck his head as he added, rather in the style of a confession, that perhaps he had helped the good doctor's ideas along a bit. "It did seem a shame to be so close to a world-famous resort and not get to see it, so I rented a car," Zack finished with a shrug as if to show what a natural thing it was to do.

Close? When they still had how many hours to travel? But Antony supposed that from the perspective of Eastern Canada, it did seem that they were close.

"That sounds like a really good idea, Zack," Felicity said. "I was worried about Antony being late for the conference. But I won't be able to get off with you." She explained about her responsibility to see a young novice to her convent on Vancouver Island.

Felicity and Zack continued to chatter, but Antony considered. It did seem that the decision had been taken out of his hands. It wasn't as if he hadn't thought of the possibility himself, but still, he couldn't feel easy about leaving Felicity.

Chapter Twenty-One

Felicity had gone to bed the night before, bemoaning the fact that they had to travel through the Rocky Mountains—surely the most spectacular part of their journey—at night. She had been so anxious for the morning light so she could start enjoying it that she had trouble falling asleep.

When she woke, however, she was confused. Surely she had slept for a full night, and yet it was still dark. And why did the roar of the train sound louder? In a few moments, though, the brilliant sunlight flooded the cabin and she realized they had been in a tunnel.

She turned to prod Antony awake, but he was already gone. A note on his pillow informed "Sleeping Beauty" that he was in the dome car. Felicity pulled on her clothes and hurried to join him.

They might have missed the most magnificent part, but the view was still stunning. Green forest crowded close to the edge of the track and halfway up the craggy peaks that extended upward to become sharp teeth of bare granite piercing a brilliant blue sky interspersed with white clouds.

"You know, the Sawtooths I grew up in are pretty significant mountains, but they're mere foothills compared to the Canadian

Rockies," she said to Antony without taking her eyes from the window. She might not have moved all morning had not the call to breakfast reminded her that she was hungry.

The view changed as they took their seats in the dining car. They were now traveling along the very edge of a long lake. Outside their window it was so close Felicity felt she could lean down and scoop some of the clear blue water rippling in a morning breeze. The opposite shore was ringed with dense pine while beyond, layers of granite mountains jutted skyward. On the other side of the car, the evergreen forest, punctuated with cliffs of sheer rock, rose steeply. From knowledge gained on youthful hikes with her father and brothers, Felicity identified pine, fir and spruce—or enjoyed imagining that she did. At any rate, except along the rivers where she was certain of recognizing aspen, there were few of the deciduous trees they had seen when they began their journey.

As the long lake narrowed to a rushing river, Felicity was seized with nostalgia, remembering visits to her native Snake River. These were proper rivers—wild and racing, deep blue and foaming white where they whirled past boulders. None of the slow, brownish waters one saw in the flatter eastern states and provinces.

Felicity finished her cheddar and red pepper *omelette* and was on her second pot of tea when the river widened to swirl around a rocky island topped with a huge triangle of granite and a few stately pines standing firm on their rocky base. The concierge came on with his morning travel commentary. "We are now entering Fraser Canyon and approaching the most famous stretch of rapids in British Columbia, where jagged boulders fill the bed of the mighty Fraser River. Its pent-up force reaches a crescendo at Hell's Gate, named by explorer Simon Fraser who said, 'This is a place where no human should venture, for surely these are the gates of hell.'"

Felicity and Antony returned to their room just as Lynda was leaving from having made up it up. Hoping to deflect any danger of the steward mentioning her special service for Felicity yesterday, she rushed to ask, "How long till we get to Mission?"

"About two hours." The answer was matter of fact and Lynda moved on.

Antony turned to his packing and Felicity said, "I think I'll go check on Cerise—let her know our plan."

To her amazement, Antony gave her a quick kiss. "Don't be long. I'm going to miss you."

"Silly, it'll only be twenty-four hours." Still, she was pleased.

Felicity moved through the train swiftly, not wanting to miss any more of the view than she had to. She hoped she wouldn't have to undertake a search to find her charge. Just past the heat of the coach kitchen, however, she spotted Cerise in the first coach.

With Zack sitting beside her. Felicity barely had time to wonder what was going on when he waved and called, "Look who I found!"

Not surprisingly, Cerise giggled.

Felicity was trying to make sense of this. It was hardly surprising they would see each other—there were only three coach cars—but they were carrying on like old friends after Zack had seemed barely to notice Cerise when they met briefly in Toronto.

"When I saw Cherry here I put it together. I didn't realize she was Anne-Marie's sister when you introduced us earlier."

"Would it have mattered?" Felicity frowned.

"Oh, yes, I've known Anne-Marie for years. I think I told you I had been to Saint Benoit."

But Cherry? Felicity was still mulling over Zack's familiarity when Cerise rushed ahead, almost defiantly, with an explanation of their meeting. "I was visiting my sister."

Felicity nodded. She vaguely recalled that he had said something about visiting the monastery in passing. Something not particularly complimentary, if she remembered correctly. "Well, then, it looks like I needn't have bothered coming to find you. I came to tell you that Antony would be getting off at Mission, and I'll go on to Nanaimo with you."

Felicity hoped her charge wouldn't argue with her. If the girl put up a fuss to be allowed to go on alone, Felicity would be tempted to give in—even if it would be a violation of her promise to Mother Anne-Marie. Well, at least, the promise the nun seemed to think Felicity had made.

Cerise merely shrugged, however.

"Right. I'll see you in Vancouver." Felicity turned on her heel and marched back to her compartment—and Antony.

His bag sat neatly zipped by the door and he was engrossed in a book. "Antony, how can you be reading and ignoring this view?"

He grinned. "I wanted to get this finished. But I do look up occasionally."

"Come on—let's go up to the dome for a last look." She shook her head when he glanced at the book in his hand. "You can bring it with you."

In the end, she took her papers as well. She did want to leave the whole thing behind her when they headed home. And Father Conall—that was the name of the precentor, wasn't it?—might be able to advise her on her attempts to capture a Gaelic feeling in her work. That is, if he was as Irish as his name implied.

In the dome car she pulled down her tray table and arranged her papers, glad that Antony, beside her, had opened his book. She would rather not have to explain why she was working from a photo of her manuscript on her phone.

She focused on the penultimate stanza:

Christ be with me, Christ within me,
Christ behind me, Christ before me,
Christ beside me, Christ to win me,
Christ to comfort and restore me.
Christ beneath me, Christ above me,

Christ in quiet, Christ in danger,
Christ in hearts of all that love me,
Christ in mouth of friend and stranger.

She smiled as she worked through a straightforward translation. The lines struck her as singably poetic on their own. Would it be gilding the lily to add extensions to suggest vocal runs?

Considering this, she gazed at the panorama surrounding her outside. Now they were engulfed by green, uninterrupted by jutting pinnacles of bare rock. None of the prominences rose above the timber line. Just as Felicity was noticing this, the speaker crackled on and the concierge mirrored her thoughts: "We are now approaching the town of Hope. Here the mountains fall back to form a distant ring around the lush Fraser Valley. This rich farmland is the delta, formed by the silt deposited by the Fraser River after its rush through the province. The flat green fields you will see are a reflective, pastoral interlude between the stone gorges of the mountains and the steel and glass canyons of downtown Vancouver."

Felicity smiled; her Breastplate lines weren't the only poetry flowering at the moment. She returned to alternating work and viewing the gentling landscape until the speaker informed them they were nearing Mission. "Here the *Canadian* will cross the Fraser for the last time. This area was first settled by missionaries in 1861. On the hill above us is Westminster Abbey, established in 1939."

The train rounded a curve in the track, and a remarkable structure of steel beams and trusses appeared, spanning the river. It made Felicity think of frameworks her brothers constructed from their Erector set years ago. As the view became clearer, she realized she was actually seeing two bridges. The upper, wider one, with a center arch flowing skyward like a giant roller coaster, was for cars. The lower one, with girders forming a series of arches, was the railway bridge which would take them on to Vancouver. Well, take her, she amended as Antony closed his book and stood.

They were returning to their room when the concierge added the information that this marked the beginning of the tidal portion of the Fraser. "These are popular waters for sportsmen as they contain white sturgeon, five species of salmon, and steelhead trout. Fishermen need to keep in mind, however, that the river can rise as much as three and a half metres at high tide. Anglers wishing to fish here must have a tidal fishing license," he concluded.

"Well, lucky I'll only be fishing for men—and women," Antony quipped.

A few minutes later Felicity felt the train slowing. Antony pulled his bag from their room and led the way to the end of the carriage where Zack was joking with a smiling Lynda who waited to open the door for her departing passengers.

Felicity threw her arms around Antony, surprised by the vehemence of her own emotion at their parting. Her eyes even felt damp. Goodness, she wasn't usually so emotional. Awareness of the train having come to a full stop made them pull apart. "See you tomorrow," she said.

"Good luck." Antony waved. She knew he would have said more with more time and less of an audience.

The men's feet had barely touched the platform before the train was moving again. Antony turned and waved. Felicity waved until he was out of sight, wishing this were like a train in an old movie so she could stick her arm out the window and continue waving.

Her sense of aloneness was so sharp it took her breath away. *Silly girl, you'll be in Vancouver in three hours.* Then the ferry, then the convent, then back again here tomorrow morning. And Zack had promised to meet her at the ferry and whisk her to Westminster Abbey—and Antony.

She smiled. Absolutely nothing to worry about.

Chapter Twenty-Two

A tall, blond monk in a plain black Benedictine cassock was waiting for Antony and Zack at the station. He introduced himself as Frère Sylvester and drove them through the town and up the forested hillside toward the monastery. Antony's mind was still on Felicity as he pictured the train rumbling on across the Mission Bridge.

"This area was first settled by missionaries in 1861," Sylvester interrupted Antony's musings, "but the monastery wasn't established until almost a hundred years after that."

Antony gave a vague reply and tried to focus on the present company. There was little time for more narration, however, because in less than ten minutes they crested the top of the hill. Green lawns on the hillside below rolled up to a sprawling layout of grey brick buildings with red tile roofs. In front of the buildings the smooth carpet of grass stretched down a slope and opened out to playing fields. The end nearest them was marked with goal posts for what Antony thought of as a football pitch, but he quickly amended his term to soccer.

They were just nearing the closest building when a door at the far end opened and several dozen boys in dark blue tee shirts and shorts burst out and raced across the driveway and down the hill to the playing field. Their guide smiled and gestured toward the energetic group. "Makes one feel old, doesn't it?" Although the brother himself couldn't have been much older than Antony. "Minor seminarians. We run the only high school seminary in western Canada. Then there's major seminary for university level work as well. You'll see them all in church—a considerable enrichment to our choir."

Frère Sylvester parked the car in front of what he identified as the guest house wing. Shouts from the soccer pitch floated up to them as they walked along the rose-bordered path to the guest house. In the foyer Dr. Spaulding strode toward them with his hand extended. "Ah, Father Antony, welcome. I see you made it across our vast continent from Quebec. I trust you had a good journey."

Antony replied that they did, indeed, but the director barely paused as he thrust a packet of conference materials into Antony's hands and suggested he settle in. "We'll meet back here in an hour to prepare. First session will be in the dining hall—dinner and introductory talks—similar format to Toronto. Good lot of conferees—including their major seminarians. Should be a great wind-up for all your efforts."

Antony wished he could come up with even half of the director's enthusiasm. He felt strange and more than a little disoriented in these rambling, sleekly modern buildings. Not at all what he was accustomed to in the way of monasteries. He dumped his bag and briefcase in the room Zack showed him to and turned to go out for a walk. Maybe getting acquainted with the layout of the grounds would help him feel more at home.

He paused at the door and looked back. He could hardly leave the manuscript just sitting there on his bed in its case, even in a locked room. The desk offered no locking drawers. He could see no secure place in the room. Finally, he decided simply to carry it with him. He would approach Father Conall after Vespers. He knew Felicity wanted to talk to the precentor, but it would be safest to have it the monk's keeping as soon as possible. And perhaps it would be more useful if the precentor had time to study the document before Felicity met with him.

Outside, Antony took a few deep breaths of the fresh, mountain air and began almost instantly to feel clearer-headed. The view from their mountain perch offered a panoramic sweep. The Fraser River curved at the foot of their hill and wound a silver ribbon through the valley while verdant-looking farmlands spread outward to green hills.

Antony turned back to the monastery and walked through the colorful flowerbeds toward the church, thinking how much Felicity would enjoy this scene—and how much he would enjoy having her with him. Between the guest house and the church an impressive bell tower rose to the sky, its rounded apex topped with a simple cross. Beside it, each of the accordion-staggered brick panels that formed the west wall of the church held a stained-glass window, mirroring the oval shape of the tower top.

Antony walked forward and entered the empty sanctuary. He was in a wide, vaguely circular space, formed by jutting angles and square pillars of grey stone intersected by brilliant windows of red, orange and yellow geometric patterns. Bits of blue glass in the clerestory windows of the domed ceiling suggested sky while yellow patches shone like the sun. Antony walked slowly around, observing the impressive, stylized, bas relief sculptures of Biblical characters along the wall and the crucifix hanging high over the altar. The starkness of the design and the empty space left him feeling alone and missing Felicity as if she had been gone for days or weeks, rather than a matter of hours.

He gave himself a shake. Aunt Beryl would tell him to pull up his socks and stop maundering. He smiled in spite of the weight on his chest. Good advice, indeed. He turned to prepare for the opening session of the conference.

Still, his sense of foreboding remained.

. . .

"Welcome to Vancouver, the dominant city of Canada's Pacific coast. It was named for Captain George Vancouver who discovered the area in 1792. Today it is home to half the people in British Columbia..."

Felicity barely registered the words of the concierge as he bid the passengers farewell and wished them a good onward journey. She had one goal in mind: deliver Cerise safely to the House of Bread and get back to Antony tomorrow—as early as possible.

Felicity hurried forward on the platform, hoping Cerise would wait for her, and berating herself for not being more specific about their meeting up. Losing her charge before they even got out of the station would hardly be a good omen for a successful conclusion to her commission. Fortunately, though, the girl was standing just inside the doorway of Vancouver's Pacific Central Station. Never mind the bored look she projected, Felicity was glad to see her. "Come on. Let's hope we can nab a taxi." Felicity strode ahead, assuming Cerise would keep up.

A short time later they were speeding through a forest of glass and concrete towers. Felicity watched the buildings march by outside her window, then saw what she was looking for. She moved her finger across the metal clasp on her seatbelt. "Ouch!" She stuck her finger in her mouth. "I cut my finger. Can you stop at that drug store up there? I need a band-aid."

The driver leaned toward his glove box. "Got one here, lady."

"No, I need antiseptic cream, too."

He shrugged. "Have it your way." He slowed. "No parking here. I'll let you out on the corner and go around the block."

"Great. Thanks." Felicity bounded from the taxi the moment he braked.

In a few minutes they were on their way again, crossing the peninsula that jutted into the harbor. Then back over the Fraser River, to the Tsawwassen Ferry Terminal. It had taken almost an hour to cross the city.

Their timing was good, though. They had barely purchased

their foot passenger tickets before the announcement came that they could board the ferry. The walking on was simple, but Felicity was interested to observe from the walkway the skilled precision required for the intricate dance of loading the vast number of cars and trucks lined up for the voyage across the strait. She had never given any thought to what it must take to keep a population the size of that on Vancouver Island supplied.

"Come on. Let's get a seat," Cerise urged her. A level above the car deck, a wide central stairway led them up to a passenger deck offering several styles of seating, a clothing and souvenir shop, a restaurant, and a snack bar. Felicity chose a seat at a table by a window looking out over the wide, blue, sun-sparkled water.

They stowed their bags under the table, but Cerise didn't sit. "I'm hungry."

Felicity smiled to hear Cerise's most frequent complaint. It reminded her that the girl was still a teenager. Fortunately, Felicity had some Canadian money from their time in Toronto—she hadn't needed any on the train. She gave Cerise a bill. "I'll have tea and…" She was about to say toast when she remembered that treat she had told Antony about. What was the name? "One of those Nanaimo bar thingies. Get what you want." She hoped that her easy compliance would sweeten Cerise for the journey.

Felicity wasn't sure about the effect on Cerise, but the creamy chocolate bar certainly did the trick for her. As the ferry pulled smoothly out into the wider water Felicity gazed, mesmerized, out the window. Water had always had that effect on her—any trip that included a boat ride had been a highlight of her childhood. She especially remembered going with her adored father to visit his ancient aunt on Bremerton Island in Washington. Felicity smiled. She must have been all of five years old—and Great Aunt Tennie in her fifties.

And the fascination remained—being on a wide expanse of water, and yet never out of sight of land. Most of the small islands along the coast were hilly and thickly wooded, but a little further out they passed a small, flat island with only a few white, red-roofed buildings and a lighthouse. Seagulls soared around the island and several followed the ferry. Felicity was entranced. The birds appeared so fragile, almost invisible descending from the sky, then became brilliant flashes of white as they caught the sun and glided over the water.

Felicity finished her snack and gathered her willpower to take out her work. In spite of feeling she would like simply to sit and stare out the window for the full two hours of the trip, it offered plenty of time to finish up the bit she had left to do—and the sense of relief would be well worth the effort.

Or should she try to engage Cerise in conversation? Maybe talk to her about her discernment? After all, Felicity had undergone just such a process herself...

Before she could think of an opening comment, Felicity was relieved of the obligation when her silent companion jumped to her feet. "I'm going out on deck. See ya." Her jaunty wave and brief giggle made Felicity hope the girl's mood had improved.

Felicity blinked at the departing back, then opened her folder with a shake of her head.

I bind unto myself the name,
The strong name of the Trinity,
By invocation of the same,
The Three in One and One in Three.
By whom all nature hath creation,
Eternal Father, Spirit, Word:
Praise to the Lord of my salvation,
Salvation is of Christ the Lord.

The first lines were quickly done, as they repeated the opening stanza. Felicity smiled at the next line, though: *By whom all nature hath creation...* She looked again out the window at the beauty of water, sky and distant islands. What better place to be contemplating the Creation? She felt the gentle rocking of the boat and thought of the cadence of the chant. Certainly a perfect place here for a vocal run.

In the next line she thought of the wind of the Spirit as she again took in the view and noted a few waves just big enough to produce a white edge of foam as they broke. Then a gull soared by her window and her mind filled with images of the dove of the Holy Spirit. Melisma, indeed. She smiled and wrote.

She was pondering the duplication of the word "salvation" in the two final lines—was that Gaelic repetition for the sake of emphasis, or would... Her pen stilled as her senses alerted. Was she being watched? The back of her neck tingled, making her want to turn, yet fearing it.

She took a breath and whipped around in her seat.

Passengers strolled along the wide aisle, moving every direction. The young couple at the table behind her were deeply engrossed in each other. A woman behind them gazed out at the water through binoculars. Felicity started to chide herself for paranoia, then glimpsed the back of a man walking rapidly away —his red hair exactly the shade of Professor McKinnon's.

Felicity jumped to her feet, giving in to her impulse to chase after him and confront him. He had his—her—document. What more did he want? What did he think he was up to, anyway? It wasn't as if she had any secret knowledge that would be of use to anybody. She barely knew what she was doing herself.

She sighed and sat back down. And what good would it do if she managed to catch up with him? If it even was McKinnon. He was hardly likely to tell her what he was doing.

Her concentration broken, she stowed her papers and gave herself to watching the ferry glide around a long island and into port, the doll's house buildings along the shore gradually growing to life size. Cerise returned, wind-blown and apparently invigorated from her time on the deck. "That was great. I hope I can get a boat someday." She grabbed her pack by one strap and headed toward the door.

How many nuns had boats? Felicity sighed and followed her charge down the stairs.

A short time later, their taxi was headed north along verdant Vancouver Island. Green grass bordering the road gave way to ever-thickening bushes and deciduous trees, until gigantic pines and thick undergrowth surrounded them. The driver pointed out a nature sanctuary on one side and the way to Vancouver Island University on the other, then drove on past a few scattered homes and a sign to The Westwood Lake Resort. Felicity hoped their driver knew where he was going.

Around a sweeping drive, beautifully landscaped by nature and human effort, the taxi stopped in front of a series of modern-looking, rambling wooden buildings backed by a row of tall fir trees. Through a break in the evergreens Felicity glimpsed a wide lake catching the shining gold of a sun nearing the western horizon. Had the driver made a mistake and pulled into the resort? "This is a monastery?" Felicity asked.

"Nuns, yeah." He nodded and held out his hand for his fare.

Felicity paid and followed Cerise out of the vehicle. She was glad the girl showed no reluctance to approach her new home. On the contrary, she almost skipped up the walk to the front door.

Felicity was surprised when the door opened and a woman with short, grey hair, wearing beige slacks and a floral blouse came out to meet them, almost as if she had been watching for their arrival. "Welcome, I'm Emma Grace, the guest sister."

She *had* been waiting for them. Then Felicity realized, of course—Mother Anne-Marie would have made careful arrangements for the reception of her baby sister.

"May I take your bags for you?" Emma Grace held out her hand. Felicity declined, but Cerise readily plopped her bag into the out-stretched hand. The guest sister led back along the walk to another building. At the door to Cerise's room she told both guests, "It's just fifteen minutes until evening prayers, then dinner in the refectory." She turned to Felicity and added, "Mary Joy will meet with you after morning prayers."

Felicity blinked. Did the sister think she was the prospective novice? "Oh, no, I'm—"

"You wanted to speak to Mother about spiritual direction." It wasn't really a question.

Ah, the long arm of Mother Anne-Marie again. Benedictines must have a good set of jungle drums. "Um—sure. Yes, that would be quite convenient." Actually, there was nothing she wanted more than to catch the first ferry back to the mainland. Still, a visit with the prioress might be useful. Felicity had wrestled at odd moments with the looming question of what she would do when they returned to their old life—well, new life, really. It had been all too easy to put such matters out of her mind in the face of more immediate events, but the time would come...

Throughout the brief, peaceful prayer service in the chapel and a tasty roast chicken dinner, Felicity continued trying to come to grips with the question of her future. Of course, there was one uncertainty that could change the picture considerably...

She jerked back from her daydream to the more immediate question: How serious was she about the idea of becoming a spiritual director? She had always rather fancied telling people what to do, no question about that, but it seemed that more and more she was learning how little qualified she was to do that. Could she really undertake to tell people how to run their lives? Their spiritual lives?

As always when in a quandary, she longed to talk to Antony. As soon as the meal ended—with an excellent cherry cobbler—she hurried to her room and pulled out her phone. Her disappointment was acute when there was no answer. Antony must still be in the opening session of his conference. She sighed and left a message—a rather rambling, disconnected jumble of thoughts that was sure to tell him more about how she was feeling than convey any actual information.

It was much too early to go to bed, and Felicity was far too restless to settle down with a book, so she donned a sweater and slipped out into the mild evening. Even before she was past the ring of trees behind the monastery buildings, she could hear the water of the lake gently lapping the shore. A map in her room had shown a path marked Westwood Lake Trail circling the thick woods around the lake and in a few places leading down to sandy beaches.

Hoping the waning light would hold long enough for her to see her way, she headed out, reveling in the freedom and the fresh air. This was certain to clear her mind of the chaotic thoughts creating a jumbled buzz in her head.

As she strode along the beaten dirt path, her head didn't clear, but at least some of the questions did line up—even though they were frustratingly lacking in answers. Thankfully, what to do with Cerise was no longer an item of concern. She had already sent a text to Anne-Marie informing her of their arrival.

And she wasn't certain that questions of what seemed to be going on regarding her manuscript project need concern her much longer. Tomorrow she would deliver her finished text to Father Conall and it would be in his hands from there to prepare it for next years' colloquium. Presumably, the entire responsibility would fall on him since the demise of his counterpart at Saint Benoit.

A few evening birds chirped out of sight in branches over her head, the motor of a late boater heading for the dock buzzed like a mosquito, and water splashed gently against the bank. She could have been ten years old, back at Payette Lake in a favorite campsite with her father and brothers.

She relaxed and slowed her step, enjoying reliving her childhood. When angry voices broke into the idyll, she momentarily thought she had stumbled across a spat between her parents, then realized this was occurring below her along the lakeside. She started to turn and retrace her steps when the familiarity of the female voice stopped her. Cerise?

Now Felicity inched toward the sound. If the agitated male voice belonged to the young man Felicity had glimpsed with Cerise on the train, this might give her a clue to explain the girl's enigmatic behavior. Or perhaps Cerise was in some sort of trouble and would need Felicity's help. She increased her speed.

Through the trees to her right Felicity could now see a band of sand at the water's edge, opening out into a beach, rather than the sheer drop of forest that ringed most of the lake. Two figures stood out against the white background. The shorter one, the woman, was definitely Cerise. The other had his back to Felicity, but she had the impression it was the man she had glimpsed walking away from them on the ferry.

"I tell you I don't know anything!" Cerise sounded near to tears, the giggle entirely vanished.

The man's low-pitched reply was indecipherable, but Cerise's muffled cry held a ring of fear.

"Cerise?" Felicity shouted and sprang forward.

Her voice, accompanied by the sound of crashing undergrowth, made both speakers turn toward her. Cerise rocketed toward her, but after one look, the man turned and sprinted down the beach.

But Felicity had seen. What was Professor McKinnon doing confronting Cerise?

No matter how many times Felicity asked the question on the way back to the monastery however, Cerise insisted that she didn't have any idea. "I never saw him before. I was just out for a walk and he came out of the woods."

It was Cerise's unaccustomed anxious attitude that made Felicity remember the girl's visit to their train compartment. "Cerise—when you came to us on the train and quizzed me about my project... Did the professor put you up to that?"

Cerise sighed. "I didn't think it would do any harm. He gave me ten dollars. Goodness knows I needed the money. It's not like my sister gave me enough." Now the defiance was back in her voice. "Then he wanted his money back. It's your fault—if you'd told me anything—"

Felicity gave a disgusted sigh and marched back to the convent, shaking her head.

Chapter Twenty-Three

Felicity stifled a yawn. If only she had been able to reach Antony last night she might have been able to get more sleep. As it was, she had spent half the night trying to make sense of Cerise's confession and this additional evidence of McKinnon's involvement with the manuscript. Apparently simply having his purloined copy wasn't enough. She had continued her inquisition in Cerise's room, but the girl's confused and unhelpful answers only muddied the waters even more.

Fully awake now, she grabbed her bag and headed to the washroom. At least she should get one answer this morning.

A short time later Felicity commanded herself to concentrate, and renewed her struggle to sort out Mother Mary Joy's explanation of the process of spiritual direction from the director's viewpoint. It sounded considerably different from the sessions she had experienced at Kirkthorpe with Father Oswin.

The nun sat in a comfortable chair, the mirror of the one Felicity occupied, on the other side of a low, round table where the flame of a scented candle flickered with a cheer Felicity was far from feeling. She had hoped the sister would recommend a course she should take, or give her a list of books to read—something concrete.

Mary Joy's reply to her questions along those lines, however, had been singularly unproductive. "Certainly, you could rush out and take a course." Her voice did not hold the affirmation that her words implied. And her look made Felicity feel that the nun had done a rather shrewd job of sizing up the young woman sitting across from her. "And yes, there are more books on the topic than you could read in a lifetime." Mary Joy made a vague gesture toward the over-flowing bookcases lining her walls.

"You've spent three years earning a theology degree—with a spiritual director of your own?"

Felicity nodded, feeling that the question was more for her own benefit than for her interrogator's. That might be sufficient theory to be getting on with, seemed to be the implication. Her mind filled with memories of sitting across from thoughtful, quiet Father Oswin, his hands steepled below his chin, his head tilted slightly to the side as he listened to Felicity pouring out her frustrations. Usually followed by his long, drawn-out "Yeees" with a little nod. And Felicity would be off again, rushing to the next topic.

"The most important thing is to listen. That's the first thing I do." Felicity came back to the present with a jerk. Were the prioress' words a rebuke to her abstraction? "I begin every session by asking 'What would you like to talk about?' I need to hear who God is to them, then we can go on to discuss what is going on in their lives."

Felicity nodded. That sounded so simple. Just letting people tell you their problems—as she had Father Oswin. Maybe being a spiritual director wouldn't be as complicated as she had pictured it. Although for her, there would be the challenge of being quiet and letting the other person talk.

"My job is about ninety percent listening." Did Mary Joy read her mind?

"And, of course, you learn about yourself as you listen to others and to nature," the prioress continued. "I understand you are in a discernment process yourself."

Felicity stared. Just what had Anne-Marie said about her? Then Felicity nodded slowly. Yes, she hadn't put such a frighteningly formal name on it, but she supposed that was it.

"Growing in awareness of our inner person is the key. The focus can't be outside rather than inside. If you are considering being a spiritual director, you must start with yourself: how you are with nature, God, your friends and family, people who are hurting—with everything. Listen to yourself. We carry the truth within us—if we listen."

Felicity opened her eyes wider to let Mother Mary Joy know she was listening. For a change.

"The next step is to do what we know. That's why we have each other. But take time every day to be quiet and reflect on what you have learned. If you don't, knowledge will stay in your head, not go to your heart. Just *be*."

"But wouldn't I need to be certified or something?"

"There are professional programs, certainly. Some are quite good."

Felicity waited, but no list of websites was forth-coming. Instead, something quite different was offered: "We are to become as little children. Little ones have a sense of spiritual mystery within them. Their gift to us is hope." Felicity struggled to keep up with the words swirling around her head. Did that apply to her? What did the sister mean?

"Our essence is divine. We are one with the mystery of Divine Love. No matter what we get into in our lives, He never leaves us. It's all unconditional love." Silence filled the room.

Felicity rose. "Well, thank you so much, Mother."

The prioress stood as well and moved toward the door of her office where they had been sitting. "He will bring everything together in a meaningful way. Your job is to listen and follow."

"Thank you," Felicity repeated and fled.

She inquired of Emma Grace whether she might tell Cerise good-bye, but the guest sister informed Felicity that the girl was with the novice sister and suggested that Felicity leave her a note. What a good suggestion—it would be easier for both of them—and there was no question of Cerise wanting to say thank you to Felicity. Although the girl had seemed appreciative enough to be rescued from the professor's inquisition last night.

Felicity handed her hastily written missive to Sister Emma Grace and heaved a sigh of relief. That was one job accomplished at least. She took out her phone to ring for a taxi to take her back to the ferry.

Antony pushed the end call button on his phone with a sigh. Yet again, no answer. Texting was an unsatisfactory means of communication, but that was his only option. Felicity's rather incoherent reply this morning to his message sent late last night —far too late to be ringing her in a monastery—had only served to increase his concern for her.

Professor McKinnon had followed her onto the ferry? And was talking to—or threatening—Cerise at Nanaimo? And Felicity made it sound like the professor had the manuscript— but of course that was wrong because a beaming Father Conall had received it from Antony's own hands last night and promised to keep it safe before its return journey to the Community of the Transfiguration.

Antony shook his head and hit send on his morning greeting to his beloved, which conveyed little more than the fact that he missed her, hoped she would be back in time for his talk after lunch, and that he loved her. He could only hope the fact that she didn't answer his call meant she was on the ferry. Zack had told him that cell phone service on the ferries was notoriously unreliable.

Antony picked up his notes and prepared to head to the

room where he would give his morning talk. He regretted being confined to the colorless setting of a meeting room, but he hadn't had time to sort out an appropriately evocative location. The decision to begin with Saint Andrew had been an easy one after he read that Scots comprised the third largest ethnic group in Canada and that the area's earliest explorers had been the Scotsmen Alexander Mackenzie and Simon Fraser. Thankfully, Canadians' high regard for their history should serve as a tie-in for the local interest he always hoped to evoke. And for his deeper sub-text, his desire to inspire his listeners to return to their spiritual roots.

He turned back to his desk and spent a few minutes surfing the internet for a more redolent scene for Saint Patrick tomorrow, but didn't find anything. Time to get on to the room for his morning talk anyway.

Halfway along the hall, Zack fell into stride beside him. "Why the frown?"

Antony explained his disappointment over finding an appropriate setting for his talks. "Of course, I suppose simply being in a monastery is appropriate, especially for Saint Patrick who founded his great monastic center at Armagh, but..."

Zack rubbed his beard as if to aid his thinking. "How about an Irish pub? Mission has ten of them."

Antony laughed. "You've been in the area for—what? Two days? And you already know—and approve—all the pubs?"

"Yeah. You see, I met this fellow last night—Brian—friend of one of the major seminarians... Never mind, it's a long story. Anyway, first night I was here, he invited me to a gig—plays the cláirseach, Irish harp you know." Zack shrugged one shoulder. "Anyway we did a bit of a pub crawl."

The Irish harp? It took only a moment for Antony to get the picture in his mind. That would be perfect. His frown turned to a broad smile. "Do you think he would play for my class?"

Zack shrugged again. "He'd do most things for a pint or two. I'll text him."

Antony's mind buzzed—this would make a session the conferees would never forget—and what a way to make his point of moving stories of faith out into the world... He would have to rewrite his notes yet again...

"Tell him if he'll do it I'll email him about what needs to be done. Make it two pints, even."

Chapter Twenty-Four

All the way back on the ferry Felicity went over and over the few phrases she had overheard on the beach and Cerise's explanation, without arriving at any coherent conclusion beyond the certainty of Professor McKinnon's involvement in whatever was going on. And his insistence on getting what he wanted. Her thoughts were interrupted by the captain's announcement that a pod of dolphins had been spotted from the bridge. "Take a look out the port side and you might be able to see them."

Felicity had no idea which was the port side, but the other passengers all seemed to be rushing to the left, so she joined them. She was straining to spot a foam of white that would indicate churning beneath the surface, broken by a silver streak in the blue water, when her attention jerked from the window. She whirled around and scanned the passengers behind her. Was that the heavy-breather again?

She smiled when a mother bent over to hold a handkerchief to her toddler's nose. "Here. Blow," she instructed.

Well, that seemed to be one menace that hadn't come to anything. Thank goodness. Poor man; Felicity hoped he got help for his condition. She did, though, keep looking over her shoulder for the rest of the journey and as she walked down the ramp to the dock, just in case her conclusion had been too optimistic. It *was* that child she heard, wasn't it? And yesterday on the ferry—this child or another? She certainly hadn't seen or heard anyone else that seemed to qualify.

"Zack!" She called and waved as soon as she spotted him waiting for her. "I'm so glad. I wasn't sure you got my text."

"Yeah, no problem." He took her bag and led to the abbey's SUV. "Father Conall said he hoped you could meet with him as soon as you got back. He sounded pretty excited to tell you something."

"Great. Maybe he spotted something of importance in the manuscript." Felicity sighed. "I'll be so glad to have this whole thing over. I'm tired of looking over my shoulder all the time."

"Huh?"

She explained briefly about some of the things that had been happening.

Zack was thunderstruck. "That's awful! Why didn't you tell me? We could have helped. Dr. Spaulding would have set me on as bodyguard."

Felicity laughed, looking at Zack's well-developed frame and dark, stubbly beard that had grown since the fresh trim he had given it in Toronto. "You'd be a good one, Zack. Thank you. It's all been so nebulous, though." Except for Antony being locked in the chapel, she amended in her thoughts.

"All the more reason to tell Dr. S."

"Actually, I did plan to talk to him—about his archeology. I wondered if he might know a Professor McKinnon."

"Hmm, I haven't heard the name, but he may well do. I'll ask him,"

Felicity started to tell him not to bother, but then they pulled in to the parking lot in front of the abbey. Zack looked at his watch. "Do you mind going straight to Father Conall? I know he's waiting for you."

"Lead on," Felicity agreed, although she would much rather he were taking her to Antony.

When Zack introduced her to the short, round-faced monk who greeted her with such eager delight, however, she was immediately caught up in his enthusiasm.

"I'll leave you to it, then." Zack closed the door behind himself as he exited.

"Did you learn anything from the manuscript?" Felicity went straight to the heart of the matter.

"Yes, indeed. Well, actually the find is down to Dr. Penhaligon." He waved to a figure Felicity hadn't noticed in the back of the office, bent over a small table. She was scanning a document with what appeared to be a rectangular flashlight emitting an intensely blue-red light.

Doctor Penhaligon switched off her light and came forward with her hand extended. "Ah, I take it this is our courier. Very pleased to meet you." She pumped Felicity's hand in a manner that exhibited her pleasure. "Remarkable document you brought us. Can't thank you enough." She bobbed her head toward the sheet of vellum on the table, making her steel-gray, blunt-cut hair swing against her chin.

Father Conall explained her presence. "Dr. Penhaligon and I have spent a most informative morning with her portable ultraviolet lamp. Fortunately, the University of British Columbia in Vancouver is a member of U15—a group of research universities in Canada. As their archivist, she was willing to interrupt her own schedule and come straight to us."

"Couldn't be more delighted. Opportunities are all too rare to study a treasure like this."

Felicity's heart jumped to her throat, recalling Antony's vision of golden coins spilling from the illumination. So it was true—this was a key to some Viking hoard. "Treasure?" was all she could manage.

"Treasure, indeed. To a scholar, at least." Dr. Penhaligon removed her wire-framed glasses and assumed a professorial stance. "Two Latin works survive which are generally accepted as having been written by Patrick himself. These are the *Confessio* and the Letter to the soldiers of Coroticus, known as the *Epistola*. These provide the only generally accepted details of his life—the *Confessio* being the more biographical of the two.

"*The Book of Armagh*, dating from the ninth century, contains the earliest copy of Saint Patrick's *Confessio* known to exist. However, significant passages appear to be omitted. Our earliest copies of the *Epistola* are much later. So, of course finding the actual originals, or even earlier copies, would be of inestimable value."

Penhaligon paused for a breath, almost as if she feared going on. "Beyond that, it appears there may be more—perhaps a journal and collection of poetry, although the reference is obscure."

"The Breastplate?" Felicity caught her breath.

"Perhaps. Only guesswork at this point." The archivist continued with details of contingencies and scientific processes.

Felicity struggled to make sense of what she was hearing. "So there's some sort of treasure map hidden in the illumination? That will lead to these manuscripts?" She shook her head and argued with herself: But wasn't this made hundreds of years ago? Wouldn't anything hidden—or stored—then have been moved? Just as this document had been?

Dr. Penhaligon continued as if she had read Felicity's supplementary thoughts. "My preliminary survey is far from conclusive, you understand. It will take a team of experts months—years, perhaps—to understand it fully, but it appears the original location could be indicative of some permanence. The real key is the evidence this provides that these documents actually exist."

Felicity bit her tongue to hold her questions. She needed to listen. She smiled, remembering Mother Mary Joy's advice. Could she be learning already?

"What we have here—under the illumination—is a

palimpsest—the original writing has been effaced to make room for later writing, but traces remain."

Felicity nodded. Père Denis had said something like that was possible. But he had apparently died before he could find it. Or had he found it? And the excitement brought on his heart attack?

"Overwriting was a very common practice as the sheets of animal skin were expensive and not readily obtainable. Parchment like this, which was available in Europe after the sixth century, was very durable."

"Oh, I thought it was vellum," Felicity interjected.

"Depends on what kind of animal skin this is. Tests will tell, of course, but I'm guessing it's sheep, which would have been most accessible in Ireland."

"So the old writing was scraped off?"

Penhaligon nodded. "That was often done, but in this case, I would say it was washed using milk and oat bran to remove the ink. When this method is used, over the passage of time the faint remainings of the former writing reappear enough to allow scholars to decipher them. As has happened here.

"The fact that most of this information was in the area later covered by illumination increases the challenge, but doesn't make it impossible. More than eighty percent of the undertext has been recovered from the *Archimedes Palimpsest* since modern methods have allowed retrieval of the part obscured by overpainted icons on that document."

"But why would a medieval scribe have destroyed such important information?" Felicity was still struggling to get a picture of what had happened.

Dr. Penhaligon smiled. "Medieval scribes weren't indiscriminate in supplying themselves with material from any old volume that happened to be at hand. Most often such erasures were done to sanctify a pagan text by overlaying it with the word of God, somewhat as pagan sites were overlaid with Christian churches to hallow pagan ground."

Felicity sighed. Right, so her dearly held theory—well, passing thought, at least—that this could be a missing sheet from *The Book of Kells*, was clearly not the case.

The archivist continued with her explanation. "The motivation here, however, is unlikely to have been sanctifying pagan property. I think it far more likely the information wasn't considered necessary—that is, it was general knowledge at that time. Or," she paused, "there is another possibility. The monk could have been protecting the information. If it was the only index, say, perhaps he wanted to ensure it didn't fall into the wrong hands during a time of threat."

"Do you mean Vikings?"

Dr. Penhaligon spread her hands to indicate that was entirely enough speculation for one day, but Felicity's mind raced ahead. If such a key were suspected—say perhaps an archeologist had discovered a reference to its existence... And if that archaeologist happened to be Professor McKinnon...

Chapter Twenty-Five

"What a perfect choice." Antony looked around The Shamrock and smiled. He had never been to Ireland, but had he been, he was certain this was exactly the sort of pub he would have found: dark wood paneling polished to a high gloss, a bar lined with red leather-covered stools on one side of the long room, a row of round tables under leaded colored-glass windows on the other side. Brass chandeliers gave enough light to see by, but not enough to destroy the atmosphere.

"Oh, I love it!" Felicity squeezed his arm.

Antony smiled at the joy of having her back with him—where he could keep an eye on her. On their way down the hill from Westminster Abbey she had told him a few tantalizing bits about Father Conall's discovery, but there had been no time to talk. That would have to wait until after this lecture.

Zack, who was escorting them, waved to a casually dressed young man with a dark red beard who approached them from a table in the back corner. "This is Brian. Good to see you, buddy." He clapped him on the back. "This is Antony—who is lucky enough to be married to this gorgeous creature." Zack pointed to Felicity and shook his head in wonder over how such a thing came to be.

The room was already filling with conferees placing their orders at the bar, so after a general greeting, Brian led the way to the back. He assured Antony he understood the role he was to play. "Just call me Secundinus." He grinned and suggested Antony stand against the wall to speak, while he would stay seated by the table—close to his pint of Guinness.

It was easy to see that Antony's class had enthusiastically embraced the venue. He just hoped all the good vibes wouldn't overpower the message he aspired to convey. If he could even get them quiet enough to hear him. He waited until a little after their assigned starting time for everyone to find a seat, then he nodded to Brian who got their attention with a single glissando on the harp.

Antony gave a brief summary of the first part of the story, which he had delivered in full detail outside the Saint Patrick Station in Toronto, then nodded to Brian for one more arpeggio to serve as a segue to his narrative:

Patrick heard angry shouts. A fierce band of Leoghaire's warriors stormed up the hill with drawn swords. A whirlwind chariot ride brought them to Tara. As Caelchon, the warrior captain, led the missionaries into the hall at sword-point, vast quantities of food and drink were being served up and down the long tables, while a cacophony of jugglers, clowns, magicians, bards, drummers, pipers, and harpers all performed to the honor of King Leoghaire.

So, as if the years between had not existed, Patrick stood once again, hands bound with iron chains, in the Tech Midchuarta, the Great Hall of Tara. Some six hundred fifty feet long and one hundred feet wide, the hall was the largest structure Patrick had ever seen. The age-darkened timbers held many and many a head of defeated enemies, but the gray stone walls were richly covered with embroidered hangings. Crimson and gold magical beasts and birds intertwined with leaves and trailing branches. And within the hall, colorfully-clad warriors, peasants, and nobles had gathered to celebrate their king's birthday.

Patrick thought that surely Caelchon would not interrupt the celebration. But as his captor approached the royal couple sitting at the high table, Patrick realized that he and his companions were to be part of the entertainment.

A silence fell over the top of the hall and gradually made its way down the cavernous room. Every head turned toward the high table. Revelers left their heather-honey mead cups and moved forward. Many stood on the tables to see better. These foreign-looking men in their somber brown, hooded robes, with the front of their heads shaved from ear to ear, had actually defied the High King by lighting a fire on his birthday eve? And on the Hill of the Slain? They had gone up the hill of snakes and returned alive? These strange men must worship powerful gods.

Leoghaire rose. Even in the vastness of his poorly-lit hall, he was a commanding sight. His crimson, purple, and gold cloak billowed over his emerald tunic. Gold and amber glinted on his brow, neck, and arms, but were all outshone by the exquisite Brooch of Tara on his shoulder. Although small, its very power was in its delicacy, as the animals, reptiles, and humans fashioned from filigree wire all winked and sparkled at one another in the firelight, and the contrasting colors of the gilt surface and molded dark glass reflected varying lights.

Leoghaire's shoulder-length hair, the color of age-darkened amber, flowed to the folds of his cape, adding to the fierce appearance of his bearded, mustachioed face. "Why have you dared to desecrate my birthday celebration by the lighting of your own hill-fire?" he bellowed.

Patrick stepped forward. "Bid your captain to unchain me, and I will gladly answer."

Leoghaire hesitated.

"We are unarmed. We come as men of peace. You have no need to fear us unbound."

Leoghaire made an impatient gesture toward Caelchon, and Patrick and his companions were unchained.

"I mean no disrespect to Your Majesty." Patrick spoke loudly, constantly aware that the real power was wielded by the druids behind the power-seat. "I wish you the happiest of natal celebrations. But there is One higher even than the High King of Tara whose holy day must also be celebrated."

From the indrawn breath behind him, Patrick knew he was reaching his audience. "I have come to Eire—rather, returned to the land where I served many years of slavery as a youth, brought here by your father Niall of the Nine Hostages. King Leoghaire, I have come back to tell you of the High God who offers all men what no other god can offer—love and peace and salvation. I have come to you, King Leoghaire, to seek your permission to tell the people of Eire of this God."

"No!" Before the king could answer, the chief druids Lochru and Lucetmal—the same who held sway in King Niall's day—strode forward. "There can be no other high god in Tara or in all Eire but Dagada. Those who defy Dagada must be sacrificed to him. Tomorrow you shall be given to Dagada on the very hill where you lit your blasphemous fire."

Only a short time ago Patrick had drunk of the cup of the last supper on that hill. On the night He was crucified, Christ had asked His disciples if they could drink of the cup that He would drink. Would Patrick's communion cup be to the death as that of his Lord's was?

Patrick turned to the people in the guise of speaking to the druids. "Yes. I lit the fire to my God on the very hill that you have kept your people from with fearful tales of poisonous snakes. Our God does not keep His followers away with fear, but bids them come to Him with love. The love of our God gives His followers power. He promises His followers that they may step on asp and cobra; they may tread safely on snake and serpent. That is the power of our God and His Son our Lord whom we bring to you."

A gentle murmur behind Patrick told him his message was getting through. But his triumph was short-lived.

"No! Such a God is not for the High King, not for Tara, not for Eire..." Both druids raised their hands and, swaying slightly in their multicolored robes, firelight dancing on the sacred gold moon-shaped lunula about their necks, chanted:

Dagada with his three tunes gives to the Eirran all good things.
Dagada plays on his harp of three strings:
With one pluck he grants the people sleep,
With another stroke he gives the Eirran mirth,
With yet another touch he brings mourning.

Dagada wields his club of great power:
With one slash he grants the people strength,
With another blow he gives the Eirran victory,
With yet another hit he brings mighty triumph.

Dagada holds his unquenchable cauldron of plenty:
With one bestowal he gives the people abundance,
With another favor he grants the Eirran riches,
With yet another outpouring flows life and health.

May Dagada the high god of all Eire ever be worshiped by his faithful people.
Dagada the harper, Dagada the strong,
Dagada the abundant.
Dagada, Dagada, Dagada.

As the swaying and chanting mingled with the smoke and firelight, and many behind Patrick took up the chant, he realized that the contest was not one of fires or snakes or priests. It was a contest between the cauldron of Dagada's plenty and the cup of the Lord's Supper. Somehow he must make them see that the power of Christ's sacrifice was greater than Dagada's club.

But combating the mystical emotion generated by the druids seemed impossible. Lochru waited for the perfect moment. When the chant had reached its peak, he signaled with an upraised hand to the harpers to join. The voice of the instrument most beloved by all of Eire and sacred to

Dagada soared above all other voices to the blackened rafters where the heads of defeated enemies hung by their own hair.

At the sound of the harp-voice, Patrick knew what to do. When at last the music softened and the chanting faded, he turned to Leoghaire, who had remained aloof from the frenzy. The bishop bowed deeply before the king. "O High One, I beg you to forgive any offense I have caused you by lighting a fire to honor my God. In respect for your own great occasion, may I sing you a harp-tale of our God that you may know of His love and power and better judge my act?"

The offer of a harp-song was irresistible. Leoghaire raised his hand for everyone to be seated. Lochru and Lucetmal scowled, but they had no option but to obey their king. At a signal from Leoghaire a bard stepped forward to offer his harp. Patrick signaled to one of his monks.

Antony turned to Brian and nodded. His own harper pulled his cláirseach to him.

Secundinus came forward, took the black bogwood harp of seven strings, and seated himself before the high table. He nestled the instrument against one bent knee and leaned the top in the hollow of his left shoulder. After a few brilliant, flowing glissandos, he gentled the strings to a soft background for the tale Patrick called out in a chanting voice that reached to the very end of the room: "And in the beginning, in the time before time, the Lord God created a garden."

The joy of the story was upon Patrick, and his eyes lit with the fire within him. With a bold stroke, Patrick abandoned all that had been taught him of the land of the Jewish Scriptures and described for his listeners their own land, for after all, had not the Lord God created Eire as truly as He created the Garden of Eden?

"A garden of emerald green hills spread beneath intense blue skies billowing with white clouds. And the Lord God gave rain and slanting sunlight and rainbows to declare His glory. He made joyous waterfalls to tumble from the hills and little lakes to fill every hollow of the ground.

The land He surrounded by blue sea with mighty waves that crashed against black cliffs. And set startling white seabirds to fly against the blue sky and nest in the dark rocks. And lambs and cattle and ponies and great, red wolfhounds—the Lord God created them all. And in the midst of this land of beauty and plenty and abundance, He set a man and a woman. And God told the man and the woman to be happy and to enjoy the bounty of His land."

At a look from Patrick, Secundinus struck a low, ominous note on the harp and held it until its warning of doom had faded. "But there was a serpent in the garden. And the serpent worshiped not the Lord God, nor loved the man and the woman. The wily, subtle serpent led the man and the woman from the worship of the true God by tempting them to taste of evil."

Again the death-sounding notes. When they had faded, Patrick smiled, and Secundinus changed to a joyous flight of strings before Patrick continued. "But our God would not leave His people to evil. He came to earth even as a man to live and teach and offer Himself as a sacrifice that none may ever need follow the way of the snake. This is the night of His sacrifice, of His entombment, of His victory over evil. For in the morning He rose from the grave and offers Himself even now to all who will believe on Him, just as He offered His own body for an abundance of life. Oh come, taste and see that the Lord is good; blessed is the man that trusts in Him."

Patrick paused for a celebration of harp-song, then continued. "Come to the banquet table of our Lord. Drink of His cup of the new life. Turn away from the cauldron of Dagada that the wily serpent in the garden would offer you." Patrick was exhausted. He let the harp finish his story.

Patrick and his companions spent the rest of the night in chains on a pile of animal skins in a locked room—perhaps one of the rooms where Niall's nine hostages had been kept, and not unlike the room where Patrick spent his first night in Eire long years ago. Patrick knew he should be praying and leading the brothers in devotions, but he was too weary. He could neither pray nor sleep. He could only be grateful that, whatever the outcome, he had been allowed to preach the gospel in Eire.

. . .

Antony was unsure whether the applause that erupted after Brian's final chords was for the harper or the storyteller—for the musician, he suspected, but it was none the less sweet. Students rushed to refill their glasses, request songs of the harper and ask questions of the narrator in about equal numbers.

It was considerably later when Antony looked around for Felicity. He hadn't noticed her leaving her chair at their table, but no matter how hard he searched the mass of enthusiastic conferees, he could not find her.

Chapter Twenty-Six

Felicity smiled. Engaging a harper for the Patrick story had been a stroke of genius. She was so proud of Antony. His tales always gripped her, but in this setting, with the harp-song reenacted as part of the story, she had never been more moved.

She closed her eyes and could almost smell the smoke from the central fire in Leoghaire's great hall. She saw the firelight reflecting off the golden armbands and torcs his warriors wore, reminding her of the treasure she had just been discussing in Brother Conall's office. How wonderful to understand the true value of the manuscript they had shepherded across the continent.

Her imagination was still soaring with the intermingled words and music when a nudge at her arm made her open her eyes. Zack slipped a note on the table before her, then melted back to the other end of the room. She opened the folded paper.

Sorry to disturb you. Dr. Spaulding would like to meet now if you could slip away.

. . .

She sighed and looked around. Although everyone was listening with rapt attention, there was still movement in the room as conferees drifted to the bar for refills. She supposed it wouldn't be too disruptive to move through the crowd, as much as she hated to leave Antony's presentation. She picked up Brian's empty glass so it would look like she was simply going for a drink for him.

By the door she handed the glass to Zack and asked him to take a refill to Brian, then slipped outside.

"I apologize for interrupting." The conference director smiled and indicated they should walk on down the street. "But Zack said you wanted to talk to me and this is my only free time today."

It took Felicity a moment to remember what she had wanted to talk to Dr. Spaulding about. "Oh, yes, I think I remember that you're interested in archeology."

"As it relates to Bible studies, yes."

"Well, I wondered if you knew a Professor McKinnon."

"McKinnon?" Dr. Spaulding repeated the name twice, then shook his head. "I don't think so. Why do you ask?" At the end of the street he turned toward the river.

Felicity considered. Now that she knew the secret the manuscript held did she need to inquire about the professor? Or did her new knowledge make it even more important to know about the people involved in the mystery? She summarized meeting him on the train, told a bit about his interest in Viking hoards—all neutral enough information. Then, hoping she didn't sound completely paranoid she told about how the archeologist seemed to be following her—omitting the fact of her searching his room.

Spaulding bent to her in shocked concern "But that's alarming—why didn't you tell me sooner?"

"Well, it's all pretty vague..." Should she go on and reveal Father Conall's discovery? She hesitated. But what could it hurt? And Dr. Spaulding might be able to help. "This morning, though, I learned the true value of the manuscript and now I'm rather alarmed."

"Value?" Spaulding's eyebrows shot up.

She summarized what the archivist had told her. "Of course, it's not quite your field, but Christian history is pretty close to Biblical archeology."

"Yes, yes. You're quite right to tell me. Exciting discovery certainly. But one can't be too careful. Where is the manuscript now?"

"With Father Conall and the archivist."

"Archivist?" Spaulding almost shouted as the roar of the river increased.

"From the University of Vancouver. You see, I was taking Cerise to her convent near Victoria, and when I got back—"

"Yes, I see. But you don't know the location the manuscript points to?"

Felicity shook her head as they entered the trees. Before she could explain further, though, a snapping twig in the underbrush made her whip around. Was that the sound of footsteps behind them? Was McKinnon following them now? Could he have heard their conversation? She could see nothing through the thick woods, however.

Felicity returned to Spaulding's question. "Dr. Penhaligon, the archivist, might have deciphered more by now, but she said it could take a team months—or even years to do so. We were supposed to take it back to the Community of the Transfiguration with us, but I expect Father Peter will be happy to leave it with the archivist team for more study. I hope so. It would be a relief not to have to be responsible for it anymore."

Her mind filled with pleasant images of that long flight—alone with Antony and none of this disturbing mystery...

Spaulding grabbed her arm roughly. So sudden she was too shocked to cry out. "I'm afraid I don't have that long to wait. Seems I'll have to take matters into my own hands. There are faster methods of discovering that secret—but they'll be too professionally hidebound to use them—worried about damaging the original.

"I know a private collector willing to pay big bucks now— and I need that money."

Felicity's mind whirled, trying to make sense out of what he was saying as they emerged from the trees. Spaulding propelled her down the gradual gravel bank toward the river and on under the bridge.

Rocks crunched beneath their feet, adding to the tumult of the mighty, rushing Fraser. Her captor pulled her to the muddy flat that would comprise the edge of the river at high tide. "Dr. Spaulding, you're hurting me." She tried to keep her voice from coming out on a sob.

He ignored her, thrusting her further down river. Around a bend they reached a secluded spot, and Felicity saw his apparent goal: an ominous metal pole stuck in the riverbed, remains of an earlier construction. She gasped and tried to wrench away. His powerful fingers only bit deeper.

Without letting go he pulled a shiny, white rope from the pouch he carried slung over one shoulder. "I had hoped this wouldn't be necessary, my dear. But I need to take possession of that document, and I fear your friends may be reluctant to release it. You, I am sure, will provide the perfect inducement."

Felicity drew a deep breath to scream. But Spaulding was faster. He clapped his hand over her mouth. "I wouldn't advise that. No one could hear you, and you'll only force me to insert a gag. A most uncomfortable state of affairs, I assure you." Felicity clamped her lips shut.

Next she tried digging her feet into the mud as he shoved her toward the pole, but the river silt slipped beneath her feet, only making his fierce grip on her arm more painful.

When they reached the pipe he lashed her to the pole, her upper arms close to her torso, then yanked her hands behind the shaft and bound her wrists at her back. She felt the rope cutting into her ankles as he tied her feet to the rough metal.

"Fortunate that the tide is out, but we can't count on it staying much longer. Looks like it has already turned." Felicity tried to ignore his insidious voice, but couldn't resist looking at the blue waters with their whirling edge of foam. How long would it take them to reach her? She could feel the chill of the water crawling up her body, and couldn't stifle a cry deep in her throat.

Spaulding smiled as he whipped out his phone and began taking pictures of her and the rising tide. She struggled, then realized she was only adding to the drama of what was undoubtedly to be his ransom note.

Her captor almost purred as his thumbs danced over the keys to send his message. He followed the text with a phone call which Felicity couldn't hear plainly, but he seemed to be making an appointment. Brenner? Was that the name he gave? Or Brennan?

Felicity heard a soft squishing sound, then a crunch of gravel as her captor departed across the bank. She twisted her head around enough to be able to see him pick up the bag he had dropped there and take something from it.

A moment later he returned to taunt her for a final time. "I'm afraid I must leave you now, my dear. You might try praying that your friends will prove cooperative."

Felicity gasped and her eyes widened at the sight of the disguise he had donned. "You!"

The man she saw in Thorpeside Wood stood before her. "In England. And at St. Andrew's. But why?"

"Isn't it obvious?"

She nodded as much as her lashing to the pole would allow. "The manuscript."

"Yes, it would have saved us all a great deal of trouble if I could have got my hands on it then. But that gumshoe interfered."

"You had this in mind all along? That's why you wanted Antony to speak at your conference. And you were behind the suggestion he bring the manuscript with him?"

"Good improvising, don't you agree? So sorry I can't stay to chat, but puzzling out all the answers can help take your mind off the rising tide." He smiled. "Yes, I heard your husband's most affecting telling of the story of the two Margarets. I'm sure you'll appreciate the irony of being allowed the honor of a re-enactment. Although it won't be you being called on for the cooperative answers."

He started to move away, then paused. "With any luck someone will find you before the tide is fully in, although I can't make any promises. And I'll be well away by then anyway." He gazed up at the rusty ring near the top of the pole. "Yes, the high water mark is fully over your head. I was a bit worried when I realized how tall you are."

And he was gone. She heard him crunch away, then twigs snapped as he crashed through the heavy vegetation along the river. She looked at the swirling water. Yes, the tide was definitely rising. She had no markers to tell her how much it had risen in the time she had been there, but it was definitely creeping toward her.

She tried to pray, but a strangled *help* was all she could manage. She was all too aware of the unlikelihood of anyone finding her in time on this deserted stretch of riverbank. And with an icy clutch at her heart—far colder than the approaching waters—she realized that, no matter what promises Spaulding might make to Father Conall to exchange her for the manuscript —she could identify her captor. If he did return it would not be to rescue her. Hopelessness engulfed her.

Then she felt a vibration. Was the pole shaking in response to the rising water? Maybe it was looser than Spaulding had guessed. She struggled to shake it loose from its foundation, but there was no give.

Then she realized it was her phone in her back pocket. The vibration stopped, but she struggled to get hold of it anyway. Maybe...

She focused her will; strained every muscle. Her upper arms were bound so tightly the ropes cut into her flesh. Especially when she moved her arms. Yet she did manage some movement. She could feel the top of her pocket. Inching her fingers around she managed to slip two inside the pocket and clamp her phone as if with tongs.

She paused to gasp for air, realizing that she had been holding her breath. She glanced at the water, then wished she hadn't. How could it rise that fast?

Inching the phone upward ever so carefully and praying she wouldn't drop it, she managed to ease it higher. Inch by inch. She tried to block the sense of a tidal wave rushing toward her. She knew hurry would be fatal. One careless move...

At last her phone was free. Carefully she made the two-fingered transfer into the secure palm of her left hand. She felt to be certain she held it screen outward and ran her fingers around the edge to determine which side was up. She closed her eyes to focus better, trying to picture her screen in her mind. If she pushed here, swiped here, then tapped here, would that get her the connection she so desperately needed? And how would she know?

Repeated fumblings seemed to produce no effect. "No!" She gasped when she felt the first cold splashings hit her ankles. Now she did scream. Although she knew the likelihood of anyone hearing her was minimal, she drew breath to try again.

Her phone vibrating in her hand brought her focus back. Praying she had judged the position of the bar correctly, she swiped. By a miracle, she must have hit it because the vibration stopped. "Antony! Is that you? I'm in the river. Beyond the bridge. He—Spaulding—" The next wash of the river brought a log with it. A branch whacked her shins so sharply she dropped her phone.

The despair that washed over her as she saw her phone whirl away downstream, then disappear, was blacker than any depth of water could be. And now, of all times—when she was just sure—and she hadn't even had a chance to tell Antony yet...

That thought invigorated her. No! She jerked her head up. She wouldn't let that scoundrel rob her—them—of that future. She struggled against the ropes. It seemed that the bonds at her ankles loosened a bit as the water soaked into them. Or was that just wishful thinking?

She tried flexing her toes. Yes, there was some movement. Certainly not enough to get her feet free, but hopefully enough to manage an awkward sort of *relevé*. It would gain her a few blessed inches—she wasn't sure what good that would do—but she knew she wouldn't let go of any possibility.

She began concentrating on her feet. *Don't think about how fast the water is rising*, she commanded herself as she realized it now covered a higher set of the eyelets on her shoes than just moments ago. *Concentrate on your exercise*. In an effort to forget the onrushing danger, she focused her mind back. She was standing at the barre just as she had done at the end of every class. "Loosen and stretch," Miss Lydia commanded. "Roll through your feet."

In a see-saw fashion, moving from one foot to the other, Felicity struggled to curl first one foot up to stand on the ball. Then down, and up on the other. Back and forth, as if she were pedaling. At first she managed to raise her heels only a fraction of an inch, but gradually she felt herself gaining more altitude. Perhaps the rope was stretching more, or perhaps she was building up strength. If she kept at it she might be able to make some difference. If her feet didn't go numb in the icy water.

She refused to panic as she felt the water reach her knees. She continued the rhythmic pedaling with her feet, but now she focused on her wrists. Would the rope that bound her hands together also stretch when it got wet? If it did... She dared to hope—always hope. She strained against the ungiving dry bonds.

The sound of a bell, faint over the tumult of tumbling water, came to her. Not from the abbey. Surely that was too far away.

Perhaps from a local church. Yet it must be marking evening prayers. Is that where Antony would be now? Where did he think she was? Was he worried about her? With a jerk of hope she realized he might have become worried enough to call the police. If only she hadn't dropped her phone.

The water now reached her fingertips. She tried twisting her hands, but didn't get any movement. The dry rope only bit deeper into her flesh. She made one more attempt then stilled. She could make no headway.

Until the water reached her wrists. The wet rope definitely eased a fraction. She was terrified by the speed with which the water was rising, yet encouraged by the loosening of her bonds. Now she could maneuver her hands. Twist side to side; pull up and down. Make it a rhythm in time with her feet. Keep at it.

Water engulfed her neck. Felicity stretched. Water lapped her mouth. She clamped her lips and prayed for strength. It was time to *relevé* with increased earnestness. Her head emerged from the river. The water receded to her neck. She smiled at the small victory, even though she knew it would only last for minutes at best.

The water was soon back up to her mouth. She put all her effort into a final stretch, her soggy tennis shoes supporting a full *en pointe*. She could stretch no higher.

Her final elevation gained her perhaps thirty seconds. She clenched her lips more firmly shut and tilted her face upward, stretching her neck in her best *tendu*. One last lungful of breath before the water reached her nose.

Then the miracle. The bonds at her wrists stretched another inch and she pulled a hand free. Then the other.

Yes! She could almost reach the knot at her left shoulder. She began plucking at it with her left hand. Still too tight. She maneuvered her right hand to assist. But the knot didn't give.

The next wave washed over her nose. *Don't breathe*, her brain commanded. She strained her arms against the ropes. If she could get them to stretch maybe she could push them up and wriggle free.

Her lungs burned. Surely they would burst. A vague idea that most people could hold their breath under water for two minutes floated though her mind. It seemed like it had been two hours already. But perhaps only a minute in reality. Surely she could hold out no longer.

Was this the end? After she had come so close?

She put everything she had into one final struggle. She knew this was the last.

Her shoulders slipped from the rope. It sank and she felt it tangling around her feet.

She didn't have enough breath left to bend down and untie her feet. But perhaps she could maneuver to get herself higher. With one final *en pointe*, her arms reaching upward toward the heavens, her fingers curved over the top of the pole.

The metal cutting painfully into her fingers, she heaved herself upward. Her head broke through the water. She pulled huge gulps of fresh air into her lungs. She hung there, panting, until she felt her breathing calm. Then her fingers begin to slip on the pipe.

With a final deep breath she let herself slide back into the water. Now she could bend down to wrestle with the rope binding her ankles.

Her hands were sore and numb. They were undoubtedly bleeding from the raw edge of the pipe. She fumbled. She was so close, but her searing lungs insisted she surface again. She grappled for the top of the pipe and heaved upward. Anger at being so near her goal—yet still so far.

"Felicity!"

Was she delusional? Had she heard her name? She swiveled around the pole to scan the shore.

"Felicity! Felicity!"

"Antony!" She yelled, longing to wave as well, but didn't dare loosen her grip on the top of the pipe.

He plunged into the raging waters and reached her with a few strong strokes. They clung to one another, the pole between them.

"Come on, let me take you in." He tugged at her shoulder.

"My feet. Still tied," she gasped.

He dove under. She was free in less than a minute.

They swam to shore side by side and sank onto the shingle next to each other. Both were too exhausted to talk, but alternated laughing and crying—Antony joyously, Felicity hysterically.

Chapter Twenty-Seven

Felicity was aware of nothing but overwhelming relief—and Antony's arm tight around her. She pulled a deep breath of air into her lungs for the pure joy of being able to. Then the wail of a siren broke into her consciousness. Moments later they were both engulfed in warm blankets with mugs of hot, sweet coffee in their hands.

"How did you know?" Felicity asked after her first scalding gulp.

Antony answered. "I knew that garbled message had to be you—then I heard the splash. I thought maybe you had said something about the bridge, so I called emergency, then headed this way with as much speed and prayer as I could muster."

A medic approached Felicity with stethoscope and blood pressure cuff. She submitted to his ministration for as long as she could. Finally the question desperately pushing at her mind burst out. "Is the baby alright?"

Antony gasped. "What did you say?"

Felicity nodded, but held her breath as the medic moved his stethoscope to her abdomen.

When he nodded and looked up with a smile, she squealed.

Antony engulfed her with another hug. "Why didn't you tell me?"

Still a bit hysterical, Felicity wavered between laughter and tears, but struggled to answer. "I wasn't sure. Then I was—this morning. I got a kit at the drug store." She looked at her bleeding fingers. "Now I have a use for those band-aids I used as an excuse. I planned to tell you at the right time. Then when I thought there wouldn't be any more time..." She burst into sobs, still punctuated with laughter.

It was some time until either of them was calm enough to answer the questions for the police officer who stood patiently by, clutching his notebook. Finally Felicity took a shaky breath and forced herself to quiet. She nodded at the officer. He came forward and identified himself as Inspector Langdon of the RCMP. "Can you tell me what happened here?"

Felicity struggled to give a coherent account. She could see by his frown that she wasn't doing a very good job.

"Officer," Antony interrupted "She's had a terrible shock. Can't this wait?"

Before Langdon could answer, however, a police diver emerged from the river carrying the rope. He held it out, dripping, to the investigator. "Lucky, it tangled around the pole, otherwise it would be in Vancouver by now."

"What does it tell us?" Langdon asked.

The diver smiled. "Tells us the guy was an amateur. Good thing for you, ma'am." He nodded at Felicity. "Nylon. Strong enough when dry, but it has a lot of stretch—up to forty per cent, even. And when it's wet it can lose up to a quarter of its strength."

Langdon nodded and turned back to Felicity. "So you say you know who did this?"

"Yes—his name is Spaulding. I think he also goes by Brennan or something like that, too. He seemed to be making an appointment in that name. It's a long story."

Felicity started to repeat her account, intending to start at the beginning. Then she gasped. "The manuscript! It and Father Conall are in danger. Probably Penhaligon, too. We know he's willing to kill for it. We need to get to Westminster Abbey now."

Langdon ushered Antony and Felicity, still clutching their blankets, to the top of the bank and into his white car with the multi-colored stripe down the side. As he drove he radioed for back-up to get to Westminster Abbey as fast as possible.

On the way Felicity explained to Antony that it had been Spaulding—or Brennan—in Thorpeside Wood and at Saint Andrews. She paused. "I wonder why he saved me from the fall there? Do you suppose he meant it as a threat?"

Antony moved his arm to encircle her shoulders again and pulled her toward him, as much as their seat belts would allow. "He probably calculated that he needed you in order to get his hands on the document."

Felicity nodded. "And he was secure enough in his disguise that he didn't worry that I could identify him, even then."

Before they could explore further, Langdon pulled up in front of Westminster Abbey. Felicity jumped out of the car, dropping her blanket and not even waiting for Antony or the police. After all that had occurred she had no intention of letting Spaulding win now.

She was so intent on racing toward the door of the monastery she hardly noticed two figures coming toward her until she almost collided with the shorter one. "Professor McKinnon!"

Then she looked in horror at the tall man accompanying him. McKinnon and Spaulding were in cahoots? Would they try to take her hostage now?

She whirled, but McKinnon caught her arm. "Don't run off. You'll be needed to identify this scoundrel."

Then she realized McKinnon was leading a handcuffed Spaulding.

"What..." Felicity began, but she couldn't even form a question.

"I've been following Spaulding for days—weeks, really. I heard you in the woods by the river and rushed back here to Conall." He looked at her apologetically. "Sorry, it appears you've had a spot of bother. I wouldn't have left if I'd realized you were in danger."

"You ran off and left her alone with a criminal?" Antony had joined them just in time to hear McKinnon's last words.

He made a shamefaced grimace. "Afraid I got it wrong—I thought Cerise and her boyfriend were the guilty parties. I was sure when she swore she didn't know anything about the manuscript. I didn't think that was possible, given her ties to Saint Benoit..." He shook his head.

"That's why you were on the train? You were following Cerise?" Antony asked.

"When she showed up back here I was convinced—until I rushed into Conall's office, expecting to accost Zack, and found this scuzzball."

"Cerise and Zack?" Felicity and Antony said together.

Felicity nodded. "She told me you questioned her." She smiled. "That's why I thought you were guilty."

"Now I realize why I didn't get anywhere. But at the time I thought she was just being stubborn. Nothing else seemed to make sense to me. It was obvious the girl had no intention of becoming a nun."

Felicity laughed. She couldn't agree more. "So what *is* she up to?"

Just then the bells in the lofty bell tower chimed forth joyfully and the door of the chapel opened. Cerise and Zack exited hand in hand, she carrying a handful of daisies and both wearing radiant smiles.

Zack's smile got even broader, making his beard curl upward, when he spotted Felicity and Antony. Pulling Cerise, he strode to them. "Sorry I couldn't stay for the end of your lecture, Father A, but I, er, had a prior appointment."

He smiled down at Cerise who held out her left hand to let

the evening sunlight catch the gold band on her third finger and set it aglow.

"You're *married?*" Felicity was the first to respond.

Cerise tilted her chin up and gave her saucy grin. Followed by a full trill of a giggle. "World's strangest elopement, huh? But I couldn't think of a better way to get free from Anne-Marie's control. It's been the same all my life. Ever since our parents died. 'Cerise do this; Cerise do that.' You know, I don't think she ever once asked me what I wanted."

"But, Zack," Felicity protested. "You hardly knew each other."

Zack grinned and pulled a rope of heavy, wooden beads from his pocket. Felicity stared. She was sure she'd seen them before, but she couldn't place the memory until Zack bowed his head, piously clasping the beads to his chest.

"The tall nun in the strange habit? You made retreats to Saint Benoit as a *nun?*" No wonder his beard was just growing out again when they saw him that night at the Toronto hotel. "And you were on the train all the time, weren't you? When you made us believe you were already here."

Zack grinned and winked. "Worked, huh?" Put his arm around his bride. "Sorry, got to run. We have a ferry to catch— bridal suite at the Empress."

Felicity realized her mouth was hanging open as she watched their departing backs. What in the world would Mother Anne-Marie say? Whatever it was, though, Felicity was certain those two would be equal to standing up for themselves.

Felicity was brought back to the present by Inspector Langdon taking Spaulding into custody. "I'll need a statement from all of you later." He included Felicity, Antony and McKinnon in his gaze. "I'd appreciate it if you could come to the RCMP office in Municipal Hall in Mission tomorrow." He held out cards with the address.

"Professor McKinnon," Felicity turned to him as Langdon ushered Spaulding toward his patrol car, "I want to know—"

Antony held up his hand. "Yes. There's lots we both want to know, but you need to sit down. And we both need dry clothes. Professor, could we meet in the dining hall and continue this over dinner?"

"An excellent idea. Half an hour?"

As much as she hated the delay, Felicity had to admit her husband was right—as usual. A hot shower and a warm snuggly sweater felt heavenly after her clinging, river-soaked garments. And she was hungry. She smiled. Eating for two was going to be fun.

Fortunately, at Westminster the guests ate apart from the community and there were no restrictions on talking. In spite of her niggling fears that he might disappear, they found Professor McKinnon waiting for them at a table in a far corner of the large dining room. And he had a surprise guest with him. "Father Conall, I'm so glad to see you," Felicity cried.

"And I you. I understand you've had quite a day of it."

"Enough to make me ravenous." She eyed the dishes set out buffet style where several other guests, most of them conference attendees, were filling their plates. They joined the queue. After everyone had filled their plates and returned to their seats, the brother assigned to host the evening meal led in prayer.

Only after she had devoured several large bites of a tasty pasta dish, creamy with cheese, did Felicity voice the question that had been burning in her mind. "So, who are you working for?"

McKinnon put down his fork. "Ah, I've rather been expecting that question. I can only answer it for you up to a point, as my client—and professional ethics—both require anonymity. I can tell you, though, that at first I was working for myself." He took a long drink of water, as if taking time to get his thoughts in order.

"When my brother George was murdered—by that villain, as

it turns out—and the police seemed helpless to solve it, I took up the gauntlet on my own bat. When George's client learned what I was doing they hired me in his place."

Felicity frowned. "I don't understand. So you're a private detective? I thought you were an archeology professor."

"Both it seems. George was the licensed detective—had his own agency for some fifteen years—well established. I helped him on a few cases, especially one a few years ago when an artifact was stolen from a museum. The case required my archeological expertise.

"Turns out, when he was killed I learned he had willed the agency to me. It was almost like he knew he'd be needing me to follow up."

The professor was quiet for a moment, as if recalling his dead brother.

"Um, the client?" Felicity prodded.

"Yes, well, as I say—no names. You'll have to take my word for it that they are a thoroughly reputable—um, group—with a long-established interest in documents of this sort—even more so in the ones it points to. I might even go so far as to say they have a demonstrable right to those historic documents of the faith in Ireland."

Felicity's mind buzzed. Trinity College, Dublin? The Irish Government? The Catholic Church? A Monastery in Armagh?

"This pasta is excellent, isn't it?" McKinnon said, indicating that the topic was closed.

"But—" Felicity persisted.

"I've already said too much." McKinnon took another bite of pasta.

Father Conall turned to Felicity and spoke for the first time. "Would it be too much to hope—with all you've had on your mind—that the chant might be ready to leave with me?"

The relief of returning to a pleasant topic, disassociated with murder and skullduggery, was so great Felicity almost laughed. "Not at all too much. I even brought it with me. I was hoping to see you after dinner, but this is even better." She reached into the bag at her feet and pulled out several pages. "I hope you can read these. There are quite a few mark-outs. I did a lot of it on the train."

The precentor scanned the pages she handed him. His lips moved as he read. Then he brought up one hand as if marking time, and finally he began humming a line of chant softly. "Oh, yes, excellent."

"I hope I didn't take too many liberties. I was trying to make room for vocal runs..."

"Yes, yes. I see exactly what you were aiming for. A very Gaelic feel, indeed. I think we might even insert a bit more repetition just here." He pointed to a line. "I can't wait to begin arranging the setting and training our choir—as the successor to Père Denis, God rest his soul," he paused and crossed himself, "will be training his. It will be the high point of the colloquium. I can't thank you—and Father Peter—enough."

He looked through the papers she had handed him again. "Is something missing?"

"Well, I wonder, might I have your copy of the manuscript back?"

Felicity gave Professor McKinnon a meaningful look. "I'm afraid I don't have it. It went, er—missing on the train."

"Missing?"

"Yes. I finished my work from a photo I took of it. I could send that to you if it would help, but can't you make another before you send the original off to the university?"

"No. I mean, yes, I could, but that's not the point. You see, it's just that the further the copy is spread abroad—um, well, the less unique our offering will be. We hope to get some real recognition for the society—produce a CD, perhaps. We need to build broader interest or the art of chant will die out."

Before Felicity could think of a reply the professor spoke up. "I am certain my client would agree with you one hundred per cent. I suggest Mrs. Sherwood send her photograph to you. A reproduction should be adequate for your promotion of the colloquium."

Felicity realized she would have to be content with assuming her purloined copy would be in the hands of McKinnon's clients —unnamed as they were. She found the idea of it being Trinity College or a monastery equally appealing.

She was still pondering when a sound behind her almost made her drop her fork. Surely she was free of that heavy breather. Was he still dogging her steps? She whirled to face a small, balding man with a cherubic face that she was certain she had never seen before. Especially not the bright plaid shirt he was wearing. That was definitely something she wasn't likely to forget.

"What do you—" she began indignantly.

The intruder held out his hand to Antony. "Please, do forgive me for intruding, Father. But I did so want to thank you for your most enlightening lectures. I have been so privileged to be able to attend both sections of the conference."

He turned to Father Conall. "And I'm intensely looking forward to the colloquium next year. My readers will be enthralled. Especially when they find I've brushed shoulders with a murderer. What a thing to become involved with. Well, not exactly involved, of course, but to be able to observe at close hand... I've never had such a story before." He let go of Antony's hand and paused for a gasping breath.

"Readers?" Felicity asked.

"Oh, yes. I have a modest, but quite devout following. It's something of an esoteric subject, after all—saints, chants, church history—but that makes my followers all the more avid. If I might," he placed a small card in front of each of them, "You can follow my blog here. I know you'll enjoy reading it." He finished his speech by drawing a raspy breath.

"Wait a minute." Antony frowned. "It was you. I remember that sound just before the chapel door slammed shut. You searched my room at Saint Benoit for material for your story."

But he was gone. He had simply melted into the group of guests around the desert table.

McKinnon picked up the card the man had placed on the table, then put on his glasses to read. "'The Phantom Blogger.' Well named, indeed."

But Felicity was staring at McKinnon. In his glasses—if his mustache were blackened—"Monsieur Laurent!"

"Père Denis called the archeology society for an expert. It was my best opportunity to get a look at the manuscript."

Felicity felt the blood draining from her head. She couldn't take much more. "You killed him to get the manuscript for your client." She put her head in her hands.

"Absolutely not. Natural causes, like they said. My goal was to track my brother's killer. My client was quite happy with my report of the whereabouts of the manuscript—as they will be to know it's in Dr. Penhaligon's capable hands. They are responsible to take up their own negotiations with Father Peter."

Felicity didn't know whether to be more angry or more amazed, but she settled for laughing until she cried.

That evening, under the pink and gold light of a glorious sunset, Felicity and Antony strolled across the green expanse of hilltop that comprised the grounds of Westminster Abbey. Antony put his hand on Felicity's still flat abdomen and shook his head. "I simply can't believe it."

"I hope you're pleased."

"That's hardly the word. Thrilled, ecstatic…" he searched his vocabulary. "Euphoric probably comes closest. That, and unspeakably grateful." He turned and took her in his arms.

After a lengthy kiss they pulled apart. "I hope that rectory will have room for a nursery." She paused. "And an office for me." She launched into telling him all about Mother Mary Joy and her decision to become a spiritual director. "It will be perfect with the baby, my time will be flexible and—"

He cut her off with another kiss.

They stood arm in arm for a few moments, then turned to ascend the bank. At the top, they paused to observe a pair of totem poles. Many of these symbolic carvings, illustrating the family lineage and cultural heritage of First Nations peoples, were topped by Thunderbirds. These, though were different. This pair bore enormous white birds, a band of black feathers on the tips of each wing accenting the breadth of their wingspread.

Antony considered. "Snow Geese, I think. A sign of fertility, domesticity and lifelong partnership—so I've read."

Felicity smiled and rested her head on his shoulder with a contented sigh. "Tomorrow—home."

About the Author

Donna Fletcher Crow, Novelist of British History, is a former English teacher and a lifelong Anglophile. She is the author of 50 books, mostly novels of British history. The award-winning *Glastonbury, The Novel of Christian England,* an Arthurian epic covering 15 centuries of English history, is her best-known work. Besides the Monastery Murders, she also authors The Lord Danvers Victorian true-crime mysteries and The Elizabeth and Richard literary suspense series. Donna and her husband of 55 years live in Boise, Idaho. They have 4 adult children and 15 grandchildren. She is an enthusiastic gardener.

To read more about all of Donna's books and see pictures from her garden and research trips as well as subscribe to her newsletter, go to: www.DonnaFletcherCrow.com

You can follow her on Facebook at: Donna Fletcher Crow, Novelist of British History

BOOKS BY DONNA FLETCHER CROW

The Elizabeth & Richard Literary Suspense Mysteries
The Torch Ignites
Elizabeth and Richard's strife-filled first meeting in a New England autumn
The Shadow of Reality
Elizabeth and Richard at a Dorothy L Sayers mystery week high in the Rocky Mountains
A Midsummer Eve's Nightmare
Elizabeth and Richard honeymoon at a Shakespeare Festival in Ashland, Oregon
A Jane Austen Encounter
A second honeymoon visit to Jane Austen's homes turns deadly
A Most Singular Venture
Murder in Jane Austen's London
Watch for: ***A Prodigious Supply of Corpses***
Deception and death at Jane Austen's seashore

The Monastery Murders, Clerical Mysteries
A Very Private Grave
Legendary buried treasure, a brutal murder and lurking danger—
an itinerary of terror across a holy terrain
A Darkly Hidden Truth
Ancient puzzles, modern murder and breathless chase scenes
through a remote, waterlogged landscape
An Unholy Communion
An idyllic pilgrimage through Wales becomes a deadly struggle between good and evil
A Newly Crimsoned Reliquary
Murder stalks the shadows of Oxford's hallowed shrines
An All-Consuming Fire
A Christmas wedding in a monastery—
if the bride can defeat the murderer prowling the Yorkshire moors
Against All Fierce Hostility
Is Felicity and Antony's spectacular train journey across Canada
carrying them away from murder—or toward it?

The Daughters of Courage Family Saga
Kathryn, Days of Struggle and Triumph
The unique story of Idaho's desert pioneers in the early days of the twentieth century.
Elizabeth, Days of Loss and Hope
Kathryn's daughter finds her way through the challenges of the Great Depression and World War II
Stephanie, Days of Turmoil and Victory
Strong family ties help Stephanie achieve success in the turbulent days of the 1970s

(continued on next page)

Lord Danvers Investigates, Victorian True-Crime Mysteries

A Most Inconvenient Death
The brutal Stanfield Hall murders shatter a quiet Norwich community and pull Danvers from deep personal grief into a dangerous investigation.

Grave Matters
Lord and Lady Danvers' honeymoon in Scotland is interrupted by the ghosts of Burke and Hare-style grave robbers.

To Dust You Shall Return
Catherine Bacon is murdered in the very shadow of Canterbury Cathedral but Charles and Antonia are overwhelmed with their own problems.

A Tincture of Murder
William Dove is on trial in York for poisoning his wife while Lord and Lady Danvers struggle to assist in a refuge home where fallen women continue to die mysteriously.

A Lethal Spectre
A glittering London season set against the horrors of an Indian mutiny

Where There is Love Historical Romance

Where Love Begins
Can Catherine Peronnet find God's purpose for her life when her beloved Charles Wesley marries another?

Where Love Illumines
Mary Tudway must choose: a life of pleasure amidst London's high society or a life of faith and service with the devout Rowland Hill?

Where Love Triumphs
Charming, brilliant and lame, Sir Brandley Hilliard believes he can do very well without love of any kind in his life—until he meets Elinor Silbert—and then Charles Simeon.

Where Love Restores
Granville Ryder must struggle to find his place in his illustrious family, in God's work and in Georgiana Somerset's heart

Where Love Shines
Blinded in the Charge of the Light Brigade, Richard, inspired by the Earl of Shaftesbury, gropes through physical and spiritual blindness to the light of Jennifer's love

Where Love Calls
Kynaston Studd is on fire to carry the love of God to the ends of the earth with Hudson Taylor; Hilda Beauchamp adds fuel to another kind of fire.

Epics

Glastonbury, The Novel of Christian England
An Arthurian Grail search from the birth of Christ through the Reformation

The Fields of Bannockburn
Scotland's story from the Coming of Christianity through Independence

The Banks of the Boyne
A Quest for the Soul of Ireland

Printed in Great Britain
by Amazon